PRAISE FOR LAN

Exciting Stuff

Heart pounding from start to finish. A unique plot and strong, believable characters, who you find yourself rooting for right from the start!!

Very impressive - New Author for me

Wow my first read in this series first read of this type of fiction actually. Really enjoyed it will definitely be carrying it on with next book and be sharing this series with other readers.

Loved It!

As an avid zombie genre fan this was right up my street. Yes, it does resemble 28 days later (virus outbreak) and World War Z (zombies climbing on top of each other) but still a good story on its own. Well written, nice level of description and gripping. I've already ordered the next set of books.

5 Stars, A Must Read!!!

I really enjoyed this book and can not wait to read more. It is fast paced and written very well. This is the first book I've read by this author and really, really enjoyed it!!!

Lance Winkless was born in Sutton Coldfield, England, brought up in Plymouth, Devon and now lives in Staffordshire with his partner and daughter.

Lance is a member of the Society of Authors

For more information on Lance Winkless and future writing see his website.

www.LanceWinkless.com

By Lance Winkless

FOUNDATION DAY

CAPITAL FALLING - THE SERIES

THE Z SEASON – TRILOGY

KILL TONE
VOODOO SUN
CRUEL FIX

Visit Amazon Author Pages

Amazon US- Amazon.com/author/lancewinkless
Amazon UK- Amazon.co.uk/Lance-Winkless/e/B07QJV2LR3

Why Not Follow

Facebook LanceWinklessAuthor
Twitter   @LanceWinkless
Instagram @LanceWinkless
BookBub www.bookbub.com/authors/lance-winkless

FOUNDATION DAY

- BOOK TWO -

LANCE WINKLESS

FOUNDATION DAY
RECAP

A deadly conspiracy has taken hold of the city. One dead body followed another, each with the life sucked out of them. The investigation fell on Detective Calum Chambers and his partner Mike.

Quickly, the appearance of dead bodies turned into brutal attacks in the city by ferocious zombified creatures. A hideous massacre at Trinity Square in the Chinese quarter by two of these horrific undead creatures left dozens dead and the investigation escalated to higher authorities.

As Chief Arnold took over the investigation, with Cal at her side, Police Headquarters were disastrously infiltrated by Merle Abital, the lone 'patsy' of the conspirators. Merle, controlled by the shadowy figure named Janus, finally proving his worth…

Following a toxin release, the police investigation team became infected and the ensuing slaughter wiped out the majority of the team, including Cal's partner, Mike.

Despite this awful body blow, a vital witness came forward that led Cal and Arnold to Merle Abital's apartment where they found his assassinated body. This is when

Cassie Sutton, a Secret Intelligence operative joined the investigation.

Information of an attack in the Arena District then led the three investigators to the city's concert arena where another massive attack broke out, but this time the infection began to spread. In the resultant carnage, Chief Arnold was attacked and killed just as Cal received word that his estranged wife Kim was in danger.

Cal managed to extract Kim from the infected area but at the terrible cost of Kim's sister Lauren's life. To take Kim to the relative safety of her father's house, Cal was forced to leave Cassie alone in the danger zone. Cassie returned to the Secret Intelligence offices at Mercury House to continue the investigation into the conspirators. Conspirators that she is soon reporting sensitive information to, at Janus' behest and his co-conspirator Doctor Francis Arnoult.

Chapter 1

Inside the arena, the alarm continues to sound. The general public are completely unaware of what has triggered the incessant noise. Kevin follows the lead set by Richard, the head of security and his boss. Richard ushers concert-goers forward towards the escalators that will take them down to the exits and Kevin does the same. He does it with a smile, as he was trained to do, and tells people to "Keep moving" should they ask awkward questions about what the emergency is.

Kevin looks through the crowd to see if he can still see the three police officers that they have just evacuated the security office with. He tells himself that he is looking to see how they are getting on, even though the real reason is to try to get one last look at the commanding and smartly dressed beautiful female officer before she disappears from sight completely.

"Keep moving," Kevin repeats absently as he strains his neck to see but he only manages to glance at the back of the woman's head, much to his disappointment.

"Keep your mind on the task at hand," Richard orders Kevin, who quickly pretends that is what he has always been doing, despite his reddening complexion.

1

Both men drift along with the crowds heading towards the escalators, continuing with their crowd control as they go. Kevin is unsure what to make of this latest emergency. Can it really be as bad as the police officers made out? Every week now there is a new emergency. If it's not COVID then it's prices skyrocketing or public services about to buckle under the strain. Kevin is only young, in his mid-twenties, but he is sure that life never used to be as complicated or expensive as it seems to be now. The world appears to be moving backwards not forwards and one inept government after the other seem powerless to improve matters. Unless their underlying plan for the world is to change the dynamics of civilisation, the very fabric of life.

I need to keep off social media, Kevin tells himself, *and stop watching the news. It's making me paranoid!*

Nearing the top of the escalators, Kevin waves a few more people through as he waits for Richard to catch him up. He looks around for Julie, the CCTV operator, as he waits, but she seems to have disappeared into the crowd. She has probably made a beeline for the exits to escape the danger. Crowd control isn't her job after all. Kevin continues to stand waiting for Richard, mindlessly scratching his ear as he does.

At first, Kevin thinks that it is the ear-scratching that has produced the strange sound he hears. He takes his hand away from his ear just as a nervous hush falls across the crowds of people. People still move onto the escalators, but they look around in confusion as they go, wondering if it was a scream they heard or if the sound came only from their imagination.

Just as Richard arrives by Kevin's side everyone inside the building receives their answer. A loud, chilling screech rings out across the vast interior near the arena's main entrances.

"What the fuck was that?" Kevin asks Richard, his eyes searching for the source of the ominous noise.

"The fight must have flooded out of the arena," Richard replies nervously. "We need to get down there to help out!"

Kevin looks at Richard in disbelief. The police need to attend to a major incident, that's their job. *A zero-hours contract with a few hours of training in crowd control and a rate of pay marginally above the legal minimum rate of pay doesn't make it my job*, Kevin thinks. Especially if what the police officers said is true. That this isn't a normal crowd disturbance but an outbreak by some kind of zombified creatures ready to slaughter. That definitely isn't in his job description.

"We can't fight zombies," Kevin tells his boss timidly.

"It's our job to keep the public safe, Kevin, and that's what we'll do. Do you understand?" Richard insists.

Richard doesn't wait for an answer from Kevin. Instead, he turns and forces his way onto the escalator. "Follow me," he orders Kevin.

Reluctantly, Kevin does as he's told and follows Richard onto the escalator. The moving staircase they find themselves on is on the far right of the bank of escalators and it overlooks the throngs of people coming out of the arena below. As soon as they begin to descend, more screams and unholy screeches ring out. Kevin has a bird's eye view of the crowd below and immediately sees that scuffles and panic are breaking out. *Whatever Richard is planning to do is up to him*, Kevin thinks. *I'm not paid enough to go into battle with the undead.* He decides there and then that he will head straight for the exits as soon as they reach the bottom of the escalator.

Suddenly, Kevin's plans to escape the rising threat turn to ruin as, just shy of halfway down, the escalator grinds to a halt. Cries of panic instantly ring out all around Kevin and Richard from the masses of people on the escalators. Kevin turns his head to see that the whole bank of escalators has stopped, stranding everyone in limbo.

Kevin is pushed from behind, threatening to topple him forward into Richard, but he pushes back, his hands grabbing onto the plastic handrails to save himself. *What now, boss?* Kevin thinks as a head rises from the crowd on the escalator next to them, a few feet down.

The attractive police officer that Kevin strained to catch one last look at climbs up onto the central reservation between the two escalators. He now stares at her, not for sexual gratification but in fascination as she begins to shimmy down towards the ground. She is carrying her shoes in one of her hands and a gun in the other. Kevin watches on in awe as the policewoman descends, followed now by her two colleagues, who have decided to follow her lead.

"What we gonna do?" Kevin asks his superior, suddenly inspired by the actions of his newly found female crush.

"We need to get off this escalator," Richard replies but he offers no suggestion of how to achieve that.

The two men remain packed in like sardines, the chaos below building. Kevin involuntarily cringes back from the side of the escalator in terror as hideous creatures burst into the crowds from the arena behind them. Shock rips through him and he struggles to process what he is seeing. Depraved monsters fling themselves at the poor people below, who have no means of escaping the onslaught. Men and women are viciously attacked from behind as they try to barge their way out of the line of fire. The crowd surges

4

forward in a panicked crush and Kevin sees heads swallowed in the crush to be trampled on, whilst blood flies into the air.

Any inspiration that Kevin had felt vanishes, buried by his shock and fear. The only thing he cares about now is escaping with his life if he can manage to free himself from the damned escalator he is trapped on.

Chaotic panic ensues below and the fever spreads to the people trapped around him as they also witness the barbarity unfolding in the crowds below. People begin to fight to free themselves from the escalators. Some climb onto the central reservations between the escalators, just as the three police officers had done. These people kick and fight to try to descend as others head in the opposite direction, trying to get back up to the level above. Shouts and screams bellow into the air, punches are thrown and faces are gorged on as the fight for survival escalates.

Kevin searches for a way to free himself from the approaching chaos. Richard, who is in front of him, has joined in the melee and tries to push his way forward. Kevin doubts whether Richard still plans on sticking around to try to help people. Richard has a look of panic etched across his face.

At the base of the bank of escalators, the fighting has become fierce and horrific creatures surge forward to take advantage, some scrambling over each other to find their targets.

Kevin turns back to see if there is any possibility he can find a way back up to the level above. There is no way he wants to descend into the carnage below. He needs to find another way out of the building. But just as he turns the escalators judder and then start moving again. Screams of panic reach new heights as the stairs below the feet of the crush of people begin to carry them down towards the chaos and the waiting, terrifying monsters.

With no alternative but to slowly be taken down into the slaughter below, Kevin decides to try to fight his way back up to the level above. Using the central reservation beside him is his only possibility. He isn't the only one who has decided that that is their last resort and he is forced to use all his strength to pull himself up and over other people who are fighting for the same space.

Finally, Kevin fights his way into a space above. He glances behind him to see if Richard is also taking evasive action. As he finds his superior, who has already been carried further down towards the chaos below, Kevin sees something flying over the side of the escalator on a direct trajectory with Richard. The creature slams into Richard, enveloping him instantly, its gruesome teeth darting forward into the side of Richard's neck. Kevin turns away; he has no desire to see the blood of his colleague spray into the air as the creature rips his neck apart.

Kevin scrambles forward an inch or two in fright, the narrow stainless-steel platform threatening to slide away beneath him at any moment. He spreads his hands as wide as the surface allows to try to gain purchase, his feet bent behind him to try to help his cause. Kevin scurries slowly forward a few inches more. On each side of him, the plastic runners travel in the opposite direction, hoping to catch him and pull him down into oblivion. Kevin gains a bit more height, his optimism growing that he might actually escape when someone grabs his leg, pulling him back in desperation. His head turns to see who has interfered with his progress and is threatening to pull him away from his only chance of escape.

A young woman peers back at Kevin, her legs running up the moving steps, her hands grabbing his leg to try to prevent herself from being dragged to certain death. The woman's eyes plead with Kevin to help her, her face stricken with stifling fear. For a heartbeat, Kevin thinks how he could help the poor woman, but the thought is fleeting. This is survival of the fittest and Kevin must save his own skin. He is beginning to slip. His leg kicks out to try to release itself from the woman's grip. Inadvertently, his foot smashes into the woman's terrified face and her grip on him is broken. She tumbles away from Kevin, her arms flailing to find something else to stop her fall but there is nothing. The woman falls head over heels down the unforgiving metal steps and into the people below, where she is carried down into the midst of the slaughter waiting at the end of her journey.

There is no time for Kevin to feel guilt for his part in the woman's demise, there is only time to try to escape. He pushes himself up the narrow slippery surface, looking ahead for other threats that might want to try to pull him down. The escalators on either side of him have cleared though. Their downward motion has seen to that. Above, a crowd of petrified onlookers stare down at the shocking events taking place below, all of them steering well clear of the entry points to the escalators.

Sweat runs down Kevin's back as he tries to climb whilst keeping his balance. *Why doesn't someone hit the stop button on the escalators?* Kevin wonders urgently, as one of his feet hits the moving handrail, causing him to slip back a few inches. He pushes up again, his hands straining to find purchase on the smooth metal. He still has over half of the steep mountain to climb.

Suddenly, Kevin's prayers are answered and the downward motion on either side of him ceases. It only takes a second for Kevin to make his decision, despite the risk of the motion starting again. He jumps down onto the metal stairs, his legs pumping immediately. Within moments, Kevin reaches the top of the escalators and finally makes it to safety.

Kevin gasps for breath as he looks at the crowd surrounding him, his legs burning from the exertion. People stare back at him as if he has the answers they are looking for and all because he wears a security uniform. Little do they know that he has no answers to offer, that he is in the same boat as them. He wishes he wasn't wearing his uniform. There isn't anything he can do for these people and he doesn't want the responsibility.

However, everyone continues to look earnestly at Kevin, waiting for him to act. He turns away from their pleading eyes, unable to take the pressure. Gradually, his lungs calm after his escape and he finds himself staring down the escalators at the mass of squirming bodies. He could be peering into the bowels of hell: everywhere he looks, bloody slaughter is taking place, now even on the lower rungs of the escalators. He suddenly realises that the butchery won't remain below. The gruesome creatures will move upwards to find fresh hunting grounds.

From out of nowhere, Kevin finds his courage and a compulsion to save as many people as he can. He needs to find safety for himself, so why not take as many other souls as he can with him? He knows what he must do and he turns around.

"Follow me!" Kevin bellows to the watching crowd and takes a step forward.

Miraculously, as if he were a messiah, the crowd of people part in front of him to make a corridor through which he can move. Each and every face suddenly holds hope that they might escape their horrific fate.

8

Kevin doesn't move for a moment, as he tries to understand the strange feeling that has crept upon him. *Is this what pride feels like?* he wonders, *or is this something else? Could it be power perhaps?* His moment is ripped apart almost immediately when an ear-piercing screech rings out from below and the strange feeling is overwritten by another more familiar feeling: fear.

Without further delay, his fear pushing him forward, Kevin rushes into the parted crowd.

"Follow me," Kevin shouts again, as he leaves the escalators behind.

People deeper in the crowd hear Kevin's call and also move aside to let him past. Behind him, the gap closes as quickly as it appeared as the people move to follow their newly found saviour. He shouts again to create more space to move into as he strides on. Eventually, as he moves deeper into the upper level of the arena complex, the crowds begin to thin and Kevin increases his speed until he is jogging towards his goal.

A wave of people follow Kevin as he continues onwards, following the path towards the rear emergency exits, which are positioned towards the end of the narrowing corridor.

One blood-curdling scream from behind is followed by another, the sound ricocheting off the ceiling above. Kevin knows instinctively that the attack on the upper level has arrived, the motionless escalators allowing the monsters to ascend to the higher level. He might not be able to save everyone but, God willing, he will at least allow some to escape with their lives.

The emergency exits on this side of the arena consist of three stairwells, hidden behind heavy grey doors.

Emergency exit signs are mounted above the doors but, unless one knows where they are, they could easily be missed. The stairs will lead his flock down and out into the grounds behind the arena, where they will be able to find roads and pathways away from the cursed arena and into the city.

With one last push, Kevin rounds the final part of the corridor and sees the emergency exits just ahead. One of the grey doors has already swung open and people are moving through it and onto the stairs beyond.

Some of the people behind see the goal and sprint past Kevin without a by your leave to make good their escape. Kevin doesn't take offence; he is just happy that he has shown them the way.

"Down the stairs!" Kevin shouts, as he reaches the open door and moves aside to allow people past. Instead of using the door himself, he slams into one of the doors next to the open one, hitting the horizontal bar of the opening mechanism. The door swings open and more people pile through it.

"Keep moving!" Kevin shouts, as the crowds pile past him as he stands to the side to let people in and to shout more encouragement.

An overwhelming feeling of accomplishment washes over Kevin as he ushers yet more people to their safety and only now does he admit that he is proud of himself. He has taken action and shown so many people to safety, people who otherwise would surely have been slaughtered by the fearsome zombified creatures. He looks back up the corridor to see how many more people there are for him to save. The crowd is thinning, and it is almost time for him to join the stampede down to safety.

Kevin sees something sinister move in amongst the far reaches of the approaching people, something that terrifies him. His vision of the hideous creature shocks him into action. He turns for the door beside him. He has played his part, and now it is time for him to make his escape.

He moves for the door but a thickset man barges into Kevin's space, knocking him back. A deathly scream screeches out from close by, stabbing fear into Kevin's guts. *Have I been too generous, too heroic?* he panics. *Have I delayed my own escape for too long?*

Regaining his balance, any compulsion for heroics has vanished from Kevin's mind. All he cares about now is escaping with his life. He sees a gap in the flow of people and forces his way into it, using his elbows to keep any interlopers at bay. Finally, Kevin moves into the stairwell, pushing his way towards the stairs and the promise of escape.

Horrific screams resonate continuously from behind at the doorway, where there is a bottleneck of people fighting to get into the stairwell. There is also a bottleneck on the entry onto the stairs in front of Kevin. People are almost coming to a standstill. He pushes against the people in front of him to try to get things moving, but he gains no more than a foot. He pushes again, inching forward, the heat inside the stairwell closing in on him. *Keep moving forward*, his mind begs, as a high-pitched scream rings out from just behind Kevin. The hideous sound is coming from inside the stairwell.

The terrifying sound causes panic all around and now Kevin is pushed from behind. He transfers his weight forward to gain more ground and his foot finds the first step down, which brings a glimmer of hope. Elbows dig into Kevin's ribcage as screams echo around him and his foot reaches to find the next step that will take him away from the horrific danger behind.

Kevin stretches to find the next step just as a wave of pressure comes from behind. This time the push is overwhelming and, with his foot in mid-air, he cannot counteract its force. He cannot stop his forward motion.

Falling forward, Kevin feels his stomach drop. He grabs onto anything he can in a desperate attempt to stop himself. All that he manages to grab onto are the people around him. His weight continues to travel and the people he has hold of fall with him.

In a blur, an avalanche of bodies falls down the flight of stairs, with Kevin in amongst them. The screams of terror that erupt cannot hide the sounds of cracking bones and smashing heads as dozens of people crash into each other and into the steps. Only the solid wall at the bottom of the staircase stops the cascade, leaving a pile of crumpled bodies and groans of pain.

Towards the top of the pile lies Kevin, stunned and waiting for the agony of his broken bones to register. Moments pass and his wits begin to return. He realises that, whilst his body aches, there is none of the excruciating pain that he would expect from broken bones.

Is this my reward for helping and saving so many people? Kevin thinks, as his eyes flicker open. *Has somebody in the heavens above witnessed my good deeds and spared me from my fall so that I can rise and make good my escape?*

Kevin believes that he has been spared and begins to try to push himself free of the mangled bodies he is tangled up with. He sees the contorted bodies and strained faces all around him as he moves. His heart goes out to them, but he must look after himself now. He looks up to see if there is an anchor point he can use to help pull himself free. A handrail or even another body will do, but what he sees drains all of his faith from him.

Evil eyes, which are sunk into the hideous face of a depraved beast, stare down at Kevin. The vicious creature's grizzly mouth prises open in the instant in which it leaps into the air to fall on a direct collision course with Kevin.

Terror and panic tear through Kevin as the beast falls, swooping down until it lands with terrific force on his stomach. The blow knocks every ounce of air from his lungs and any scream that might have been festering there. Kevin's entire body strains against the agony, his head falling rigidly backwards, exposing his throat, which the beast's teeth clamp onto until they bite and tear through the soft flesh. Blood splatters into the air as Kevin's throat is torn from his neck. His eyes stare in disbelief at the flesh between the creature's teeth. Horror is the last thing that he feels, until his pain and fear are completely forgotten.

Chapter 2

Cassie's mouth is dry. Her tongue feels like dried leather that cracks as she speaks. Her account of the chaos that has taken place in the city, and specifically in the Arena District, begins from when she placed herself in the middle of the police investigation. She understands that it was no coincidence that she was assigned to be the liaison between the police department and Secret Intelligence. Her orders were facilitated by another unknown operative of S.I. The order could only have been given by someone high up in authority, but she knows not who.

The burner phone she is holding was handed to her only two nights ago and this is the first time it has rung. At first, she had just stared at the flashing screen, displaying an unknown number, her heart thumping and her stomach churning. Cassie's exhausted mind had struggled to decide what to do. Whether to press the illuminated green button or the red button. The wretched man dressed in a trilby hat who had forced the phone upon her had made it very clear what would happen if she did not comply with his instructions.

Cassie might believe she had dreamt the sinister encounter that had taken place in the dead of the night. She had been summoned to a small park situated in the centre of the city under false pretences and in relation to another case she was working on. The vile man had appeared as if from nowhere, from the shadows, hovering towards her under his old-fashioned hat. The meeting was no dream, however. The phone in her hand tells Cassie that much.

The words coming out of Cassie's mouth are privileged. She should not be uttering them to anyone outside the official investigation. Her stomach churns again as she continues with her account of the butchery she has witnessed for whoever might be listening. Trying to console herself by reminding herself that she is not telling her audience anything that they cannot hear on the news channels doesn't ease her somersaulting belly. Not one iota.

Questions are asked throughout by an insistent male voice, as Cassie talks into the burner phone. Her attempts to keep her report as vague as possible only have limited success. She quickly realises that she isn't dealing with people who can be easily fooled. Details of Chief Arnold's demise, nay slaughter, are reluctantly surrendered by Cassie. Still, she tells herself that newscasters will be reporting the same information, if not now then soon. She doesn't mention Cal. She won't offer his name up. She does not want to involve him in this sordid affair. He must be protected.

"And who is taking over the lead in the investigation?" the vile voice asks out of the blue, as if reading her mind.

Cassie falls silent for a moment, her head spinning, her tired mind racing to think what to reply.

"I don't have that information at this time," Cassie says coolly, hoping her momentary pause was not detected by her interrogator.

"Our sources inform us that Detective Callum Chambers has been instructed to take the lead," the voice questions suspiciously.

"Really? That information surprises me as I understood that he is off-grid, taking care of a family matter, but I have only just got back to the office," Cassie replies instantly, her usual quick wits finally resurfacing, if only momentarily.

"Then it would appear that we need that question clarifying, Operative 21. Please make the appropriate enquiries and confirm who is leading the investigation when we have finished here. You may message the answer to this number," Cassie is advised.

"I will confirm," Cassie replies.

"Thank you. Now please hold for a moment," the voice instructs.

As the line goes silent, Cassie's eyes flick to the closed door of her office and to the window beside it, where she sees her colleagues going about their business. At any moment, any one of them could walk in to speak to her. Would they see the guilt on her face as she tries to disguise the damning phone call she is participating in? Would they demand to know what she is up to? Or voice their concerns to her superiors? She knows her concerns are unfounded. No one would guess what is transpiring. She is too well trained to allow that, but it does not stop the feeling of nausea rising within her.

Cassie's impatience grows as the line remains silent. She wants to be released from the call as soon as possible. She guesses that discussions are taking place on the other end of the line to see if they want any further information from her.

How dearly Cassie would like to know who is involved in the discussion. But how can she know? To know would be to know who is blackmailing her and forcing her to reveal privileged information. If she knew who was forcing her hand, she might be able to gain leverage to fight back and possibly free herself from their grip, or even bring them down. The line is completely silent, however, so there is no opportunity to eavesdrop and garner any information that might help.

"Thank you for holding, Operative 21," the voice reappears, just as Cassie is debating her other options.

"Can I be of further help?" Cassie replies submissively.

"Not currently, thank you. We will await your confirmation of who is now leading the investigation and will be in touch if we need anything further. Keep your phone switched on," Cassie is instructed.

"I will confirm," Cassie agrees.

With that, the call is ended by the other party. Cassie breathes a sigh of relief but her stomach flips again as her nerves settle. Bile seeps into the sides of her mouth, her belly protests and suddenly she feels that she is going to be sick. Just as the feeling builds and Cassie panics that she is going to vomit all over the desk in front of her there is a knock on her office door.

"Cassie, how are you?" Director Khan asks, as he walks into Cassie's office, taking her by surprise.

"I'm fine," Cassie manages to say as she swallows down her bile and tries to keep her stomach in check. Her concentration on not vomiting, especially in front of her superior, has made her forget to rise out of her chair to meet the director of Secret Intelligence.

"Are you sure? You've had a shocking day today and you look pale," Khan asks with genuine concern.

"It's been a horrific day, sir, and very sad," Cassie replies, laying it on thick in the hope that it might mask her current condition, which thankfully is subsiding.

"So much carnage and so many deaths," Khan replies sorrowfully.

"Chief Arnold is going to be a big loss to us, Sir," Cassie adds regretfully.

"Indeed," Khan agrees. "Do you think Detective Chambers is up to the task?"

"Detective Chambers is very capable, Sir. If anything, he knew more about the case than Arnold, as he was the original investigator on the case," Cassie tells Khan.

"Where is he? Why isn't he here?" Khan asks, puzzled.

"He will arrive shortly, Sir," Cassie replies, stretching the truth. "He had a family emergency that he had to attend to."

"A family emergency!" Khan protests. "We have a city-wide emergency! He should be here, front and centre."

"Yes, Sir," Cassie concedes. "Detective Chambers knows that. He will be back on the case as soon as he has dealt with his family emergency."

"He had better be, or he will be replaced," Khan insists.

"Sir, there is nobody more qualified than Chambers in this matter. We need him," Cassie counters.

"I couldn't agree more, Agent Sutton. My point precisely. But he is of no use if he isn't here working on the case. Wouldn't you agree?" Khan argues.

"Yes, Sir," Cassie is forced to agree.

"Then I suggest you contact him and remind him of that," Khan says.

"I will do that, Sir," Cassie agrees. "How is the containment in the Arena District going?" she adds, hoping to change the direction of the conversation.

"Progress is still unclear," Khan replies, taking the bait. "The military are struggling to cover such a large area. Reinforcements are inbound to bolster their numbers but the situation is extremely precarious."

"It doesn't bear thinking about if they don't hold the line," Cassie warns.

"Let the military worry about that, Agent," Khan orders. "Your job is to uncover who is behind these attacks so that we can put a stop to them."

"Yes, Sir," Cassie acknowledges.

"Everyone is looking over their shoulders, Cassie. Another attack could happen anywhere and at any time. You have the full support of this department to put a stop to this. So, I suggest you use it."

"I will, Sir," Cassie insists.

"And get Detective Chambers back on task!" Khan growls, not forgetting about him for a moment.

"Sir," Cassie replies, finally standing up from her chair.

With that, Khan does an about-turn and leaves Cassie's office without uttering another word. He has said his piece and sees no reason to labour his point. Cassie is still taken aback that the director has seen fit to travel down the building to visit her. Normal etiquette would be for her to be summoned to his office in the higher reaches of Mercury House, many floors above. Cassie has only had that privilege on one previous occasion and that was as a junior member of a team. On that occasion, she had been ordered not to talk unless she was addressed directly, which she wasn't.

Perhaps Khan decided to make a detour as he was travelling up or down the building or maybe he had a spare ten minutes? Both options are unlikely in the current situation. Khan must have decided that her work was the present priority and didn't want to stop her working by summoning her. If only he knew what she was actually doing was reporting sensitive information to the conspirators behind the attacks.

A wave of nauseating guilt hits Cassie again and she flops back down into her chair. Her head moves forward to take refuge in her hands, but she stops herself before her hands close around her face. *There is nothing to be gained from self-pity*, she insists to herself. *Think about it. How can this be turned to my advantage? Am I going to allow myself to be controlled by a group of maniacs, hell-bent on bringing death and destruction, or am I going to fight?*

To hell with it! Cassie decides. *If they want to blackmail me and bring me down, let them try. I have a lot to lose, but so do they, and I'm not going to allow myself to be dragged down to their level. Some things are more important than the individual and this is one of those times.*

A plan forms in Cassie's mind. *I'm an agent in the intelligence services, a spy. This is my opportunity to become a double agent. Now is the time to play them at their own game and use their hold over me to my advantage, and to the advantage of this investigation.*

Cassie knows that, if she is serious about becoming a double agent, she should rush across her office, catch up with Director Khan and call him back to talk. She should tell him everything. Lay all her cards on the table and confide in him. But she doesn't. She doesn't move from her chair.

Somebody in authority assigned her to become the liaison between S.I. and the police and that person is also a double agent. Only this despicable person is working with the maniac conspirators and, who knows, they could be the mastermind behind the heinous crimes that have been perpetrated. Could Director Khan have given the order to reassign her? Could he be the mole?

Khan appeared concerned for her welfare and mightily determined that the investigation should proceed at pace. After all, he came all the way down to see her to reiterate his points. Could that have been a test? Was his real purpose to determine if she is towing the line, doing as she is told?

Cassie cannot take the risk. Her future and the future of the investigation might depend on it, and should the investigation fail...

There is only one person Cassie knows that she can trust and yet she must betray him. She has no other option other than to message and confirm that Callum Chambers has indeed taken the lead in the investigation. Cassie picks up her phone to do just that, whilst telling herself she isn't telling the conspirators anything they don't already know. The information will be of little use to them, but it will help gain their trust and help embed her cover within the group.

Cassie taps out a short message, with a feeling of guilt as she writes Callum's name. She ends the message by saying "If there is anything more I can do," and clicks 'Send'. Appearing willing to help, but not looking over-eager is the best course of action at present, she feels.

Cassie imagines the phone that receives her message bleeping and the man with the well-spoken, commanding voice clicking on it. She wonders who the man is and where he is. These are the questions that need answers if the investigation is going to move forward. The man on the phone is not the same man who she'd met in the park in the dead of night. Cassie is sure of that as he was in his senior years. Cassie might not have got a good look at the man's face in the darkness, and under the shadow of his trilby hat, but his voice confirmed that much.

The only evidence Cassie has is the phone number that is now stored in her burner phone. She doesn't hold out much hope that the phone number will lead anywhere, however. These people are professionals. The number will be routed through the internet and be almost impossible to trace. There is a chance that the supercomputers at S.I. could trace it, but there's a bigger chance that any attempt to do so would trigger red flags at the source of the number and blow her act of cooperation. The risk is too great. She will have to find other evidence to progress the investigation.

Cassie needs someone to confide in, to bounce ideas off. She needs Cal to return, needs him back on the team. Will he understand what she has been forced to do? Will he forgive her and continue to trust her? Nerves begin to rise within Cassie once more as she scrolls to find Cal's number in her phone.

Chapter 3

"Hello, Cassie," Cal answers wearily, after clicking 'Answer' on his phone.

"Hi, Cal. I'm so glad to hear your voice," Cassie replies earnestly, taking Cal somewhat by surprise.

"Really? We only split up a few hours ago," Cal tells Cassie, feeling his face blush.

"A few hours seems like a lifetime at the moment, partner. I need you back," Cassie insists.

Cal's face reddens further, something he is conscious of as he notices Kim's father watching him as he speaks. Tom is still sitting on the sofa in his kitchen with Kim, who is still resting. Cal sees the sadness in Tom. His life has been turned upside down. Next to him is one distraught daughter and, in the adjacent room, his eldest child lies dead. Cal wonders if his father-in-law will be able to cope alone if Cal leaves.

"What's happened? Has there been a development?" Cal asks Cassie, turning away from Tom.

"Yes, you could say that. I need to discuss it with you," Cassie replies.

"Go ahead," Cal responds.

"I need to discuss it with you in person, not over the phone," Cassie replies cryptically.

"Why? What's happened?" Cal tries again.

"Not over the phone," Cassie insists. "When can you get here?"

"Things are tough here, Cassie," Cal replies, unsure what to do.

"I'm sure it is, Cal. I'm sorry about that, but these are desperate times and I'm sure I don't need to explain why. Director Khan has already been to my office asking where you are but, more importantly, I need you back here. You're the only one I can trust," Cassie tells Cal, suddenly worried that someone might be listening to their conversation, "trust to help me with this case," she quickly adds, to try to cover her tracks just in case anyone is eavesdropping.

"Okay, Cassie, I hear you," Cal says, turning to look at Tom and Kim again. Tom attempts a reassuring smile for Cal but fails miserably. Cal is loathed to leave Kim in her current state. He wants to be here for her in her time of need, but she won't thank him if the attacks escalate though. Nobody will if there was something he could have done to stop them.

"Cal," Cassie says earnestly, adding to the pressure he is feeling.

"I'll speak to Kim and her father," Cal tells Cassie. "Once they're settled, I'll leave."

"Thanks, Cal. I'll be waiting for you," Cassie says, relieved.

"Should I come straight to Mercury House?" Cal asks.

"Yes. Show your ID at reception and they will phone up to me to come and meet you. We will sort out your entry

ID for Mercury House when you arrive," Cassie confirms. "How long will you be, do you think?"

"I won't be long here. I'll message you when I'm leaving," Cal replies.

"Okay, great. Thanks, Cal. See you soon," Cassie says, before ending the call.

"You've got work to do then," Tom says, giving Cal a knowing look as the call ends.

"I'm afraid so. Are you sure you're going to be okay here?" Cal asks, as Tom prises himself out from under Kim's legs.

"We will manage," Tom replies, moving away from Kim to let Cal say his goodbyes to his wife.

Kim is in a daze when Cal tells her he must go back to work. She nevertheless becomes upset as he goes to leave her. She grabs hold of Cal's arm, tears rolling down her face, as she begs him not to go. In any other circumstances, Cal would relish his estranged wife's attention, wrap his arms around her and hold her tight. He cannot though. He must leave her. For her own sake and the sake of untold others.

Thankfully, Tom comes to Cal's rescue. He takes hold of Kim's arm to release her grip on Cal. Tom soothes his daughter as only a parent can, taking Kim in his arms.

"Kim, I…" Cal tries to speak.

"Please, Cal, you need to go," Tom cuts Cal's words off as he tries to console Kim.

Cal turns away and, before he knows it, he is sitting behind the wheel of the old BMW that they arrived in. Tears fill his eyes, hindering him from finding the car's ignition. Cal's free arm wipes away most of the water that blinds him just as the key finally slips in to start the car. Before he can change his mind and rush back to Kim, Cal's foot floors the accelerator. The car's back wheels churn into the gravel surface of the driveway and Cal wrenches on the steering wheel, sending the BMW into a 180-degree spin.

The beam of the car's headlights pierce through the darkness of the long driveway as Cal speeds down to join the highway at the bottom. Turning sharply left out of the driveway, Cal floors the accelerator again when the car straightens onto the road. He races away from his wife with no consideration for the speed limit. *The sooner I get back to work, the sooner this nightmare will end and the sooner I can return to be with my wife*, Cal tells himself.

Traffic on the road is quiet and Cal pulls his phone out of his pocket. He clears his vision again with his sleeve before he starts writing a message. In between keeping an eye on the road, Cal types a short message to Cassie, which simply reads, "I'm on my way."

Cal doesn't put his phone away. Instead, he sticks it between his legs so that he can feel it vibrate. Cassie is bound to reply to his message and he doesn't want to miss Kim or Tom trying to reach him, or anyone else for that matter. Too much is going on right now to miss anything coming through to his phone.

Virtually no traffic is heading towards the city. The public seem to have been scared of approaching the epicentre of the outbreak. Plenty of vehicles are on the opposite side of the road, however. Cal guesses that not many of them will stop until they are well outside the city's limits and beyond. Well out of harm's way. He completely understands their logic and would join them if he could. He would take Kim as far away from the danger as he possibly could, would even lock her in the car if she protested, although Cal is certain that Kim wouldn't object after the horror she has been through this evening.

Sure enough, as Cal speeds towards the city, Cassie messages him back and her message is short and simple. He slips the phone back between his legs, wondering what the development she mentioned in their conversation is. He hopes that there is a break in the case, but something tells him that's wishful thinking.

The journey back into the city goes quickly and inbound traffic is still thin on the ground as Cal heads into the centre. Mercury House is situated in the very centre of the city, only a couple of blocks away from the police headquarters building and a twenty-minute drive from the Arena District. Cal has driven past the clandestine home of the Secret Intelligence Service on almost a daily basis, but he has never entered what he imagines is the murky world inside. There is no indication to the unsuspecting eye that the tall, glass-clad building houses the offices of the intelligence services, offices that are hidden amongst other businesses that occupy the building's floor space, such as advertising agencies and accounting firms. Cal would have no idea himself if he weren't in the police force.

Cal dispenses with formality and parks directly outside Mercury House, ignoring the parking restrictions that are clearly displayed. He realises that the BMW he borrowed from Lauren's neighbours might be reported, towed away in no time and impounded. The car pound is the best place for the vehicle, which is looking even more battered now after its multiple escapades and, if Lauren's neighbours ever want their car back, Cal will know where it is.

After looking at his phone to double-check if there is anything from Kim, Cal gets out of the car. He is immediately taken by how different the city feels now that he has its breeze drifting over him. This is not the city he remembers, Cal is positive about that. He isn't sure what hits him first: the strange smell in the air or the constant and disturbing crack of gunfire in the distance.

A loud blast of gunfire suddenly erupts from nearby, making Cal duck in reflex as a wave of fear courses through him. He panics that the fight with the undead has somehow spread to Mercury House already, his head spinning. Turning in the direction of the gunfire, Cal sees movement, a figure running. This is no zombie, however. Cal quickly realises it is a man. The man chases across the road and away from a small convenience store, his arms bursting with looted stock. Behind the man, in the doorway of the store, what must be the store's owner stands with his arm in the air, his hand gripping an old, smoking revolver.

Cal finds his right hand tightening around the grip of his service-issued Glock sidearm. Under normal circumstances, his gun would already be up and aimed at the man standing in the doorway of the store holding the revolver, but these are not normal circumstances. His hand loosens around the Glock in unison with the store owner turning around in defeat to return and tend to his shop.

Every citizen of the city will have gathered whatever weapon they have for protection, lawful or not. Cal feels the tension in the air. The entire city is on edge. The outbreak in the Arena District won't be the only cause of death and injury tonight, that much is guaranteed.

Cal attempts to put the approaching chaos out of his mind for the time being at least. His concentration is needed elsewhere. He turns towards the entrance of Mercury House, preparing himself to get back to work.

Even though the hour is late, the door to Mercury House swings open. Cal is slightly surprised that such a sensitive building doesn't lock its door at night.

"Can I help you, Sir?" a deep voice asks the moment Cal enters the building's foyer.

Now Cal sees why locking the doors is unnecessary. Across the foyer, behind a large, heavily constructed reception booth, three fierce-looking security guards are waiting. Two of the men are sitting down, unconcerned about Cal's sudden appearance, whilst the one who addressed him has stood to greet him.

"Yes. Tell Cassie Sutton that I've arrived," Cal replies in an authoritative manner, showing the guard his police ID as he arrives at the reception booth.

"Certainly, Detective," the guard replies. "I won't keep you a moment."

The security guard, who is taller than six foot and built like a brick shithouse, smiles at Cal as his attention moves to a computer screen positioned in front of him. The man is ex-military, Cal can tell easily, as are the other two guards, who all but ignore Cal's presence. The guard has obviously been instructed in how to greet visitors to the building though and Cal wonders if his polite manner comes easily to him. Cal suspects not and that the guard would dearly love to grab one of the guns that are surely stored within close reach behind the booth and stick it in Cal's face as a welcome.

"Ms Sutton is on her way down," the guard tells Cal, after a quick phone call. "Please take a seat in the waiting area."

Cal turns towards the seating area just off reception that the guard points at without saying a word. He imagines that there are advantages for the other businesses occupying the same building as S.I. Added security for one, but there are bound to be disadvantages too.

Choosing a seat that gives him a view of the entire foyer, Cal sits down, not expecting to have to wait too long for Cassie's arrival. The security guard who attended to him has sat back down with his colleagues, and Cal has been forgotten about. In fact, none of the three men glance out from the reception booth until a door slides open in the bank of lifts off to the left and Cassie appears. The moment she appears, all three men take a sudden interest in what is going on outside their booth. All three pairs of eyes watch her as she walks across the foyer.

Cassie looks relieved to see Cal as he gets up from his seat to meet her. She looks quite emotional, as if she might even burst into tears.

"Are you okay, Cassie?" Cal asks, as he approaches her.

"Yes, I'm okay, thanks," Cassie replies, steeling herself. "There's just a lot going on."

"You'd better tell me all about it then," Cal insists.

"When we get to my office," Cassie replies, turning back to the bank of lifts.

"How is your wife?" Cassie asks on the journey up.

"Not good. I've left her with her father," Cal replies miserably.

"At least she is with someone," Cassie offers.

"Tell me what's going on then?" Cal asks, trying to change the subject.

Just as Cal asks, they come to a stop and the door opens with a ping. Cassie steps straight out and heads towards a security door. She swipes a security card through a panel next to the door and then looks up at a camera mounted beside the door. A loud click sounds and Cassie pulls the heavy door open.

"Detective Chambers," a female voice sounds the moment Cassie is through the door.

Cal turns in surprise to see Tilly, Chief Arnold's former assistant, approaching across the busy office. The poor young woman looks drained. Cal had suspicions that there was more to her and Chief Arnold's relationship than a purely professional one. He wonders if the loss of her superior is hitting Tilly harder than it might have.

"Hello, Tilly. What can I do for you?" Cal asks.

"Commissioner Jackson has assigned me to you, as your assistant," Tilly tells Cal.

"Really? He didn't mention it. Are you sure you're up to it?" Cal asks gently.

"Yes, Sir. Commissioner Jackson asked me the same. I'm determined to continue and help put a stop to this barbarity and bring those responsible to justice. For Chief Arnold's sake, if nothing else!" Tilly assures forcefully.

"Cal," Cassie says impatiently.

"Okay, thanks Tilly," Cal says, seeing the urgency on Cassie's face. "We plan on doing just that. Agent Sutton and I just need to catch up, so can you gather the latest information on the case and be ready to update us as soon as we're finished, please?"

"Sir, I'm afraid that Commissioner Jackson asked me to take you straight to a briefing the moment you arrived. He has been notified that you're in the building and he is waiting with Director Khan, top-ranking military officials and representatives of the government. I need to take you there immediately," Tilly insists.

"I won't be long. I need to speak to Agent Sutton first," Cal replies.

"She is needed in the briefing too, Sir. The Commissioner was insistent. They are waiting for you both before they start," Tilly pushes.

Cal looks at Cassie, undecided what to do.

"Let's go, Tilly. We can talk later," Cassie says, rolling her eyes.

Cassie does an about-turn and strides over to the door that they have just used to enter the offices. Cal knows that she is unimpressed as he and Tilly chase after her, but what can he do?

Cassie stomps straight over to the lifts and presses the button. Only then does she turn around. She has a face like thunder and her eyes are like daggers as she looks at Cal. Cal raises his eyebrows, giving her a sympathetic look, and eventually her face breaks although there is still an underlying anger there.

"Is it something I've said?" Tilly asks boldly to break the silence while they wait.

"No, it's not you. We just have things to discuss and deal with," Cassie answers.

"Anything I can help with? That's why I'm here. I think you'll find me very capable," Tilly offers.

"We have no doubt about that, Tilly," Cal replies. "There will be plenty for you to do but not on this occasion."

"I understand. Just let me know when you have something for me," Tilly insists.

With that, the lift arrives to take them up to the briefing.

Chapter 4

Cassie is first out of the lift. She takes them over to another security door, which is a carbon copy of the one on the previous floor. She passes the security checks smoothly again and the door opens to allow them through. The area beyond is different to the floor where Cassie is based, which consists of a large open-plan office with a peppering of contained offices around its perimeter. This floor, by contrast, is closed off by walls and corridors. The only open section is a reception area immediately in front of them.

"Hello, Agent Sutton," a well-mannered middle-aged female greets Cassie from behind a desk as they arrive on the floor. "Director Khan is waiting for you in conference room A. Is this Detective Chambers with you?" the woman asks, looking directly at Cal.

"Yes, this is Detective Chambers," Cassie confirms.

"Excellent," the woman smiles. "And this is?"

"My assistant, Officer Tilly Madison. She will be accompanying me," Cal insists.

"Very good. Then let's not keep the director waiting any further, shall we?" the woman says, rising from behind the desk. "Please follow me."

Cal sees Cassie roll her eyes again at the woman's performance as she turns her back to lead them into one of the corridors. Cassie follows nevertheless and, within moments, they are led into a room with a sign mounted outside reading CONFERENCE ROOM A.

Inside the conference room, the lights are dimmed and silhouetted figures are sitting looking at a large television screen. The screen shows a high-quality, black-and-white, night-vision stream of a battle. Constant bright flashes of tracer gunfire and explosions leave no doubt that the footage is of a firefight. The only things Cal isn't sure of are whether the footage is a live stream or recorded and the location of the firefight. He assumes and hopes that the location is the Arena District, but he wouldn't be surprised if the threat had spread out into other areas, unfortunately.

"Director Khan," their female chaperone says timidly after a short pause. "Agent Sutton and Detective Chambers have arrived."

Almost immediately, the television freezes just as a large explosion all but whites out the screen. The shadowy figures turn away from the screen's blinding light in unison and a commanding voice simply says, "Lights." A switch clicks on a wall and the room illuminates, causing Cal to squint slightly despite the bright television screen.

"Thank you, Madeline, that will be all," a man says, who Cal recognises as the director of Secret Intelligence, Director Khan.

As Madeline retreats from the conference room, Cal sees that next to Khan sits Police Commissioner Jackson and next to him is the city's mayor, Mayor Roberts. There are eight other people in the room who Cal is unfamiliar with. Five are sitting around the same table as the other men whilst three others are sitting in chairs away from the conference table, looking over proceedings. Tilly sidles over and sits in a chair with the people who are sitting away from the table, which makes Cal assume that they are assistants to the others at the table.

"Nice of you to join us, Detective Chambers," Director Khan greets Cal sarcastically.

"And you are?" Cal retorts in the same vein.

"You know very well who I am, Detective," Khan growls.

"I do, Director, so shall we dispense with the sarcasm?" Cal replies.

"Detective Chambers..." Commissioner Jackson begins to scold Cal for his insubordination.

"No, Detective Chambers is quite right, Commissioner," Khan concedes. "My apologies, Detective. We are just very keen to bring this threat to an end and we need you on-board."

"As am I, Director, and I apologise for having to take a step away to deal with a family emergency," Cal admits.

"Please take a seat both of you and let's get down to business then," Khan offers. He directs Cal and Cassie to take seats near the head of the table, in between the others who are already sitting.

"Let me introduce you to everyone," Khan continues once they are both in position. "I'm sure you both know Police Commissioner Jackson and are familiar with Mayor Roberts."

Cal and Cassie acknowledge the two men who are sitting to their left and are closest to them. Khan's attention then moves to the people sitting on the opposite side of the table from him, people who are not familiar to either Cal or Cassie.

"This is General Peters," Khan says.

His hand moves out in a presenting motion towards a man with a stern but intelligent appearance who is kitted out in a meticulously pressed and immaculate combat uniform that has never seen the battlefield.

"General Peters is in command of the troops currently in the city, and next to him is Colonel Medlam," Khan continues.

Cal eyes Colonel Medlam, who peers back at him unforgivingly. Cal wonders what the buzz-cut officer's role in proceedings is. This man has definitely seen action and Cal would guess that he lives for the fight, judging by the menacing look in his eye.

"I'm sure I don't need to tell you that this is Secretary of Defence Martha Dunguard," Khan says, moving his focus across, "and her chief of staff... Sorry, I didn't get your name," Khan fumbles, without embarrassment.

"John Mulry," the younger man confirms.

"John Mulry. Thank you," Khan repeats, as if to imprint the chief of staff's name in his mind.

Cal nods at the two at the far end of the table, suddenly recognising Martha Dunguard from the Secretary of Defence's appearances on television. She is obviously here representing the government, Cal decides, and will no doubt be reporting back to its very top.

"And, finally, this is Julia McCormac, director of Disease Control."

"Who's behind this attack on my city?" Mayor Roberts demands, staring at Cal and almost interrupting Khan's introductions.

"Our investigations led us to one of the perpetrators of the attacks, Mayor," Cal blurts finally, after being taken aback by the mayor's sudden demand. "We are confident that the suspect, one Merle Abital, carried out the attack at police headquarters and the one in Chinatown. He was also more than likely responsible for the attacks of my original investigations into the bodies that were turning up in the city. Although we cannot confirm that yet."

"But you've hit a dead end as far as Abital goes? Literally!" Mayor Roberts presses.

"Yes. Unfortunately, by the time we found him, he had been murdered. But that doesn't mean we've hit a dead end," Cal replies.

"It sounds pretty final to me!" Roberts exclaims.

"We are still gathering evidence from the crime scene, Mayor. There is a wealth of digital evidence that we are combing through and we're confident we will discover new leads to follow," Cal improvises, hoping that Cassie's colleagues are indeed doing just that.

"We need results, Detective, not conjecture. As far as I can see, these people are running rings round you while my city turns into a war zone of undead monsters!" Roberts protests.

"Please calm yourself, Mayor," Khan interjects. "This investigation is wide reaching and extremely complicated. The investigation has proceeded well but at great cost to Detective Chambers' colleagues. They discovered Abital and are following up on new leads as we speak. I realise that the stakes are high but people like this don't just roll over ready to be caught."

Cal is grateful for Khan's defence of the investigation, especially considering what the director has pointed out is all too true after all. Mayor Roberts is left hanging by Khan, almost embarrassed. He soon retreats back into his chair, holding his hands up. Cal wonders how often the city's mayor is put in his place and wonders how many other people would dare to even try.

"Please update us on where the investigation is currently," a female voice asks from the opposite side of the table.

Cal turns his head to see that Martha Dunguard has decided to join in the interrogation and she fixes Cal unwaveringly in her sights. He buys himself a few seconds to prepare his answer by shifting around in his chair so that he is facing the Defence Secretary.

"We believe that, whilst Abital carried out the horrific attacks, he was not the instigator or the brains behind the plans. It's our understanding that he was merely following orders. We suspect he was a loner, drawn into the conspiracy by people exploiting his loneliness and lack of confidence. Our forensics teams have combed through Abital's apartment to see if there is any clue as to who had drawn him in and directed him. The evidence is still being compiled and steps are being taken to try to retrieve information from his computer and phone which have, unfortunately, been deliberately destroyed."

"Is it looking promising that data will be retrieved from the damaged drives?" Dunguard enquires, asking a question that Cal doesn't know the answer to.

"We are hopeful, but we can't give a definitive answer until our tech guys have completed their work," Cassie replies, coming to Cal's aid.

"So, exactly what leads are you following up on presently?" Dunguard demands.

"Again, our experts are following Abital's internet usage trail. We've discovered he was using the dark web, and we are confident that is where he was communicating with his co-conspirators. If we can find what website they were using to chat there may be a chance we can trace the origins of the communications," Cassie replies.

"And we are attempting to trace the origins of Abital's deliveries," Cal offers. "It appears the same courier company was used to deliver Abital the tools he used in the attacks. This will probably be a dead end, with false addresses and cash payments, but a mistake might have been made."

"I see," Dunguard says. "Are there any other leads?"

"We are investigating the release system used at police headquarters to see if any of its components can be traced," Cassie replies.

"Has the main complex in the Arena District been secured?" Cal asks.

"More or less. Why?" General Peters replies, speaking for the first time.

"Because there is another release system on site which needs to be taken into evidence," Cal points out.

"I will get a squad to retrieve it," Peters volunteers.

"Absolutely not," Julia McCormac, the Director of Disease Control intervenes.

"Excuse me?" Peters responds, as if offended.

"The risk to your troops is too great. The release system is probably still contaminated and precautions will need to be taken to remove it," McCormac explains.

"And there is the question of documented evidence. We can't risk forensic evidence being contaminated," Cal adds.

"Do you not think that the army is prepared for all scenarios, Ms McCormac? Because let me inform you that it is," General Peters insists. "My troops are on the ground, fighting back against this outbreak. I have units inside the complex mopping up any threats, helping survivors and monitoring air quality. I can assure you they are fully equipped and ready to undertake any operation they are ordered to."

"Whether they like it or not!" Colonel Medlam adds with a snarl.

"I didn't mean to suggest otherwise," McCormac says, defensively. "I just meant that precautions need to be taken."

"And they will be. Rest assured," Peters replies. "If Detective Chambers needs the release system retrieved to aid his investigation, the army will see that it's done."

"We need all the evidence we can get," Cal states.

"Then Colonel Medlam will make the arrangements," Peters replies.

"I must request that the release system be delivered to my department before it is entered as evidence," McCormac demands. "Samples will need to be taken and the system decontaminated and made safe. The samples could prove vital."

"I am sure General Peters will facilitate that," Secretary Dunguard replies, giving the general little choice in the matter.

"I would like to accompany the retrieval team, if that's possible," Cal asks out of the blue.

"I'm not sure that's a good idea, Detective," Dunguard replies.

"Nevertheless, Secretary, there may be vital evidence other than the release system that needs to be gathered from the site," Cal insists. "We cannot afford to lose anything."

"General?" Dunguard questions.

"I don't see any reason why Detective Chambers cannot be in attendance. My men will secure the site and will be able to kit him out," Peters replies.

"Very well," Dunguard agrees. "But if there is any sign of danger then withdraw, Detective Chambers."

"Of course, Ma'am," Peters acknowledges.

"I'm going too," Cassie says, and nobody argues.

"When will your team be ready?" Dunguard asks.

"We have everything onsite to proceed immediately. We just need to get the two officers there," Colonel Medlam answers, looking at Cal and Cassie. "I can have a helicopter here to transport them within 20 minutes."

"Make your arrangements then, Colonel," Dunguard orders.

"Ma'am," the colonel replies, rising from his chair, phone already in hand.

"Don't take any unnecessary risks out there," Khan says to Cal and Cassie as Medlam leaves the room.

"We won't, Sir," Cassie assures.

"We should be back here quickly and Officer Madison will keep us appraised of any progress with the evidence already under scrutiny," Cal adds, looking over at Tilly.

Chapter 5

"You like living close to the edge, don't you?" Cassie says above the sound of the city and the crack of gunfire in the distance.

Cal looks at her while they wait on the roof of Mercury House for the helicopter that will transport them back to the Arena District. He swallows down the acrid taste in his mouth before he answers her, a taste caused by the invisible smoke of battle that's in the air.

"Believe me, I really don't," Cal replies.

"You could have fooled me," Cassie smiles. "Volunteering us to go back to the arena tells me otherwise."

"You volunteered yourself, remember?" Cal grins back at Cassie. "These people have got to have made a mistake somewhere. We just need to follow the evidence. It's not my fault that it's in that godforsaken place."

"I'm not looking forward to going back there, I must admit," Cassie says.

"It's not too late to change your mind," Cal replies, his grin widening, knowing full well that she won't.

"Who'd be watching your back then?" Cassie retorts.

"Nobody that I'd rather be with," Cal admits.

"Well then," Cassie replies, victoriously.

"Seriously," Cal says, changing the subject, "we still haven't discussed what's on your mind."

"We will, but not now. It'll wait until we get back," Cassie replies.

"Are you sure?" Cal asks, seeing a wave of anxiety cross Cassie's face.

"Yes, let's concentrate on the task at hand for now. We will talk later," Cassie replies.

Cal leaves the subject and gazes around, reaching into his pocket for his pack of cigarettes. *His lungs are already full of smoke so what difference is a bit more going to make?* he tells himself. Whilst the smoke and the sound of gunfire might not be blocked by the other tall buildings adjacent to Mercury House, their view towards the Arena District is. The part of the city they can see appears normal and he wonders what view they will receive of the battle zone once they're airborne.

"Those things will kill you," Cassie jibes, as Cal puts a flame to the end of his cigarette.

"That's the least of my worries right now, don't you think?" Cal replies, letting out a long stream of smoke into the air.

"I do, to be fair," Cassie agrees, as a chopping sound begins to resonate in the night sky.

"Here we go," Cal says, drawing on his cigarette vigorously whilst grabbing the holdall at his feet and throwing it over his shoulder.

A flashing landing light becomes visible against the lights of the city before the silhouette of the helicopter presents itself. The hovering black shadow quickly zooms towards the roof of the building until Cal and Cassie begin to be buffeted fiercely by the downdraft from the helicopter's rotors as it approaches to land on the helipad fixed to the roof of Mercury House.

The moment the aircraft touches down, Cassie moves forward. Cal wonders how many times she has caught a lift from the roof of her workplace. A few times at least, he decides, by the way she handles the situation.

Cal follows Cassie's lead as her legs take her up the low stairway onto the helipad, her head ducked down slightly, lest it be taken off by the unforgiving rotors above. He finds himself noticing that she is wearing more suitable footwear for this expedition, in the form of white training shoes. She has matched them with jeans, a casual top and a windbreaker jacket. He, by contrast, looks like he's dressed himself from the bargain bin at a superstore outlet. He still has his work shoes and suit trousers on but has added a government-issue navy T-shirt that Cassie provided for him when he took five minutes to clean up in the staff washrooms. Thankfully, she also provided him with a black windbreaker, again government issue, which, if zipped right up, makes him look half presentable.

Cassie keeps moving forward towards the waiting helicopter as she mounts the platform, undeterred by the assault of the spinning rotors. The side of the aircraft slides open and a man dressed in a flight suit and helmet appears, his hand reaching out to help Cassie on-board. She expertly grabs the hand and eases herself through the opening with the aid of a foothold sunk into the side of the fuselage below. The hand is quickly offered to Cal and he climbs up into the helicopter. Cassie is already sitting in a flight seat wearing a headset. Cal takes the seat opposite and finds a headset of his own, the holdall once again at his feet.

"Everything okay?" Cassie's voice comes through Cal's headset.

"All good," Cal replies. "You look like you've done this before."

"A few times," Cassie admits, as the hold door slams shut and the pilot powers the engines.

"ETA, five minutes," another voice sounds in their headsets as the helicopter lifts off.

Cal wonders if they are on the right side of the aircraft to get a view towards the Arena District as the helicopter begins to rise and his stomach drops. Within moments they are hovering above all the surrounding buildings and, sure enough, out of the window next to him he gets a look towards their destination.

The view doesn't last as the pilot manoeuvres the helicopter around, pointing it at the Arena District. What he did manage to see didn't tell him much, the darkness and the distance put paid to that, not to mention the smoke haze.

"Let's hope that the site is as secure as Colonel Medlam suggested," Cassie says, taking her sidearm out to double-check it before they land.

"I'm sure he wouldn't allow us in if it wasn't," Cal assures.

"You've got more confidence than me," Cassie replies, her gun moving expertly through her hands.

"If we're not sure, we won't go in," Cal offers.

"We might not realise until it's too late," Cassie counters.

"We'll be okay as long as we stick together," Cal replies, unconvincingly and Cassie peers back with an expression that's far from reassured.

In no time, the helicopter begins to lose altitude and the pilot positions to land. Out of the window, Cal sees the sprawling arena complex below and, to his relief, he cannot see any flashes in the immediate vicinity that might suggest fighting is still taking place in the surrounding area. The fighting would appear to have moved away from the epicentre. Bright flashes in the distance and other helicopters in the sky seem to confirm that. The evidence doesn't calm Cal's nerves though. Anything could happen once they land and he needs to be prepared.

With a jolt, the helicopter touches down and, almost immediately, the hold door is whipped open. Air wafts into the hold, the draught heavy with smoke, and both Cal and Cassie cough as they exit the helicopter. Dozens of troops man the open area outside the arena complex, which the pilot has landed a safe distance from.

Cal and Cassie move away from the helicopter automatically, but neither is sure where they are supposed to go or who they are supposed to meet. Before they are fully clear of the helicopter's rotors the pilot powers the engines and begins to take off, leaving the two in no-man's-land.

"Detective Chambers!" a voice calls.

Cal turns to see a rugged, bearded man in combat dress moving towards them from underneath where the helicopter has only just taken off. The soldier looks like he has just come from manoeuvres in the jungle, deep behind enemy lines, and is armed to the teeth. He is also flanked by three other troopers, who are equally combat-ready.

"Detective Chambers?" the fearsome soldier says again as he arrives.

"Yes, I'm Chambers," Cal remembers to say, as the man straightens his back as the helicopter flies away.

"I'm Sergeant Locke, Detective, and these are my men," Locke announces, towering over Cal. "We've been ordered to escort you into the complex. If you'd follow me."

Cal finds himself lost for words again as the intimidating Sergeant Locke turns towards the complex.

"He's a big chap," Cassie whispers towards Cal, as they follow Locke, whose men take up positions around them on either side, with one to the rear, in a protective formation.

"You can say that again. He's not like any soldier I've seen before," Cal replies quietly.

"They're Special Forces," Cassie informs Cal. "I've dealt with them before. They play by different rules."

"I see," Cal replies absently, studying the soldiers again in awe.

As they draw nearer to the complex and the arena's main entrances, the troops on the ground increase in number, as do the dead bodies littering their path. All the troops move out of Locke's path, giving him a wide berth. None of them dare to hinder the Special Forces sergeant's progress as he steps around and over the corpses in his way.

Cal concentrates on keeping pace with Locke, trying to ignore the mutilated bodies he must traverse. Inevitably, he finds himself peering into the eyes of the dead faces on the ground, praying that he doesn't find himself locking eyes with Chief Arnold's gruesome remains.

"Shocking, isn't it?" Cassie says from beside Cal.

Cal can't bring himself to answer her. He is too traumatised to speak and they haven't even got inside the complex yet. He can only imagine how badly things deteriorated after they managed to escape and the horrors that will be waiting inside.

"This way," Locke orders over his shoulder.

Cal follows without question and is relieved to realise that they aren't being led towards the main entrances of the arena. Locke is heading right, passing the main entrances and taking them towards another unknown destination. Cal isn't sure where they are going but surely anywhere will be better than the carnage in the main foyer?

Circling around the side of the complex, Locke stops suddenly when he reaches an open door with an emergency exit sign above it.

"This is the stairway up. We've cleared it, but it's not pretty inside, so be prepared," Locke informs them, repositioning his rifle as though he might expect trouble.

Locke's men tense up, ready to follow their leader inside. Cal feels their tension, reaches inside his jacket and pulls out his Glock from his shoulder holster. Cassie doesn't need an invitation; her sidearm is already gripped between her two hands.

Locke steps through the breach, followed by one of his men. Cal allows Cassie in next before following her, with the remaining two men at his rear. The stairwell is well lit but that does little to stop the feeling of dread Cal feels rising as he enters the enclosed area.

The walls seem to close in as Locke starts to climb. The first flight of steps is clear and they follow Locke around to the next. Cal sees the blood splatters on the next flight of steps almost immediately. He knows they are a precursor to the horror awaiting them as they climb higher and he doesn't have to wait long before he sees the first mangled corpse.

Just around the next corner, a broken body is draped over the steps above. Locke steps over it without a pause, his rifle pointed forward, searching for danger. Cal reaches the body and carefully chooses his way over it. The young man's face is filled with pain although Cal can see no sign of torn flesh, suggesting it was a fall that extinguished the lad's life rather than the teeth of the undead.

More bodies follow, one after the other, their numbers increasing the higher they climb. Male and female bodies are entwined on the steps as they move. Some show no signs of blood trauma, but others have their necks torn apart or lumps of flesh ripped from other points on their upper bodies. Each of these bodies also sports bullet wounds. All of them have been shot in the head at least once as the battle moved into the complex.

Locke and his colleague who is leading the way take extra precautions not to disturb a body dressed in a military uniform as they circumvent it. The dead soldier has flesh wounds to his face and neck, together with a single bullet wound in his head. Cal wonders if one of the men escorting them had the thankless task of firing that bullet. It's a horrible feeling that Cal knows all too well.

Nobody utters a word as they climb, even the hardened Special Forces soldiers are stunned into stony silence by the grim spectacle. They concentrate on scanning for danger while Cal concentrates on keeping his stomach down and not falling into despair.

Locke takes them around another corner and visibly slows his progress as he does, moving more deliberately, his focus down the sights of his automatic rifle. He keeps moving steadily forward though and Cal soon sees why he is taking extra precautions. A door stands open into the complex, raising the threat level. Cal guesses that it is the same level as the security room they visited earlier, at the top of the escalators.

Locke's comrade covers the opening while Locke leads Cal and Cassie past the open door and onto the next flight of steps. There is a wide concourse on the other side of the door. It is littered with bodies and the walls are pockmarked with bullet holes. Cal sees many more bodies in military uniforms lying on the ground in amongst the civilian bodies, too many to count. The battle to clear the complex was bloody and extremely costly.

Past the open door things become easier and the body count reduces to almost zero. Progress becomes quicker and, only a few flights up, Locke comes to a stop next to another door. After looking over his shoulder to make sure everyone is accounted for, he knocks three times against the wooden panel.

The moment the third knock sounds there is a clunking noise and the door swings open. On the other side of the door, a face appears behind the muzzle of a rifle and below a combat helmet. The relief on the young soldier's face when he sees that the people knocking still have blood pumping through their veins is obvious, although whether the undead would knock politely is another question.

Locke visibly relaxes slightly when he sees the soldier guarding the door and takes them through.

"Any developments?" Locke asks the young trooper as he passes.

"Nothing, Sarge. All quiet on the home front," the young man replies enthusiastically.

"Well don't expect it to stay that way, fuckwit," Locke growls. "Keep your guard up!"

Any notion that the young soldier had of impressing the fearsome Special Forces sergeant is blown apart by Locke, who saunters past, unimpressed. To add insult to injury, one of Locke's men laughs and slaps the poor lad on the chest, telling him to "Keep up the good work" as he arrives. *Tough love*, Cal decides, as Locke's three colleagues stop to tease the young soldier further while Locke continues to lead them on.

The door leads out into a fairly narrow corridor which Cal assumes leads to their destination: the complex's ventilation system.

"That was horrific," Cassie says, as they follow Locke.

"Worse than I was expecting," Cal agrees.

"I suddenly miss the office," Cassie replies.

"I think we're going to have to get used to it," Cal points out.

"I'll never get to that point," Cassie argues.

"Let's hope we don't have to," is all Cal can think to reply.

There are several adjoining corridors that Locke ignores as he passes them. Cal, on the other hand, peers down each length with suspicion, half expecting to see zombified monsters waiting to pounce. *Relax*, he tells himself, *the area is obviously secure, or Locke would be taking more care and his men wouldn't have stayed behind at the fire exit entrance.* Cal sees Cassie also eyeing each one nervously, but Locke still appears unconcerned.

Finally, Locke looks left into an opening and makes a turn and Cal and Cassie follow him round and immediately see a team of four people ahead. The people are military personnel, their green, camouflaged attire tells them that much, and two of the personnel are dressed in light-green plastic bodysuits, suggesting that this is a military biohazard team.

"I'll wait for you here," Locke says, stopping well short of the people further down the corridor, as if they were lepers.

"Thank you, Sergeant," Cal says, as he passes Locke.

Cal approaches the team with trepidation after Locke's seeming reluctance to take them any further. He glances back over his shoulder to see the sergeant with his back against the corridor wall, lighting a cigarette. The sight stirs a deep craving in Cal's lungs, but he resists the temptation and heeds the 'No Smoking' signs that are mounted on all the surrounding walls.

"Detective Chambers, I presume," a voice says, diverting Cal's attention away from his craving.

"Yes," he replies to the man dressed in a plastic suit with its hood draped down his back.

"Good. We've been waiting for you. I'm Major Doctor Patel and this is my assistant, Lieutenant Doctor Bergman," Patel says, as the woman next to him, who is also dressed in a plastic suit, nods her greeting.

"I'm pleased to meet you. This is my partner, Agent Sutton," Cal replies.

"Excellent. Shall we proceed?" Patel asks. "I think time is of the essence."

"By all means, Doctor," Cal agrees, hoping he is referring to Patel by his correct title.

"Will you both be joining us?" Patel asks.

"If that's acceptable," Cal replies.

"We have two extra suits. So yes, that's acceptable," Patel agrees.

Approximately ten minutes later, Cal and Cassie are encased inside the biohazard suits, as are Patel and his assistant. Patel has given them clear instructions on how the suits work and a list of dos and don'ts as the suits were fitted. His instructions were quite simple. They basically have 30 minutes of air in the small oxygen tanks the suits are fitted with. Thirty minutes in which to do their work.

Cal looks over at Cassie, whose face looks back at him through the large, clear-plastic front of her hood. She gives him a nervous smile. It appears that even her extensive experience in the field has fallen short of donning a biohazard suit.

"Follow me," Patel's voice sounds through the built-in communication device in the suit's hood.

Cal bends down to pick up his holdall, which contains the forensic equipment he might need to check for evidence in the release system's vicinity. The rubber gloves on his hands aren't as cumbersome as he first thought they would be, but the real test will come when he is handling the equipment.

Patel and Bergman pass the other two support staff they have with them, who are also now wearing suits, and head towards an adjacent door. Patel made it very clear that the conditions are not entirely ideal for handling such delicate material but, under those conditions, their precautions would have to suffice.

The speakers in Cal's hood go quiet as they move. There is only a faint hiss of air feeding into the suit to keep him company as he approaches the door. Now he understands why Locke decided to keep his distance from proceedings and enjoy a cigarette instead. Another pang of nicotine craving hits Cal as he follows Cassie through the door.

The area inside opens out into a large industrial-type room, with pipes and machines positioned around the walls. Patel seems to know where he is going and takes them straight across to a wide pipe that emerges out of the floor and crosses the room horizontally before disappearing into a wall.

"This is the release system," Patel's voice announces as he steps aside.

On the floor next to the pipe is a contraption no bigger than a business-type briefcase. The system appears to have a round chamber, which Cal assumes held the gas or whatever the contaminant was, with what might possibly be a small pump below the tank. The entire apparatus looks to be made of black plastic, including a pipe that protrudes from the round tank and has been inserted into the ventilation pipe at the other end through a crudely drilled hole.

"We will leave you to do your investigations before we remove the system," Patel announces, moving further to the side.

"Thank you," Cal replies, setting the holdall on the ground, ready to open.

"What do you want me to do?" Cassie asks.

"Can you search the surrounding area for anything that might have been discarded or left behind by whoever put this here?" Cal replies. "Put anything into one of these evidence bags using these."

Cal hands Cassie the bags and a pair of small tweezer-like tongs out of the holdall to use to handle any evidence she finds. He also gives her a small torch and a UV lamp to use. He doesn't need to explain to her what to use them for. Cassie takes the equipment and goes about her work.

Cal concentrates on the release system itself and the area immediately around it. He searches for anything on the floor around the system that might be considered evidence. He uses another pair of tweezers to pick up a few bits of fluff and hair that could hold clues for the labs to investigate but he doesn't find anything too exciting. He then moves on to the system itself, but he finds even less that could be considered evidence. His specialist UV lamp and other paraphernalia from his holdall show no fingerprints to cling on to in hope, and no other bodily fluids that might offer a clue. All he identifies is a few fibres of material that have probably been left behind by the bag the system was transported in. He places the fibres into evidence bags but holds no hope that they will prove significant to the investigation.

After double-checking his process, Cal is satisfied that he hasn't missed anything. He puts his equipment and the meagre pieces of evidence into the holdall and stands up.

"Thank you, Doctor. I've finished," Cal says, looking at the two doctors standing nearby.

"Are you sure?" Patel replies.

"Yes. It's all yours," Cal confirms.

Cassie arrives back at Cal's side with her findings, which don't amount to anything more significant than those Cal has identified. She hands over a few evidence bags containing some fibres and hairs, and another with several cigarette butts in it. Cal guesses that the only evidence they will find on the cigarette butts is that the security guard they met earlier was smoking in a restricted area. The guard will have to be brought in to provide a saliva sample... If he is still alive, Cal suddenly realises.

With their job done, Cal and Cassie watch the two military doctors do their work. They take even less time to pull the pipe out of the ventilation duct and to lift the release system off the floor to place it into a containment bag. Once inside the first bag, they put that inside a second bag for good measure and then apply silver duct tape across the closed zipped opening as an extra precaution.

After the release system is secured, Patel produces a canister from his holdall and proceeds to spray the area with the canister's contents. He pays particular attention to the hole in the ventilation duct, spraying all around it and giving a good blast of spray into the hole itself. Cal assumes that the spray is some kind of disinfectant. Not the type you can buy from your local supermarket, he is sure of that, and he's relieved to be enclosed in his bio-suit as the vapour from the canister spreads.

"Are you ready?" Patel asks, when the canister has emptied its contents.

"Yes, Doctor. We've finished," Cal confirms.

"Can you please give me the evidence bags you need to keep and leave everything else here?" Patel asks, taking Cal by surprise.

"Why?" Cal asks.

"Contamination, Detective. Anything we've touched or taken could be contaminated with the contagion," Patel answers. "We will take the evidence and give it to Disease Control with the release system. We cannot risk taking the evidence out without it being decontaminated."

"But we need to process the evidence," Cal protests.

"I understand that, Detective, but not at the risk of spreading the disease. I'm sure you understand," Patel insists, as he takes another containment bag out of his holdall. "This room and the arena below will need to be decontaminated."

Reluctantly, Cal reaches into the holdall and takes out the evidence bags they have filled. He then throws the holdall onto the floor before placing the evidence bags into the small containment bag Patel holds open for him.

"Thank you, Detective. I'm sure Disease Control will work with you to get this evidence processed," Patel assures, as he seals his bag.

With that, Patel moves towards the exit, he too leaving his holdall behind. Between the four of them, all that they carry are two containment bags. Cal realises that the doctor is correct in taking his precautions, he sees that now.

"You two first," Patel says, referring to Cal and Cassie, "but one at a time. You will be decontaminated on the other side of the door."

Before Cal can let Cassie proceed first, she pushes him back towards the exit door. *There is obviously little time for chivalry in her book*, Cal thinks, as he finds himself on the other side of the door and back in the corridor.

Cal is shocked by his greeting and becomes disorientated for a moment. A metre or so outside the exit, Patel's two support staff wait in their bio-suits holding something in their hands, like executioners. Before Cal can regain his wits, a cloud of gas envelops him entirely. He stumbles backwards away from the threat, hitting the door behind him. He finds himself holding his breath for dear life as his vision becomes completely impaired by the thick vapour, which shows no sign of abating.

Breathe, you idiot, he tells himself, as his reasoning returns and he realises that he is being decontaminated and that his suit is still providing oxygen for him. Cal finally relaxes somewhat and lets the process take its course. Eventually, his vision outside his protective hood begins to return but, just as he thinks that the process is over, hands begin to move vigorously over his body. He manages to remain relaxed as the two support staff wipe his bio-suit down completely, leaving no nook or cranny untreated. He winces as his crown jewels are given the same vigorous treatment.

With his vision now returned, save for a misty haze in the air, Cal sees the two staff step back away from him when their task is complete. They discard the large material wipes, which are probably soaked in some chemical or other, into a waiting, open containment bag.

"Please step outside the curtain, remove your suit and then pass it back to us," Cal is ordered through the speaker in his hood.

Curtain? What curtain? Cal asks himself in confusion. Then he sees it: a clear-plastic curtain behind the two support staff. Only then does Cal realise that he is actually standing in a plastic decontamination-tent structure that the two support staff must have erected while he and Cassie were inside the ventilation room.

Cal does as he's told and moves past the two staff. On the other side of the curtain, Cal finds the zip to his suit and pulls it all the way open so that he can step out of it. Once extracted from the suit, he passes it back through the curtain, where it is taken from him.

"Please use the wipes to wipe off your hands," a muffled voice bellows from beyond the curtain.

While he waits for Cassie to have her decontamination assault and to appear through the curtain, Cal wipes down his hands deliberately. He doesn't need to be told to take his time to ensure that his hands are clean. The constant medical advice given during the recent COVID pandemic has instilled that necessity in everyone's psyche.

Through the clear-plastic curtain, Cal can see a blurred vision of Cassie receiving her treatment. He wonders if she was as taken aback as he was when she arrived on the other side of the door. If she was, she doesn't show it when she arrives at his side of the curtain and goes through the same process as he did, extracting herself from her bio-suit. Cal stands well back and lets her get on with it. There is no need to risk cross-contamination.

"I wasn't expecting that," Cassie says, as she turns round after passing her bio-suit back through the curtain. "You could have warned me."

"What, and spoil the fun for you?" Cal smiles.

"You've got a twisted idea of fun," Cassie replies, taking a handful of wipes to clean her hands.

"It's not the first time I've been told that," Cal retorts.

"I'm sure it isn't," Cassie smirks. "Where's Sergeant Locke?"

"I'm not sure," Cal replies, turning, having not realised that he has disappeared from the end of the corridor.

"We need to get back to Mercury House," Cassie says, picking up her jacket. "There's no point hanging around here. We can't take the evidence with us anyway."

"I'm sure he'll be back in a minute. He's probably gone to relieve himself," Cal replies.

"Not very professional if he has," Cassie points out, as Doctor Bergman appears through the plastic curtain.

"Maybe it couldn't wait," Cal wonders.

"I hope you're right, but I don't like it," Cassie replies, the tension in her voice obvious.

"Is everything okay?" Bergman asks, taking her wipes.

"Our escort seems to have disappeared, Lieutenant," Cal replies.

"These Special Forces' types are a law unto themselves. Major Patel will find out what's going on when he's through," Bergman assures.

Moments later, Patel arrives through the curtain, carrying the two containment bags with him, and goes through the same procedure as the rest of them after putting the bags down. He is followed through by the other two members of staff and all three simply throw their suits back through the curtain. The curtain is then sealed closed and a warning sign is stuck across the opening.

"Where is Sergeant Locke?" Patel asks without prompting.

"We were about to ask you the same question!" Cassie replies.

"Bloody Special Forces!" Patel growls angrily. "Pass me the radio," he orders.

Bergman picks up a radio from one of the equipment cases and goes to hand it to Patel. Just as Patel reaches for the radio, Locke bursts into the corridor.

"Drop everything!" Locke shouts. "We're evacuating. NOW!"

Cal and Cassie look at each other with fear etched on their faces. Neither can believe that they are in the arena again and about to go back into battle with the undead.

Chapter 6

"What is going on, Sergeant?" Patel asks calmly, as Locke grinds to a halt.

"I've just heard that our right flank has been overrun. A wave of zombies is coming back this way," Locke barks in reply.

"Gather our things," Patel tells Bergman.

"Fuck your things, Major! We're going... now," Locke shouts, taking Major Patel aback.

"Grab the two containment bags, Lieutenant Bergman," Patel orders, despite Locke's instructions.

"Major..." Locke growls.

"Hold your station, Sergeant. That is an order!" Patel cuts Locke off. "We cannot afford to leave the evidence behind."

Cal watches on. *Patel is right and it won't take a second to grab the two containment bags*, he decides, as he pulls his Glock from its holster.

"With me, Cal," Cassie shouts.

Cal turns to see Cassie heading back up the corridor, her gun held by her side at the ready. Cal understands immediately that she is going to take up a defensive position at the end of the corridor. A wise precaution and he moves to back her up.

Cassie reaches the end of the corridor and immediately takes up a defensive position at the corner with the main run down to the emergency exit where they entered. Her back is against the wall, her head looks around the corner and her gun is gripped in both hands near her chest, ready to bring it to bear at the first sign of danger.

"What can you see?" Cal asks urgently, as he arrives by her side.

"Nothing much. The men by the stairs have formed a defensive perimeter. It looks like they're expecting trouble," Cassie answers.

"I can hear gunfire outside," Cal points out nervously.

"Yes, I've heard it. It's constant," Cassie replies.

Cal scoots across to the other side of the corridor so that he can see without disturbing Cassie. His sidearm is next to his right thigh, pointing at the ground, as he takes a look down their exit route. Locke's men all have their rifles poised as they defend the opening to the stairs, two rifles aiming directly at the stairs beyond. The young trooper that they'd met guarding the door has joined them. He looks nervously first in one direction and then the other.

"On me," Locke orders, as he glides past Cal and Cassie, his rifle across his chest.

Cal follows Cassie as she joins the rush to follow Locke. Cal sees that both Major Patel and Lieutenant Bergman are each carrying a containment bag. Patel's rank gives him the prerogative to overrule Locke. Cal would prefer to see weapons in their hands right now, if he is honest with himself, rather than the evidence.

"Report," Locke demands from his men as he approaches them.

"Nothing yet, Sarge. Two extraction helicopters are inbound, ETA five minutes," he is told by the man nearest the stairs.

"Okay, let's move. Atkins and Bubba, you lead us down," Locke orders and the two men nearest the stairs immediately step forward. "On the double and check your blind spots," Locke adds.

Before the men have taken their second step, gunfire erupts from the rifle of the soldier on the left, the man Locke referred to as Bubba. Bubba doesn't stop or look for congratulations when his rifle stops firing. Instead, he presses forward. Cal didn't see what Bubba fired at. His aim was downwards, but he can imagine Bubba's bullets ripping into the undead target.

Almost instantly, more bullets erupt, bringing progress to a stop again. Cal aims his Glock at the stairs, ready to fire, as he wonders how many creatures are coming up at them. The sinking feeling in his gut tells him there are too many and they haven't even reached the first step down yet. How are they possibly going to make it outside and then to the waiting helicopters?

Locke obviously has the same concern but, instead of wondering about it, he acts.

"Grenade," Locke shouts, as a metal lever springs into the air and Locke's arm throws the grenade down the stairs.

Cal almost panics. He has never been in the vicinity of an exploding grenade, much less one in such an enclosed space. He dives against the wall on his left, hoping that the doorframe and wall will give him some protection. For a moment he feels embarrassment rising inside him. Has he overreacted in front of all these battle-hardened soldiers? His embarrassment is forgotten when he sees Major Patel land against the wall next to him and Cassie dives to the floor on the opposite side.

Cal's thoughts are totally obliterated a second later when the explosion hits with unimaginable ferocity. He ducks his head in reflex, his arms moving over his head as the wall and the very floor below his feet shudder as the boom of the grenade bellows up from the stairwell. Moments later, smoke and dust billow out from the door next to him to sting his eyes and choke his lungs. He trembles against the wall, feeling as though the building is collapsing in on him.

Through his ringing ears, Cal hears a shout, an order. His stinging eyes gush water, blurring his vision. He blinks to try to clear his vision, his hand moving to wipe away the water and dust. He manages to see something; he blinks again and his vision clears enough to see the Special Forces men ready to move. None of the men have moved from their positions to take cover from the blast. They stayed where they damn well were, prepared to face the onslaught and to be ready to move as soon as the explosion dissipates.

"Move!" the order comes again.

Cal forces himself off the wall, his legs wobbly beneath him. The smoke and dust thin and he sees Cassie scrambling to get to her feet, as all the medical staff are to one degree or another. Cal manages to reach her and he grabs her arm to try to help her up.

"I've got it," she tells him, as she finds her feet.

"Move forward!" a voice barks from behind Cal and a hand shoves him towards the entry to the stairs.

Cal doesn't protest at being shoved. He understands that they are in the hands of the professionals. The Special Forces team are their only chance of making it to the safety of the helicopters. He stumbles forward, dragging Cassie with him, her hand held tightly in his left hand and his Glock in his right, held just as tightly.

Gunfire sounds from the stairwell. It rings up from below and out of sight, assaulting Cal's ears. The shots cause him to duck again in reflex, as do Major Patel and his team, who have wound up in front of Cal and Cassie. Even through the smoke, which is beginning to clear, Cal sees the fear on their faces, the same fear that burns inside him.

"Keep moving forward!" a voice bellows from behind Cal and he suddenly realises that it is Locke shouting the orders, that it is the sergeant who is now bringing up the rear.

The people in front of him begin to descend the stairs and Patel forces his way to the head of them, just behind the heavily armed men leading them down. More shots ring out and Cal hears grizzly sounds of undead creatures just beneath the din of the gunfire. He has no idea how many beasts are attacking. He doesn't want to know, even though he knows he must face them.

Still Locke pushes them forward, not letting them fall behind his men, who are creating a pathway down. The gunfire is almost constant and Cal imagines the flood of creatures piling through the door at the bottom of the stairs that lead outside. They follow Patel and his team down and around the first corner, where bodies begin to appear on the stairway, mutilated bodies blasted apart by the grenade's frightening explosion.

"Watch your footing," Cal warns Cassie, who has retrieved her hand from his grip so that she can take full control of her weapon with both hands.

Cassie doesn't acknowledge Cal's warning. Her concentration is fixed ahead, on where the danger is. Her eyes search as they keep descending and approach the doorway that leads to the arena's higher concourse. Cal sees the change of light in the stairwell, caused by the opening that Locke's men have passed to continue down, just out of Cal's sight.

The light coming from the concourse changes subtly just as Patel's team draw level with the open doorway. Cal only just notices it but something in his gut warns him of danger and he slows his descent.

"Cassie," Cal says urgently, but she doesn't respond. "Cassie!"

"What?" Cassie replies impatiently, turning to scowl at Cal.

Cassie's back is facing the doorway when the creature flies through the opening, appearing as an apparition at first. As the beast slams into one of Patel's support staff, just below Cassie, any notion that the creature isn't real crumbles to dust as the ear-splitting scream that erupts from the woman dispels any lingering doubt.

Behind Cal, Locke moves to intercept the enemy almost instantly, knocking into Cal as he moves. Cal himself is trying to bring his Glock to bear on the creature but the woman's head is the only target he finds. The creature is attacking her from the other side, out of his range.

Cassie's face is a picture of confusion when Locke barges past her, knocking her sideways and against the adjacent wall. Cal's aim is obliterated when Locke lands on top of the woman and the creature, with seemingly no concern for his own safety. Locke hits the pair hard, knocking them off their feet sideways and they slam into the ground, landing across the doorway's threshold.

Blood splatters across the floor as the woman and creature land together. The creature has already torn into the woman's flesh, and her fate is sealed. Locke lands expertly on his feet next to them, ready to make his next move, his compact rifle clutched at the ready. The creature flails wildly to separate itself from the woman, who is stunned and in shock. Locke makes his move before Cal can even steady himself to bring his gun to bear on the threat again. Cal watches on in awe as Locke springs into the air, landing on the ground next to the creature's head. His boot slams down onto the creature's throat as his free hand whips out a combat knife. In a flash, Locke swipes the knife through the air in a downward motion. The knife's blade cracks through the top of the creature's skull, disappearing up to its grip.

Instantly, the creature's body goes limp, its threat extinguished, but Locke doesn't finish there. He knows what must be done next. Cal sees the anguish on his face as Locke slides the knife out of the creature's head. Cal moves to cover the tormented soldier as he wipes the blood from the knife across the clothes on the beast's body. Locke slides the knife away on his hip, deciding to use his rifle for his next kill.

Locke's bullet kills the infected, suffering woman instantly. The woman may not have been Special Forces, or even familiar to Locke, but she was a soldier, a comrade, and Cal feels Locke's pain as he fires on his sister in arms. Cal knows the hideous feeling all too well and a vision of Matt flashes sadly through his head.

Gunfire echoes from below, pulling all of them out of their turmoil, which will have to wait for another time.

"Move out," Locke orders, turning to cover the concourse beyond the doorway, in case another attack comes.

Major Patel is nowhere to be seen. He has made his escape from the attack and Lieutenant Bergman must have followed him. Cassie nods at Cal to indicate she's okay as she heads down the next flight of stairs, with Cal right behind her. Cal keeps an eye out for Locke and sees him pull his rifle in and move to follow as soon as Cal reaches the next turn.

In front of Cassie, the other member of Patel's medical support staff stumbles on the steps. The man is clearly shaken by the attack on his partner. Cassie grabs his shoulder to try to steady him as more shots ring out, the sound deafening as it ricochets around the enclosed space.

In front of them, Cal sees that Patel didn't escape far. The doctor stands trembling on the steps just around the next (and last) corner, with Bergman by his side. Just below them is the exit from the stairwell and the open ground of the complex beyond it. Taking cover around the doorway are Locke's men. All of them are searching for the enemy with their rifles and looking longingly into the night sky for their escape route: the helicopters.

"Atkins, Ken, cover the rear," Locke orders, as he pushes past on the stairs.

One of the men swivels away from his position to do as he's ordered and Cal lets him pass. The other pauses for a second and releases a salvo of bullets as Locke arrives and taps him on the shoulder. Feeling Locke's tap, the man brings in his rifle and rises to follow the first man to cover the rear.

"Anything?" Cal hears Locke ask Bubba, who remains covering the door.

"They're out there, Sarge, in the darkness, but no sign of the transport," Bubba replies, as Locke aims his rifle out beyond the stairwell.

"They'll be here any time now, so be ready to move," Locke says confidently.

To the sound of fighting and gunshots outside, they wait. Cal hopes that Locke is right and that the transport will arrive at any moment. Patel obviously wishes for the same. He hasn't moved from his position on the stairs and looks petrified, ready to lose his shit at any moment. Bergman next to him looks fearful too, but not as shit-scared as Patel.

"In the sky at eleven o'clock, Sarge," Bubba announces.

"I see them," Locke confirms. "Be ready to move on my order," he barks over his shoulder to them all.

"Stay with me," Cassie says calmly to Cal, glancing up at him.

Cal hears the now-familiar sound of helicopters approaching through the doorway and above the sound of gunshots. He prepares himself to move, his hand gripped tightly around his Glock as apprehension churns his belly. They will need to fight to reach the helicopters and they stand with one dead already, after only descending the stairs.

"Get ready!" Locke barks over his shoulder to everyone, reaching for a grenade that is attached to his combat vest.

Cal sees Locke point at something outside the door, speaking to Bubba as he does. Cal cannot hear what is said, the sound of approaching helicopters and gunfire muffling the words. Bubba nods his head and takes hold of a grenade himself, readying himself for action. Cal switches to the other side of the stairwell to try to see outside, to try to see what is waiting for them.

From the partial view of the scene outside that Cal does manage to obtain, all he learns is that it is totally dark, apart from the flashes of light from the battle taking place out there. He has no view of what Locke was pointing at and decides to move forward to a position behind Locke and Bubba to give himself a better angle. Just as he arrives, a bright light illuminates the darkness and, as gusts of wind arrive to blast the ground, the helicopters come in to land. Cal's stomach drops as the light shows him what is waiting for them outside. Creatures are out in the open, with more appearing from a treeline straight ahead.

"Atkins, Ken, we're moving," Locke shouts. "Form a perimeter."

The two men guarding the rear move back down the stairs, shepherding Major Patel, his team and Cassie down with them. Cassie looks at Cal anxiously as she arrives. He tries to give her a reassuring smile but knows that he has failed miserably.

"Stay together," Locke orders in the moment before he and Bubba move out into the open.

Upon leaving the shelter of the stairwell, both Locke and Bubba heave grenades into the air, their target the treeline from where the zombie attack is coming. As soon as the grenades are released, their rifles are up and firing at the creatures already out in the open.

Cal follows the two Special Forces men out, his own gun up and ready for action, but he doesn't know where to look first. Ahead of them, the grenades explode, ripping into the treeline, but a safe distance away. Light pours over the scene of chaos for a moment, illuminating the creatures that have escaped the explosions. Locke and Bubba's rifles fire on those creatures continuously and, behind them, Atkins and Ken open up on targets.

Away to the right, two helicopters hover off the ground at a safe height from the battle below, but ready to land. Cal looks for the other soldiers who are fighting and sees muzzle flashes in the distance on the far right of the grounds, in front of the arena complex. The only fighting in their vicinity is being done by Locke and his men. The other soldiers must have been pushed back.

Locke keeps them moving, undeterred by the odds against them, and keeps firing. Creatures are all around and closing in, drawn closer by the movement, gunfire and the scent of fresh meat. Cal fires his first shot at a creature that appears in between the four men forming the stretched perimeter. The bullet hits the beast in its snarling mouth. Teeth shatter and blood sprays from the dark cavern. The creature's head explodes and it hits the ground out of sight.

Next to him, Cal hears Cassie's gun fire a second before he is hit hard from behind. With no idea of what's hit him, Cal falls forward and out of the perimeter. Unable to save himself from falling, terror overwhelms him. Another body falls next to him and something squirms on top of him. In total panic, Cal twists and turns to try and fight off whatever is on top of him. He waits for the pain as the inevitable teeth slice into him.

Cassie stumbles as she is knocked, her feet scrambling to keep her upright. Cal and Bergman fly forward and hit the ground. The creature is on top of Cal. Cassie panics, bringing her gun up instantly and firing into the creature's body. There is no headshot for her to take as Cal fights underneath the creature to free himself. He twists and turns violently as Cassie sees another shot to the body and takes it. The bullet smashes into the beast's ribs and, together with Cal's writhing, it falls off Cal's back, ending up face to face with Bergman, who is stunned on the ground. Cassie rushes to find another shot as Ken, next to her, swivels to bring his rifle around but, in a flash, the creature's head shoots forward. Bergman's eyes bulge in terror when the beast's mouth snaps around her nose and its muscles bite down.

Cassie hears a crunch rise from the ground and vomit threatens to erupt from her stomach. The creature bites through Bergman's nose in an instant and pulls its head back to feverishly take the nostrils into its gullet. She cannot bring herself to look at Bergman, her belly won't allow it. Instead, Cassie concentrates on the beast's face and pulls the trigger on her sidearm. In unison, Ken opens up with his rifle, filling the beast's head with bullets.

On one side of the now limp creature, Cal scrambles to his feet with a look of both shock and relief fixed on his face. On the other side, Bergman's body twists and contorts. Cassie isn't sure if Bergman is squirming in shock and pain or because she has been bitten and is infected. The question is academic. Either way, Bergman is doomed and, thankfully, the Special Forces operator, Ken, comes to the same conclusion. He aims and shoots Bergman twice in the head, putting her out of her misery, a misery that would have only become a living nightmare. Cassie sees Bergman's nose-less face as the bullets kill her. She doesn't feel sickness any longer at the awful sight, just relief that it wasn't her who had to shoot the poor woman.

"You're okay, Cal," Cassie assures as she grabs Cal by his arm to pull him back into the fold.

Cal doesn't answer her and Cassie continues to keep hold of him. Locke doesn't pause for a moment. He continues on, pressing closer to the landing area. It is up to them to keep pace, whatever happens, and Cassie pulls Cal back into formation with her.

"Where is Bergman?" Cassie hears Patel squeal as the formation is restored.

Cassie ignores the major's pathetic question. She is positive that Patel saw Bergman and Cal go down, but it didn't stop him from clinging onto the coat-tails of Locke. There was no thought to see if he could help his doomed assistant. Cassie knows Patel is playing stupid to try to mask his cowardice. *Fuck him*, Cassie thinks, *he's nothing but a scared little weasel.*

Locke carries them on, his rifle firing constantly. He pushes them right to the very edge of the landing area. The downdraft from the two helicopters that finally begin to land does nothing to deter creatures from attacking. Locke's men take no prisoners; their skill with their weapons is awesome. Every vicious creature that dares approach their position is despatched without mercy. Thankfully, the grenades that exploded by the treeline stemmed the tide of beasts for a time, but that time has now ended, Cal sees, as his disorientation after the attack on him dissipates.

As the helicopters drop to the ground, a new wave of the undead begins to appear out of the treeline. The creatures surge towards the noise of the helicopters and their position. They fight amongst themselves as they clamour to fulfil the promise of slaking their gnawing hunger but, still, they close in fast.

"On to the helicopters!" Locke bellows above the din.

Major Patel doesn't need to be told twice and runs for the closest aircraft, the last remaining member of his staff scrambling behind him. Cassie doesn't hold back either, but she steers clear of the major and sprints for the other helicopter, which has landed metres away to the right. There is no choice for Cal and he chases after Cassie, letting the Special Forces men continue to cover them.

At the hold door, one of the helicopter's aircrew is positioned. He doesn't offer Cassie a hand into the hold on this occasion though. He kneels on one knee with a rifle in his hands. The weapon is aimed and ready to open fire to cover their retreat should it be needed. That doesn't hinder Cassie from launching herself at the helicopter and climbing in at speed. Cal is inside just as fast and he turns immediately with his Glock at the ready to help cover the Special Forces' retreat.

The men split apart from each other, two going for each aircraft. They don't turn and run, however, instead they move backwards, deliberately facing the enemy and continuing to fire. The two men aiming for the other helicopter arrive and load on first and, as soon as they do, the helicopter's rotors power and it lifts straight up.

Locke and Atkins close in on the second aircraft as the wave of undead creatures arrives in the area vacated by the other helicopter. Next to Cal, gunfire erupts as the crewman fires to help cover the approaching men. Cal follows suit, just as Locke and Atkins turn to board.

"Cleared for lift-off," the crewman shouts the moment Locke's feet leave the ground and he's pulled on-board by Atkins.

Cal grabs onto the closest handrail as the pilot rapidly takes them up and off the ground, seconds before the horde of zombies reach their position. Cal watches as the closest creatures launch themselves into the air in a futile attempt to catch their prey, their animal instinct unrelenting.

Quickly, the ground drops away, leaving Cal to watch the horde of zombified creatures go berserk as their prey rises out of reach. Vicious fighting breaks out as frustration replaces their hunger. Bodies are littered on the ground in front of the arena complex and whether they are infected or not, they were all human souls only recently. Cal feels deep sorrow for all of the fallen as his view changes when the pilot manoeuvres onto his flight path.

The change of direction alters Cal's view of the turmoil taking place below. To his right, the complex begins to shrink and disappear from view, until muzzle flashes grab his attention instead.

Cal focuses on the fighting taking place towards the perimeter of the complex's grounds, near the shimmering water of the canal skirting them. The fighting is fierce. Cal guesses that the troops down below were taken by surprise by the undead's counterattack. The area was supposed to have been secured and Cal wonders what drew the army of the undead back to the complex.

Cal finds himself staring into the shimmering waters of the canal, almost in a daze, as the events of the day take their toll. He stares at the water, which continues its flow towards the city, and suddenly his concentration focuses again. The water is being disturbed. The light of the moon is being displaced by something in the water. Only after a moment's consideration does Cal decide what is disturbing the water and his realisation is terrifying.

Chapter 7

"Are you okay?" a voice shouts in Cal's face as he falls back from the open hold door, his mind calculating. "Cal… Cal, speak to me. You've had a shock but you're safe now!" Cassie barks into Cal's ear over the din of the helicopter.

Cal ignores Cassie's concern and pushes himself up and into the nearest seat, reaching for a headset as he does. He quickly sees that nobody else is wearing a headset. Everyone is hunched over, busy catching their breaths after their fight to reach safety.

Cassie plonks herself in the seat opposite Cal and Cal waves his arms at her, indicating for her to put a headset on. He leans over to Locke, who is staring at the floor of the helicopter, processing what has happened and breathing heavily. Locke's recovery will have to wait, Cal decides, and he taps the fearsome fighter on the shoulder to get his attention. Locke rises and looks at Cal wearily with an expression on his face that says, *What the fuck now? Haven't I done enough for you?*

Ignoring Locke's look of annoyance, Cal signals for him to also put on a headset. Reluctantly, Locke complies and reaches behind him.

"What is it, Detective?" Locke says tiredly.

"We have a problem," Cal tells him. "We need to go to Gas Street Basin immediately," Cal demands.

"What? Why?" Locke interrupts.

"Cal?" Cassie questions.

"Will you shut up and listen!" Cal shouts in frustration. "They're in the canal," he continues, as silence finally falls over the comms system. "The fighting at the complex has moved near the canal and bodies are in the water. They could be soldiers that have fallen in, but I don't think so. The infected are in the canal."

"How do you know?" Locke asks.

"Because I saw them in the water as we were lifting off," Cal insists.

"But it's dark outside. How could you have seen clearly?" Locke questions.

"The moonlight was reflecting off the water. Do you think I'm making this up, Sergeant?" Cal growls in reply.

"If the infected are in the canal, they could drift into the city," Cassie offers.

"Not could, Cassie. They will!" Cal insists. "They will float towards Gas Street Basin. The canal syphons off through an outlet into the river there and if they manage to climb out of the canal, the basin and the whole city is vulnerable."

"I'll alert my commanding officer," Locke offers. "He will send a unit immediately."

"By all means inform him, Sergeant, and get him to send a unit, but we need to go straight there," Cal insists. "We don't know how long they've been in the water. They could be washing up in the basin already. Inform the pilot of our new destination."

"Let me speak to my commander," Locke replies.

"He's right," Cassie interjects. "If these fucking things are in the canal we need to move to intercept. Tell the pilot to change course. Now!"

As the words come out of Cassie's mouth the floor beneath them tilts and the helicopter changes direction.

"Changing course to Gas Street Basin," a voice says through the helicopter's comms system. "I don't know if I'll be able to land there though," the voice continues, confirming that it's the pilot speaking.

"As fast as you can please, pilot," Cal replies. "We'll worry about landing once we're there."

"Affirmative. ETA three minutes," the pilot confirms.

Locke forgoes any more debate, finally realising the severity of the situation, and gets on his radio to speak to his commanding officer.

"Have you got any heavier weapons on-board?" Cal asks, looking at the crewman, who stands over them gripping an overhead handrail.

Without saying a word, the airman turns to the bulkhead behind him and pulls open a door mounted into it. Behind the door, in a rack, are three automatic rifles, together with one empty space. As he gets up from his seat, Cal assumes that the empty space was previously taken up by the rifle in the crewman's hand.

Cal is unfamiliar with the type of rifles stored in the rack, but he takes one out. After giving it the once-over, he turns and passes it to Cassie, who takes it gratefully. He pulls one out for himself but, just before he goes to return to his seat, he sees a row of ammo magazines stored below the rifles. One of Cal's hands is steadying himself on a handrail so he is forced to put his rifle back before he can help himself to the magazines.

Again, Cassie takes Cal's offerings of magazines gratefully. After stuffing a quantity into his own pockets, he grabs the rifle again and returns to his seat to check over the weapon and to familiarise himself with its function.

"Do you two know how to use them?" Atkins asks suspiciously.

Cal and Cassie look at each other for a second before Cassie answers.

"Don't worry about us, soldier. We have some experience," Cassie replies, with a hint of disdain.

"I'm not worried about you, missy. I'm worried about getting shot by a misfire," Atkins replies, in a condescending but serious manner.

For a moment Cal holds his breath to see how Cassie will react to Atkins' tone and to him calling her 'missy'.

Cassie doesn't rise to the bait, however. Instead, she goes to work on her rifle, releasing the magazine to check it, she then tests the action of the weapon before reinserting the magazine and pulling back the action to load her rifle.

"I see you've played before," Atkins concedes. "Fair enough," he adds.

On the other side of the aircraft, Cal is not as confident with his weapon. He is almost embarrassed when he tries to copy Cassie's performance to check his rifle. He has trouble identifying its functions but clumsily manages to complete his check… eventually. Thankfully, Atkins has lost interest in him and Cassie and has taken to looking out of the window.

"Command is despatching troops to the basin," Locke confirms, following his radio call. "They should arrive just after us."

"I doubt they will be there that quickly," Cassie replies, as the helicopter begins to lose altitude.

"I guess we're in the box seat until they do then," Locke tells Cassie.

"I guess so," she confirms.

"Gas Street Basin is below," the pilot's voice comes over the radio. "Just searching for somewhere to put down."

"There is a small square on the northeast corner near the basin," Cal says, using his extensive knowledge of the city to their advantage. "I think there is room to land."

"I see it. I should be able to squeeze us down inside it," the pilot replies before going silent.

"Did anyone get a look at the water?" Cal asks.

"Negative," Locke replies. "It's too dark down there."

"Crewman, what's your name?" Cal says to the man who is still standing over them.

"Airman Harris. Why?" the young man replies.

"We need you to come with us," Cal replies. "We must defend this position because the consequences would be dire if we don't."

"I can't just leave my position here, Sir. I'd be in trouble," Harris tells Cal.

"I'll take responsibility," Locke announces, giving Harris little option.

"Okay," Harris answers, unsure of himself.

"You'll be fine, bud. Just stick with me," Atkins grins, as the helicopter bumps to the ground.

"Are you alright to wait for us here, pilot?" Cal asks.

"Affirmative. I'll hold position," he confirms. "But take my phone number before you go."

Cal takes the pilot's phone number as the engines above their heads begin to wind down. There are messages on Cal's phone too, which he sees are from Tilly. The news of the attack at the complex must have reached her because she is concerned for their safety. One of the messages also says that they've had a development in the case. Cal can't think about that now: there are more pressing matters. He sends Tilly a quick message to say that they're okay and that they'll discuss the case when they're back. The pilot asks to be kept informed of any developments and tells them he'll be ready to go at a moment's notice if needed. Locke, Atkins and Cassie watch on, waiting, standing to move out as soon as Cal is ready.

"Open it up," Locke tells Harris, who has remained standing by the hold door and now looks decidedly nervous.

"Let's do this, buddy," Atkins tells Harris, as he passes him to jump to the ground.

Atkins, the adrenaline junkie, is relishing the new challenge, unlike Harris, who looks like he wishes he was anywhere else but about to jump out of his comfort zone and into danger. As soon as Atkins' feet touch the ground he goes into a well-drilled routine. His rifle is up and he takes a position away from the now-silent helicopter, with Locke covering their position. Harris follows Atkins down and, to his credit, puts his training into action by joining the Special Forces men to help provide cover as Cal and Cassie disembark the helicopter.

An eerie stillness hangs over the square, which would normally be bustling with people crossing it to head to their chosen destination for the evening. Nobody is out on the town tonight. Apart from the outbreak scaring people away from the bars and restaurants, nothing is open. Everything has been ordered to close apart from essential businesses like shops, and most of those daren't open their doors.

"Do you want to take us in, Detective?" Locke asks. "You know the terrain well by the sounds of it."

"I can do," Cal replies nervously.

"Don't worry, Detective. I'll cover you," Locke insists.

With that assurance, Cal moves past Locke to take the lead. Locke is right, he does know the area well. He used the square as a through road on a regular basis with Mike when they used to move through the city together. Chasing leads or chasing down criminals.

Turning left, Cal takes the team around the rear of the helicopter, which has fitted nicely into the square. Luckily the only trees skirt the outer edge of the square, giving the pilot just enough room to land. The basin is on the other side of a row of buildings just outside the square and down one of the short roads that cut through the buildings.

Gas Street Basin is an important tourist destination for the city. The basin has moorings for long boats and other river boats that people arrive in from the surrounding, adjoining canals and rivers to visit the city. Most remain on their boats for their stay and many are actually homes for the owners. They travel around the country in a nomadic style, whilst other boats are rented for a week or so's holiday. This has meant that a plethora of bars, restaurants and retail outlets have grown around the basin. These draw even more people into the area, normally, giving the basin an exciting vibe and meaning that it can become extremely busy.

Taking one of the exits out of the square, Cal knows that some of the boats currently moored in the basin might be occupied, which raises the stakes. Hopefully, most of the holidaymakers will have cut their moorings and hightailed it out of the city. If they had any sense that's exactly what they should have done.

Checking over his shoulder to ensure that Locke is behind him, Cal takes the nearest road that will take them into the basin. Locke is right behind Cal, his eyes bulging down the body of his rifle, looking for targets. Having such a capable soldier on his shoulder brings Cal a small amount of reassurance. Locke's performance at the complex was formidable.

"Slow down," Locke says under his breath to Cal, as they near the end of the road and boats come into view.

Cal doesn't need telling twice and, in fact, he slows enough for Locke to take over the lead. Cal has shown them the way and now it is his rifle covering Locke's back.

At the end of the road, Locke brings them to a complete halt to scan the basin from behind the cover of the last building. Atkins moves right to the other side of the road to cover that side of the basin. Harris backs him up, sticking with Atkins, just as Atkins had suggested.

"All clear," Locke says, looking over to Atkins on the other side.

Atkins nods his reply to Locke and scampers back across the road to move back into formation, with Harris close behind.

A short distance across from the buildings, past a walkway that runs around the basin, is an edge, with the water and boats a few feet below. Locke moves to the left, to circle around the edge of the basin and towards its main expanse. Cal is anxious to circle around. He must check the water as soon as possible, wanting to know if his suspicions are correct.

Locke stops his progress when he sees Cal break ranks, but he doesn't berate him, he just moves to cover Cal, as does everyone else.

With dread in his stomach, but with the hope that he might be wrong, Cal peers into the water as he nears the edge. The basin is relatively empty of boats. Holidaymakers and nomads alike have taken the opportunity to vacate and to float away from the perilous city. Dark waters stare back at Cal. Seemingly, the moonlight has also vacated the area. It takes a moment for Cal to focus on the black film that moves steadily under the smallest of breezes or when penetrated by a foreign body. After a moment his heart lightens when he sees nothing out of the ordinary, or of concern, in the expanse of water. He begins to feel a bit foolish for making such a fuss about the threat and diverting the helicopter.

"Anything?" Cal hears Cassie ask from behind him and he goes to tell her the good news. Just as he starts to speak something catches his eye. A piece of debris surfaces in the dark water, something that Cal struggles to identify. He keeps watching as it floats closer, the form appearing to change as it bobs in the water. Suddenly, the object morphs in front of Cal's eyes. The object grows in the water as what was hidden below the waterline surfaces and Cal realises in horror that he isn't looking at debris but at the back of a human body. At first, Cal thinks he is imagining the movement he is seeing, but larger ripples begin to disturb the water around the body, leaving him in no doubt that it is moving. Cal's eyes widen when, without warning, an arm rises out of the water, causing the body to rotate, and a hideous face appears above the surface. Cal's heart stops as dead, black eyes stare back at him and the mouth opens, releasing a disturbing hissing sound as it gargles with the water in its gullet.

A hand touches Cal's shoulder, jolting him out of his living nightmare. He turns to see Cassie behind him. Her mouth is moving but he struggles to hear her words through his horror.

"You were right then," Cal finally hears Cassie say.

"Yes, unfortunately," Cal manages to reply. "I can only see one body here. We need to check the rest of the basin, especially around the outlet and the slipway."

"I know, I heard you," Locke tells Cal, when he looks at him. "Let's move."

Locke turns to move out just as a bone-chilling screech echoes in the near distance. Cassie looks at Cal with a knowing look as the sound fades. Her look asks Cal if they should proceed in the face of such danger.

"There's nobody else here to stop them," Cal says, not just to Cassie but to them all.

Locke must agree because he is already pressing forward. Cassie raises her rifle and sets off after him, with rejuvenated determination. Atkins and Harris fall in behind and together they begin to tread the perimeter around the basin. On the right is the water below the stone quayside. Cal doubts that the creatures could climb out from there. The threat will be the wide slipway used to put boats into the water. The slope runs into the water at the far end of the basin. Creatures that arrive there on the tide will be able to literally walk out of the water.

They move deliberately behind Locke. The building and side streets on their left loom threateningly. Should the enemy have already escaped from the basin's waters, they could easily be concealing themselves in the shadows that the buildings provide, biding their time to attack. Locke takes that threat seriously. His rifle glides from one blind spot to another, searching the shadows, as does Cassie's beside him.

Cal trusts in their cover and, instead, he concentrates on the basin's waters and on the haunting silhouettes of boats floating innocently near the quayside. Unlikely as it may be that the creatures could climb out of the water or up onto a boat, Cal has learnt quickly not to take anything for granted. He has learnt to expect the unexpected and that his life may depend on taking appropriate precautions. He sees more ominous things floating in the waters, both near to and far away, but he doesn't linger on them. Seeing the floating horrors once was enough for him. Instead, he searches for anything coming over the edge of the quayside or moving on the nearby moored-up boats and leaves the floating bodies be, at least for now.

Gradually, Locke nears the far side of the basin, where the walkway turns right. He comes to a stop before they turn to regroup. The danger area is approaching where the canal syphons off into the river and the slipway, which is some distance away after the turn. Cal peers across the basin to try to view the slipway, but it is hard to see in the darkness and with the line of sight blocked by boats.

"We have movement," Locke says quietly, his eye fixed down the sights of his rifle.

"On the slipway?" Cal asks.

"On the quayside. I can't see the slipway, but they must be coming up it," Locke replies.

"How many?" Cassie asks.

"I have eyes on at least four," Locke replies.

"We need to stop them moving out into the city," Cal insists.

"Are you suggesting a full-frontal attack, Detective?" Locke questions, still staring down his rifle.

"I don't know what I'm suggesting, Sergeant. I'll defer to you on how we should defend the city," Cal concedes.

"Then we attack," Locke decides instantly. "Harris, cover the rear. Atkins, front and centre."

Atkins leaves Harris behind immediately and joins Locke, taking a knee just in front of Cal. The two men discuss tactics for a moment before Locke issues his orders. Cal hears him order Atkins to take the left flank, on the side of the buildings, while Locke intends to take the right flank, on the basin side.

"Agent Sutton, can you back up Atkins in a covering position while Detective Chambers covers me? We will hit them straight on in a pincer movement. We should deal with the ones we can see easily but we need to get closer and there could be others we can't see from this vantage point," Locke asks, but the question is more of an order than a request.

Atkins and Cassie move low to the cover of the buildings, while Locke begins to stalk forward with Cal in support. Locke aims for a stone bench secured to the quayside, which Cal assumes he intends to use as a firing position. Cal only hopes that Locke can reach it before the creatures notice them.

As they draw closer to the slipway and the congregation of creatures that have made it up the slipway and onto the quayside, Cal begins to see the enemy more clearly. He counts six beasts on the quayside and, from the new angle, he sees another four rising up the slipway. The disturbed water where the slipway disappears into the water suggests that more creatures are trying to drag themselves back onto dry land. If they hadn't arrived to check the area out, untold numbers of the infected could have moved into this part of the city unchallenged.

Locke does stop when he reaches the stone bench and he rests his arm on top of it, his rifle aimed towards the targets. He glances right to see the progress of Atkins and Cassie. Cal follows the direction Locke is looking in and sees that Atkins has also settled on a firing position and is giving Locke the thumbs up, with Cassie just behind him.

Before Cal has even redirected his focus forwards again, Locke's rifle explodes into action, sending a shiver down Cal's back. Across from them gunfire also bursts out, both men having selected their first target. Behind Locke, Cal repositions himself to bring his rifle to bear on the threat as two creatures drop to the ground under the initial burst of gunfire. He tries to catch a beast in the sights of his rifle in the hope of bringing the skirmish to a swift conclusion.

The sudden outburst of noise brings an almost instant reaction from the creatures at the slipway, the sound like an electrical shock to their systems. Locke fires again but Cal doesn't notice if he manages to hit anything. He is too busy concentrating on trying to bring a beast into his own sights but is failing miserably.

Cal looks up from his rifle to try to get a better bearing on the targets and immediately wishes he hadn't. Attracted by the sound of gunfire, the creatures have launched a counterattack of their own.

"Sergeant, they're attacking us. The ones on the slipway are coming too!" Cal warns Locke urgently.

Locke ignores Cal completely for a moment. His total focus is on his weapon and he releases bullets, one after the other. Across the road, both Atkins and Cassie are firing constantly but, from what Cal can see, their rapid fire is having little effect.

"Open fire!" Locke shouts at Cal, in between bursts of fire.

Adrenaline courses through Cal's body as he is called into action. He makes a split-second decision to concentrate his fire on the slipway and the creatures moving up it. Instead of focusing too tightly on one particular creature, Cal opens fire in their general direction, trusting that at least some bullets will find a valid target.

After his first volley, Cal raises his head to see if he has made any difference. Through the darkness, he cannot see if he has hit anything. He doesn't see any bodies on the ground and the beasts still rush to move off the slipway so that they can attack. He fires again, this time aiming for the very top of the slipway where most of the creatures are concentrated. The rifle jolts in his grip and he feels sure that his bullets strike their targets, but the shadows still rise onto the quayside.

"They're still coming," Cal tells Locke urgently, as if he didn't already know, "and more are climbing out of the water."

Locke pauses his onslaught for a moment and pulls a grenade off his combat vest. Cal goes to open fire again to cover Locke while he throws the explosive device.

"Here," Locke shouts. "Pull the pin out and throw it at them," he orders, shoving the grenade at Cal.

Having never held a grenade or even seen one in real life before, Cal hesitates for a spilt second to take the explosive from Locke. *Don't freeze*, his mind screams, *we're fighting for our lives.*

As Cal stands and his hand curls around the grenade, Locke releases it, his hand immediately returning to his rifle, which instantaneously bursts back into life. The grenade is heavier than Cal imagined, but it is compact and will be easy to throw. He sees the pin instantly and rapidly pulls it free using the wire ring at one end. Another metal piece of the grenade instantly springs away from the body and Cal suddenly panics as he realises the grenade is active. Like a hot potato just taken out of a microwave, Cal turns to get the device out of his hand as fast as possible. He sees the target area and launches the grenade into the air, hoping that his aim at the crest of the slipway is well targeted.

As the grenade leaves his hand it becomes lost in the darkness. Cal cannot see its trajectory as it flies through the air. He can only stand gawping, waiting for the inevitable result.

A blinding flash of brilliant light erupts directly above where the slipway meets the quayside. Cal's aim is good but, before he has the chance to congratulate himself, the blast noise from the explosion and its shockwave rush to assault him. Stunned by the ferocity of the blast, Cal falls back to his knees to escape it, his ears ringing.

"Good shot." Locke congratulates him as Cal tries to regather himself and the explosion dissipates.

Before Cal can bask in his glory, Locke is rising from his position and rushing forward. Moving behind his rifle to cover Locke as he uses the diversion to his tactical advantage, Cal realises that he should be up and pressing home the advantage with Locke. Staying behind his rifle, he pushes himself up and goes in pursuit of the Special Forces sergeant.

Across from him, Cal sees Atkins closing in on the target area with Locke, with Cassie close behind him in support. Gunfire blazes from the two men as they press home their advantage and Cal sees creatures fall in their wake. He even fires his own weapon sporadically, his fire aimed now at the lower part of the slipway, where yet more creatures are emerging to get in on the action.

Closing in rapidly now on the slipway, the carnage caused by the explosion and the incessant gunfire begins to become apparent. Cal checks behind to see where Harris is and immediately sees him bringing up the rear and, to his credit, his rifle is aimed behind him, covering the rear as ordered.

Locke and Atkins blitz the quayside and the slipway as they close in on it with awesome efficiency. As a priority, they work in tandem to cut down anything that still stands after the explosion but anything that moves, even the mutilated bodies on the ground, are also peppered with bullets. Cal remains in a supporting position behind Locke, taking potshots himself when he finds a target. The gunfire is controlled and deliberate. Not one bullet is wasted and, when a magazine empties, it is swiftly swopped out with such astonishing skill that it barely hinders their progress. To say that Cal is impressed by the Special Forces operatives' fighting skill is an understatement.

Cal is aware of the carnage he is treading in whilst the fighting is in full flow. It isn't until the last standing zombie's head explodes under Locke's ferocious gunfire and the fighting dies down that he realises the full extent of what is under his boots.

Cal's foot kicks something and he looks down instinctively as the thing spins away from his foot. Even before the piece of flesh and bone stops spinning, Cal sees with horror that the thing is a mangled severed head that the explosion has separated from the owner's neck. He diverts his eyes away from the disgustingly singed and damaged atrocity, hoping that the image doesn't imprint itself on his subconscious. The horror of the head that Cal inadvertently kicked is surrounded by other sights of equally horrific proportions. Wherever Cal's eyes fall there is nothing to ease his disturbance. Horrifically maimed bodies and severed limbs are scattered all around, including a selection of more disgustingly disfigured heads for Cal to fret about. The ground is plastered with blood and fleshy parts that cannot be identified. However, it is the smell that penetrates Cal's being. The stench passes through his lungs, drawing bile into his mouth. Burnt skin and hair poison every breath he takes; he cannot wait to escape the area and to breathe easy again.

"That's the last of them," Atkins states with one final pull of his trigger.

"Stay alert, soldier," Locke orders.

"Always, Sarge," Atkins replies, taking up a covering position.

Atkins stays on his feet. Taking a knee in the gruesome mess surrounding them would have to be a last resort. Harris levitates towards his new best friend, Atkins, but the young airman keeps covering his assigned zone.

"Look," Cassie says, appearing a bit green around the gills herself.

Cassie's eyes are fixed on the disturbed water at the bottom of the slipway. Nobody needs to guess what is disturbing the water: Locke already has his rifle trained on the area.

"Just when you thought it was all over," Cal jokes.

"This is far from over, Detective," Locke replies, not even cracking a smile. "For all we know, these things have already wandered off into the city. The whole area needs to be swept and it needs to be done now!"

"Where are the troops that were promised?" Cassie asks. "Detective Chambers and I can't hang around here. We've got work to do."

"I am sorry if we're keeping you, Agent," Locke growls. "We're here under the detective's direction, remember?"

"Of course I remember, Sergeant," Cassie seethes, "and it's lucky we came. But, as you said, this isn't over. Cal and I need to get back to work to find out who's behind this attack and to try to stop others before they begin. This was nothing more than a necessary detour for us. We must continue our investigation, Sergeant."

"She's right," Cal confirms.

"I know she's right," Locke concedes, "but if we leave now more of these fuckers will climb out of the water. We need to wait for the troops to arrive."

"Can the three of you hold this position until they do?" Cal offers as a compromise.

Locke takes a moment to evaluate the terrain and their position. He looks over his shoulder at Atkins and Harris, who are still covering their backs, and finally he looks at the water.

"Yes, we can hold this position until the troops arrive," Locke finally confirms.

"Thank you, Sergeant. I will make sure your superiors know what you did, both here and at the arena," Cal offers.

"Fuck my superiors, Detective," Locke scoffs. "Just do your job and put an end to this."

"That's what we intend to do, I assure you," Cassie interjects.

"Good. Now get on your way. I'll break the good news to this pair. I'm sure they'll be delighted that we get to stick around instead of heading back for coffee and cake," Locke grins.

"Thanks, Sergeant," Cal says, simply realising that Locke isn't interested in any other platitudes he may wish to offer.

"Until the next time," Cassie adds.

"Watch yourself on the way back. There could be more of them around," Locke warns.

"We will, Sergeant, and thanks again," Cal replies.

"It's been a blast," Locke says, completely intending his pun.

Harris looks over at Cal and Cassie with a longing expression as they begin to make their retreat back to the helicopter. Cal feels for him, but it's needs must at the moment and Locke needs all the backup he can get right now. Harris will surely find his way back to his station as soon as the other troops arrive. Cal hopes so anyway.

"I'll be glad to leave this place," Cassie says from behind her rifle.

"You and me both. That was gruesome," Cal agrees. "Maybe we'll never get used to the carnage. Not like Locke anyway."

"It strikes me that this is just a walk in the park for that man," Cassie observes, as they move off.

Suddenly, a deep, powerful boom rocks the quayside and both Cal and Cassie glance urgently back towards the slipway to see a plume of water breaking into the air, through the darkness.

"That's one way to keep them at bay," Cal says in shock.

"Boys will be boys," Cassie replies.

Chapter 8

The pilot jumped out of the helicopter, pistol in hand, as soon as he saw Cal and Cassie arrive back in the square. The man was at his wits' end when he asked what had been happening and demanded to know where his airman was. His concern was completely understandable: the noise from the firefight at the quayside would have easily carried back to his position, especially the explosions. On top of that, his airman was nowhere to be seen. The pilot had feared the worst. He needed some convincing that all was well before he climbed back into his cockpit after opening the hold door. Cassie used all of her skills, and charm, to eventually put his mind at ease.

Something tells Cal that their pilot will be relieved when he gets rid of his two passengers as the helicopter's engines power up and it lifts off. The short hop over the city gives Cal barely enough time to check his phone but he sees that there are no new urgent messages. He just about has time to warn Tilly that they are inbound and to send a quick message to Kim's father, Tom, to see how they are both doing before the descent to Mercury House begins.

The building's roof is empty as Cal jumps down from the helicopter following Cassie and they move off the helipad. Cal watches the helicopter rise into the night sky from the side of the helipad before he goes to head back into the building.

"We need to talk, Cal," Cassie says, just as he turns to find the way off the roof.

"What now?" he asks.

"There will never be a good time but at least we're alone up here," Cassie replies, with a worried look.

"Okay, Cassie. What is it? What's wrong?" Cal says.

"I'm..." Cassie struggles to speak. "I'm… I'm being blackmailed by the people behind this," she finally says, her head falling to look at the ground in shame.

Cal is stunned into silence as he tries to process what Cassie has just told him. *Is she in some way responsible for the terror that has taken so many lives and plunged the city into turmoil?* he asks himself in horror. Even now the sound and smell of death and destruction surround them as they stand on the roof in the night. Anger begins to build inside Cal as he wonders just how much of a hand Cassie has had in bringing this terror upon them.

"What have you done?" Cal manages to ask, without losing his temper.

"Nothing, Cal. I'm not responsible for any of this!" Cassie insists. "You must believe me," she pleads.

"Then you'd better explain, Cassie, because I want to believe you, I really do," Cal replies.

"We can use this to our advantage, Cal. This could help us beat them," Cassie blurts.

"How, Cassie? You're not making any sense!" Cal insists. "Why don't you start at the beginning and explain to me what is going on?"

"Yes, okay, I'll tell you what's happened," Cassie replies, close to tears.

"Take a breath first," Cal suggests.

"I was contacted two days ago by an unknown source in connection with another case I was working on," Cassie begins.

Two days, Cal thinks, *that's positive. At least she can't have been involved in the planning of the attacks. But was she involved in the actual attacks themselves?*

"I met the unknown source late at night two nights ago in a downtown park. He said he had vital information about my case. He knew details about the case when he contacted me, so I assumed that he was genuine. But at the meeting, another man met me and that's when things went sideways," Cassie says.

"How so?" Cal encourages her to continue.

"He hadn't come to meet me about that case. He'd come to coerce and blackmail me. He knew information that forced me to go along with what he demanded," Cassie insists.

"What did he ask you to do?" Cal asks, hungry to know.

"That's just it. Nothing. All he wanted was for me to take a burner phone off him and to answer it when it rang. I didn't know why or that it had anything to do with these attacks. Maybe I should have guessed that it was connected," Cassie wonders.

"How do you know it's connected?" Cal asks.

"Because the phone rang tonight for the first time. When I got back here after you left," Cassie continues.

"And?" Cal pushes, ignoring her mentioning that he had left.

"I was asked details about the attack in the Arena District and who was in charge of the investigation after Chief Arnold's death," Cassie replies. "It was a conference call. I don't know how many people were listening but only one person spoke to me."

"What details did you tell them?" Cal asks urgently, concerned that he or his family might be in danger.

"As little as I could reasonably say. I gave them details about the attack, sure, but nothing that would affect our investigation or put other people in danger. I said nothing that they wouldn't hear on the news in due course anyway," Cassie assures.

"Did you give my name up?" Cal demands. "Are my family in danger?"

"I said that I didn't know who had been put in charge, Cal. I told them I'd only just got back to the office and didn't have that information, I promise you, but they already knew it was you. They said as much and asked me to confirm, which I had to do in the end," Cassie says guiltily.

"Thanks for nothing," Cal replies, wondering what they have on her to make her betray him. "What about my family?"

"I have no reason to believe that they're in danger, Cal. I'd tell you if I did, wouldn't I?" Cassie insists.

"I don't know any more, Cassie. I don't know what to believe any more or if I can trust you," Cal replies honestly.

"You can trust me, Cal. I'd never do anything to harm you," Cassie promises.

"Really! How do I know that? What have they got on you, Cassie?" Cal demands.

"I will tell you, but let me continue my explanation first, okay?" Cassie asks.

"I'm all ears," Cal replies, exasperated.

"I hated that phone call, but it made me think that this is the best lead we have. Granted, it's tenuous, but it could be our only direct link to the conspirators," Cassie reveals.

"You're reaching a bit, aren't you?" Cal retorts. "What have we got: an untraceable number with a voice at the other end?"

"You're not thinking, Cal. We have a way in. They obviously think I'll be useful to them so let's lead them on and see where it leads us. Let's give them some of their own medicine," Cassie explains.

"You're right. It's tenuous," Cal replies after a moment's thought. "But you could also be right that we could use it to our advantage. What do you think our next move should be? We need to give them something."

"I phone them and tell them about today's events. There'd be no harm in that information and it would show them my commitment to their cause," Cassie suggests.

"Or they could see right through it," Cal counters.

"We have to give them something," Cassie replies.

"What if you just text them to warn them that evidence has been taken from the arena? That would be a bit more subtle. Let them contact you if they want more information," Cal suggests.

"So just throw a line in the water for now?" Cassie checks.

"Exactly. Let's see what we catch," Cal confirms.

"You're right," Cassie agrees. "I don't want to look overly keen."

"No, we don't want it to look too obvious and give the game away," Cal agrees.

"So, you'll support me on this?" Cassie asks.

"For now," Cal replies. "Have you told anyone else? Your superiors?"

"No. I did think about informing Director Khan but I'm sure there's another mole in S.I. and I don't know who I can trust," Cassie says.

"I agree. Let's keep this between us for now. Is there anything else that you haven't told me?" Cal asks.

"No, Cal. I told you as soon as I had the chance," Cassie insists. "This is the first opportunity since I found out what the phone is for."

"Okay. Thank you for telling me, but I need to know what they're holding over you, Cassie. Perhaps I could help you with it," Cal says, and sees Cassie's head drop again.

"I'm going to tell you. It's just hard for me to say," Cassie replies sheepishly.

"Detective Chambers is everything okay?" a woman's voice says from behind.

Cal turns to see Tilly exiting the stairwell from the building below, knowing that Cassie isn't going to confide in him with other ears around to pry.

"Yes, thank you, Tilly. We were just regrouping. It's been one hell of a trip," Cal lies.

"I heard. Just awful. Thank God you're both okay. I was wondering where you were. The helicopter arrived and went but then you didn't appear. I thought you'd gone off in the helicopter again or got lost. I tried to phone you," Tilly says, concerned.

"No, we were just regrouping. We're coming now," Cal replies, not wanting to raise any suspicions.

Cassie has fixed her game face back on. There is no sign of her discomfort or guilt in front of Tilly. She raises her eyebrows at Cal as he turns in defeat to follow Tilly inside. He can't help but wonder what Cassie was about to tell him. What dirty laundry has she been hiding away?

"You said in your message that there has been a development in the case," Cal asks Tilly, as they travel down to the main office.

"Yes, Sir. The forensic tech team may have traced an internet node based in the city that could possibly be the source of communications with the suspect, Merle Abital." Tilly informs them.

"They made the trace on the dark web?" Cassie asks.

"I believe so, Agent Sutton. But it's not my speciality, I'm afraid," Tilly replies.

"Who knows about this, Tilly?" Cal asks urgently.

"Everyone, Sir. There was a briefing not half an hour ago about it by the team's head of department. Commissioner Jackson and Director Khan attended the meeting, as did many other S.I. heads of department. Why?" Tilly replies.

"I was just wondering. What was decided in the briefing?" Cal asks.

"They have sent a specialist S.I. tactical unit to the site with orders to infiltrate and secure it, Sir," Tilly tells them.

"Where is the site and what's the unit's ETA?" Cassie probes.

"It's a building on an industrial park in the south of the city and they will arrive at any time now, Agent. That's also why I came to find you. Everyone is convening in the tactical room to watch the team's progress and I didn't think you'd want to miss it," Tilly informs Cassie.

"You were right to come and find us, Tilly. Well done," Cal says, his stride becoming more urgent so that he can reach the tactical room, wherever it is.

Tilly uses her security pass to gain entry to the same floor that the briefing with the dignitaries was held on before they left for the arena complex. Cal wonders whether everyone has a security pass other than him, even though it is of little consequence.

Tilly seems to have familiarised herself with their new base at S.I. very well. Anyone would think that she'd been working in the building for a long time, and hasn't just arrived in her new surroundings only this evening. Even Cassie, who works at S.I. day in, day out, allows Tilly to lead them through.

Madeline, the receptionist who had shown them through to the conference room earlier, is sitting behind the same desk and watches them approach. Tilly says "Hi" to her on her way past and, this time, Madeline stays where she is, obviously knowing that Tilly already knows the way.

Tilly takes them past the previous conference room and various others further down the corridor until she arrives at a door at its end. Outside it, a guard is standing to restrict entry into the room beyond. The guard smiles at Tilly as she arrives in front of him.

"This is Detective Chambers and Agent Sutton. They are expected," she tells the man.

"Thank you, Tilly. You can go in," he says to them with another smile, after checking a list he is holding.

Cal is impressed by his new assistant. Tilly seems to have not only familiarised herself with the building but also the staff working inside it. She also knows more than he does about the state of the investigation at present. She clearly makes it her business to 'be in the know'. There is a reason why Chief Arnold chose Tilly to be her assistant. The chief was no fool and Cal is beginning to appreciate Tilly's multiple strengths and why Chief Arnold relied on her so much. Tilly is an asset that he needs to make more use of, he decides.

Inside the large tactical room, everyone of note seems to be standing at the far end of the room. All the bigwigs who attended the previous briefing are in attendance and are mainly standing in a huddle together, chatting. There are also several other people there, people that Cal is unfamiliar with, but he guesses that they are other members of the security services, the police force and probably the government. All the chat stops as they arrive and almost everyone immediately turns to look in Cal and Cassie's direction.

"At last. Detective Chambers and Agent Sutton. Thank God you're both safe!" Director Khan announces, as they enter and Tilly ducks out of the way to take a seat. "We've been on tenterhooks waiting for you to get back here safely. A shocking turn of events at the arena."

"Shocking indeed," Commissioner Jackson agrees from beside Khan.

"It was," Cal agrees, looking at both men suspiciously. He doesn't know who he can trust any more and suddenly wonders whether he and Cassie might have been allowed to go to the arena deliberately. Was the trip orchestrated from the start to put them in harm's way? Did somebody inside the tactical room plan that they wouldn't return?

"It was lucky I assigned one of my best men to escort you," Colonel Medlam pipes up.

"Was it?" Cal snaps sarcastically, surprising himself.

"Yes. You couldn't have been in better hands than Sergeant Locke!" Medlam bites back. "You should be grateful he was there."

"Grateful!" Cal begins to rage.

"Gentlemen, please," Secretary of Defence Martha Dunguard interrupts. "Detective Chambers and Agent Sutton have been through quite an ordeal. I think we can all agree on that from Major Patel's account. So, let's cut them some slack and let them settle in. Can we get you a drink?" she offers with a smile.

"Both of them should be in quarantine," a voice announces from a television screen on Cal's right that he hadn't noticed.

Major Patel's face stares back at Cal when he turns to look at the TV screen. He is sitting behind a desk in another location, attending the meeting remotely.

"If we should be in quarantine, then so should you and half of the troops on the ground in the city," Cal replies angrily.

"I am in a secure environment, I can assure you, Detective," Patel insists.

"Lucky you," Cal fires back. "I'm quite happy to fuck off and secure myself at home if you'd prefer!"

"Gentlemen, please!" Dunguard interjects again. "Tensions are running high, so everyone calm down. Need I remind you why we are all here? We need to be working together and not at each other's throats."

Dunguard is right and Cal takes a breath to try to calm himself. He knows he shouldn't have lost his temper with Patel but, after his performance at the arena, Cal has little time for the man.

"I'm sorry," Cal says. "As you say, tensions are high. Black coffee would be good, please."

"We have an amber light," General Peters announces. "The tactical unit has arrived at the target location. I suggest we take our seats."

On the large television at the head of the room, Cal notices an amber light has appeared on the screen. Cassie wastes no time in taking the load off her feet and claims the closest chair in front of her. Cal quickly joins her around the table, noticing the state of his clothes before the lights dim and he sits down. Perhaps Patel isn't wrong and he should be in quarantine, or his clothes at least. They are covered in suspect matter of God only knows what. He consoles himself that, if this infection was transmittable by bodily fluid, he would have turned into a rabid biter hours ago.

"What are we expecting to find at this location?" Cassie asks.

"Unknown," Khan answers. "All we know is that some communication was routed through a computer at the location."

"Communications have been routed through many locations, worldwide," Jackson adds. "It may be just a coincidence that this site happens to be in the city. The computer might have been hacked remotely and the site completely innocent."

"We're about to find out either way," Khan insists.

Not holding out much hope that anything will be discovered at the site, other than a computer that a virtual private network is being routed through, Cal looks at his phone. Tom has returned Cal's message to tell him that Kim is as well as can be expected and that he's managed to put her to bed to rest. Cal hopes Kim does manage to rest. She needs it for the baby's sake, if not hers.

"Is everything okay?" Cassie whispers.

"Yes, thanks. Kim is resting," Cal replies.

"The best thing for her," Cassie says.

Thanking Tom for his update, Cal puts his phone away and looks across the table. Almost every seat has been taken around the large rectangular table that he and Cassie are positioned about halfway down, on the opposite side to Khan and Jackson. Everyone's attention is fixed on the large screen on the wall at the end of the table, waiting for the feed from the site to begin.

Cal sees the concentration fixed on people's faces in anticipation. It seems that everyone has more confidence than he that this lead will go anywhere. As Jackson said, this is only one site in a worldwide VPN network. One cog in the wheel. Cal is sure the tactical team will find a computer, but only one that is connected to the internet and contains no physical evidence of its own.

The other point that Cal is only now considering is, if Cassie is right and S.I. has a mole feeding intelligence to the conspirators, wouldn't they have warned their contact of the impending operation, to give them a chance to clear the site and destroy any evidence? The more he thinks about it, the more Cal is sure the operation will be another dead end. He watches the screen anyway and feels a jolt of anticipation when the feed flickers onto it.

Chapter 9

Computer code runs on the screen in front of Uri. Code that has become his best and perhaps only friend over the past long years. Loneliness is not something that concerns Uri. He made that choice in another lifetime when he was no more than a child on the West Bank.

His parents were among the first settlers to take the Israeli government's offer of a subsidised settlement after the capture of the West Bank in the Six-Day War of 1967. The offer had been too good to turn down for a poor family such as his. Uri understood that. Uri was far too young to comprehend the geopolitical ramifications of the Israeli occupation or the grievances of the Palestinian people. He was just excited to be living in a real home and attending a proper school where he could make new friends.

The 1970s were the decade in which he left his previous life of family and friends behind. He was just twelve years old when the bomb exploded in his school on a day when his parents happened to be attending. Uri cannot remember the reason why his parents were at school that day. He can only remember their bloody, tattered bodies after the explosion that ripped through his classroom, killing them and all of his classmates and friends.

Eventually, Uri was miraculously plucked from the rubble of his classroom and cleaned up. His saviours repeated how lucky he was to be alive, but Uri didn't consider himself lucky. To this day, he wonders if he would have been happier if he had been disintegrated by the bomb like his parents had been, along with every friend he had ever had.

Only turmoil has followed Uri since that fateful day. Turmoil and hatred. He wasn't taken away from the West Bank to somewhere where he could live in peace and heal after his trauma. He was handed around the West Bank from foster family to foster family and none of them could handle him or suffer his rage. Even the children's home he found himself in when no other foster families could be found to take him struggled to control Uri.

Only when he was 18 years old and conscripted into the Israeli Defence Force to fulfil his obligation of national service did Uri begin to channel his rage under the unforgiving discipline applied. Finally, Uri discovered an outlet for his turmoil and an opportunity to seek revenge.

His dedication to the cause didn't go unnoticed and his determination and skills were honed and expanded upon as his service continued. Uri didn't give up his opportunity when his national service drew to an end. He signed up full-time and the Defence Force were eager to have him. They trained Uri to become a specialist infiltrator and killer, training that Uri seized upon. He was offered ample opportunity to reap his revenge but, no matter how much blood he spilt in the name of the defence of the West Bank, nothing quelled Uri's underlying turmoil.

Over the years, Uri's thirst for blood became meaningless to him and his enthusiasm diminished. No matter how many bodies he piled up, nothing brought back the child he once was. The Defence Force noticed the change in Uri and conceded that his time on the front line was over, but they weren't finished with Uri, not yet, and that is when his life changed again.

It was the 1990s when Uri was transferred into communications and he found a new passion: technology and coding. The tech revolution had been building over the previous decades, but Uri encountered it when it spiralled at extraordinary speed and he immersed himself in it. He had no time for other frivolous activities. The code was his friend, his life. There was no complication or malice inside the code, only honesty, and he used it to open up the world to his whims.

After he was discharged from the military, Uri took on private contracting work. He didn't care who he was working for as long as the work interested him, and the remuneration was of equal interest. He soon found that his work in the private sector often called for his other set of skills. Skills that he was happy to offer for the right price.

The years went past and Uri became disillusioned again. He was growing older, past his prime. He knew it and, to his surprise, he found Israel calling him home. He would never set foot in the West Bank again; he had promised himself that when he first left. So, he settled on its border in west Jerusalem. Another disputed territory, but not the West Bank.

There was nothing worthy to work for any longer. Only the same old grudges and power grabs that pay handsomely but are ultimately unfulfilling. Instead, Uri spent his semi-retirement immersed in code and the dark web and often, to his surprise, discovering Jerusalem on foot. That was until his skills were called upon again, but this time by a worthy, no, inspiring, cause.

Merle Abital had been the first person Uri had executed in more than a year. Uri's pseudonym, Mr Easter, may have been the person who had knocked on Merle Abital's door, but it was Uri's skills that had carried out the fateful deed.

Uri unusually finds himself dwelling on his latest killing, despite the action having to be taken for the higher cause. Abital was a buffoon but had proved a very useful buffoon, fulfilling his function with exemplary and surprising success. The man had surprised Uri and had proved his worth to the cause on multiple occasions. Uri knows he shouldn't feel sorry for Abital, knowing he had finally found a calling in his life that gave him meaning. Abital might have felt terror at the end, but Uri is positive he would have found satisfaction in the vital work he completed before his demise. Perhaps that is why Uri finds himself dwelling on the death. Abital finally found purpose in his pointless life only to have it ultimately torn from his grasp.

Uri decides that he must be getting soft in his old age as he turns away from the screen of code. He has extinguished more lives than he can remember during his long existence. Many of them were innocent people who had never hurt anyone. Women, children, nobody was off limits to Uri if they were in his way or just happened to be in the wrong place at the wrong time. Nothing got in the way of his mission; failure was not an option he could afford. Failure was bad for his reputation and bad for business.

Other people in his line of work, or even in the military, complain about being visited from the afterlife by their victims. Uri has never been visited by ghostly figures complaining about their demise. There is no afterlife as far as he is concerned. He has searched into the eyes of too many of his victims as their life force slipped away to know that there is no soul to carry on their existence. Any notion of a soul is a fantasy, something clung onto by people too afraid to accept the only truth. That dead means dead.

Standing, Uri wanders over to the window across from his desk. The second-floor vantage point provides a good strategic view over the industrial park that he is established in. Only the odd light glows in the darkness. A security light in a factory, or a light in a warehouse that wasn't switched off at the end of the working day. The industrial park is still, which is why Uri's control hub is here. Hiding in plain sight in the bustling downtown areas of the city would have its advantages, but Uri prefers the orderly predictability of business, not the chaotic unpredictability of the general public. From his vantage point, he can easily see the comings and goings in the industrial park. The main entrance is shrouded in darkness and the only road onto the park is in full view to the left as he looks out of the window. At night the road is virtually unused and even during the day it is never overly busy.

These are the reasons Uri stops just as he was about to turn and return to his workstation. He watches three sets of headlights come to a stop just short of the entrance to the industrial park. Uri has spent enough nights looking out at the same view to know immediately that the sudden appearance of a group of headlights is unusual. Uri's honed sense of danger has been nurtured over decades of looking over his shoulder. The tingling in his fingers, together with the tightening in his stomach, are sensations he never ignores. He watches the stationary headlights, waiting for their next move with growing anxiety, praying that his instinct is wrong and that the vehicles will innocently pull away and pass by the entrance.

The lead vehicle pulls off and, for a moment, Uri thinks it is going to pass the entrance to the industrial estate, that he has misjudged the situation. The headlights swerve urgently in his direction and Uri knows that he was wrong to doubt his gut feeling. He glimpses the other two vehicles following and turning in the same direction even as he bolts away from the window.

One vehicle entering the industrial estate at this time of night is unusual but not unknown. Businesses have burglar alarms that go off. Whether they are false alarms or not, they need to be investigated by keyholders. And there are cars that might turn into the park, their drivers looking for a quiet back road in which to perform one or other nefarious activity. Three sets of headlights is definitely out of the ordinary, especially when the vehicles in question stop short to prepare and then drive into the park with such purpose. Uri's clandestine bolt-hole has somehow been compromised. He doesn't know how. Nobody else was privy to its whereabouts, not even Janus.

There is no time for debate or for an investigation into how the control hub has been compromised or the ramifications of its discovery. Right now, all Uri can do is to execute his evacuation plan as efficiently as possible.

Uri's travel bag sits on the floor. As always, it contains his essential belongings so that he is ready to move at a moment's notice. He ejects two hard drives from the two computer towers at his control station and slings them into his travel bag before collecting the few personal items that are on the desk. Uri scans the old industrial office he has been using as a work and living base for the past weeks to double-check he isn't leaving anything vital behind. He isn't. He is far too methodical to make such a mistake.

He understands that the whole area, especially the mattress positioned on the floor on the far side of the room, will be a hive of incriminating DNA evidence. He can't take it with him, not under these circumstances. The physical evidence will have to be dealt with in another fashion, along with all the other evidence the room contains.

Uri swings his travel bag over his shoulder just as the sound of diesel engines closes in on the building. He doesn't bother switching off the light as he leaves his bolt-hole and rushes down a short corridor to the building's back stairwell. Without a pause, Uri descends towards the ground floor, the route well practised in both daylight and darkness. Uri could find his destination blindfolded if needed.

The vibrations from the heavy engines outside the building spur Uri on as he lands on the ground floor, his target now only a few feet away. Uri hears boots hitting the paving outside as he reaches for the dusty pallet positioned on the ground against the wall. Pulling it aside, a black hole presents itself. The abyss is ominous and uninviting. It offers no light whatsoever to help Uri's journey, but he needs no light. He lowers his travel bag into the hole before his feet follow it down. The space below is tight. He must wriggle himself into the tubular drain, pushing his bag forward and out of the way to allow his body enough space to squeeze through. Uri hates confined spaces, that is his Achilles heel, but he has forced himself over the years to build up tolerance to his claustrophobia.

Cold water soaks into Uri's clothes as he lowers himself inside. The dampness agitates his claustrophobia. His brain tries to create more fear by asking what if it begins to rain? Would he become trapped inside the tight drain and drown before he could free himself?

Uri banishes such thoughts from his mind so that he can concentrate on the task at hand. After sliding his body into the pipe, his hand takes hold of the pallet to pull it back into place to cover his escape route. Darkness envelops him as the pallet moves, cutting off any dim light from above, while his mind once again threatens to paralyse him with fear.

An almighty crash forces his head further down into the darkness, despite Uri knowing that the pallet will hide him. The door to the building is no match for the concerted effort the intruders apply to gain entry. Uri cowers further back from the hole above, as unforgiving voices shout a warning as the team enters the building. The shouts are intended to disarm their quarry. "Armed officers" and "Lay down your weapons!" are among the favourite phrases bellowed out.

Paying no heed to the angry words of warning, Uri pushes his bag in front of him until he is at least a few feet away from his entry point. Once he is satisfied, he pauses for a moment and shuffles over onto his back. The confined space barely allows him to raise his head to look back towards the hole, but his straining neck just about manages it. His view allows him to see the screen of the phone he has struggled to take out of his pocket and, even as boots stomp on the floors above, Uri presses numbers on the phone.

Uri bears no ill will towards the law enforcement officers who are flooding into his domain above. He is sure their dedication is admirable and that their families are proud of their selfless work. But that fact doesn't stop Uri from pausing for a moment before he presses the 'Call' button on his phone. He gives the officers time to enter the building and time for at least some of them to climb the stairs to find his lair before he finally presses the green button.

The ground that he is buried beneath shakes violently, as if a high-magnitude earthquake has suddenly broken out. Water from the shallow stream below spills up onto him as dust and slime are shaken free from the top of the storm drain. Particles rain down onto his face just as a bright light flashes to illuminate his subterranean world. Uri's eyes slam shut to protect themselves from the falling particles but not before a flashing image is ingrained into his brain.

Uri searches the image while he waits for the ferocity of the earthquake to lessen. He sees past his feet and the falling particles, down the length of the tube he finds himself in. Dark shadows are imprinted onto the image in the water at the bottom of the tube. Rats stunned into shock by the explosion above recoil from the sudden burst of light and the horrendous noise. Uri hopes they will flee for their lives in the opposite direction to the hole and away from him. With any luck, any rats in his vicinity at the other end of the drain, and in the direction he needs to travel, will also scarper away.

Eventually, the concrete drain settles down as the explosion subsides but not before a massive crash is heard, which Uri reasons must be part of the building above collapsing. When Uri hammered through into the storm drain as part of his escape-plan preparations, he was satisfied that the drain would withstand the explosion. He hadn't envisaged that it would also need to withstand a collapsing building, but thankfully it has. Maybe he had been overzealous with the explosives he had set.

After his fingers have wiped away the debris from his eyes, Uri turns back over onto his stomach. The drain ahead consists of a long run before it empties out into a stream on the other side of the road that runs adjacent to the industrial park, the road where the headlights had stopped. He pushes his bag forward in front of him and pulls himself forward with his hands and elbows, pushing with his feet against the slick concrete. The tube has now become almost silent, apart from the sounds made by his efforts to traverse it and the squeaking of rats. There is no sound of movement above and Uri wonders whether any of the infiltrators have survived the explosion.

With aching joints, Uri pushes on. Moaning to himself that he is too old for this is futile. Moaning won't free him from the drainage pipe. He tries to concentrate on the feeling of euphoria he will feel when he finally slips out of the pipe and into the clean waters of the stream. The back of his mind cannot help but torture him, however, and he wonders if his brain wants to descend into madness and trap him in this pitch-black tomb. *What if tree roots have broken through the pipe and collapsed it to block his way? What then?* his mind asks. Uri had checked out the other end of the drain, the outlet, but it was impossible for him to see the entire length of the drain, not without travelling its length. There was no way he was going to do that if it wasn't completely necessary. His claustrophobia had argued against it. *Now it is necessary*, he tells himself, and so now he will find out.

An inordinate amount of time passes, the bag is pushed forward and Uri strains to follow it. Squealing rats are never far ahead, but thankfully the approaching bag seems to be keeping them at bay. Uri is soaked to the skin from the constant pool of water in the bottom of the pipe and from sweat. The exertion required to crawl along the slick, confined space is tremendous.

Uri's mind works overtime during the seemingly endless journey. One minute he panics that the pipe will become blocked and that he will be forced to turn around, although tuning around in such a tight space would be impossible. The next minute he convinces himself that the authorities have guessed his escape plan and are waiting patiently outside the outlet, with guns drawn. He tries to distract himself from such tortuous thoughts by using his brain to figure out how the authorities found his secret lair. In the end, his mind numbs and all he can manage to do is to toil and to continue on in a daze, while gasping for breath.

A gust of fresh air drifts around the bag in front of Uri. He drinks the replenishing oxygen into his lungs greedily. His mind begins to return to its task and he shuffles on again with new vigour. The fresh air must mean that he is near the end of his journey. Uri slows his progress when the sound of running water meets his ears, confirming that the end of the pipe is near. He peers around the side of the bag in front of him and, sure enough, he can see the dimmest of lights only a metre or two ahead.

Uri might be desperate to free himself from the storm drain but he knows that the end of the line is where the risk lies. He cannot see any man-made light piercing the darkness ahead but that doesn't mean that there isn't someone lying in wait for him to pop out who will stick a gun in his face.

Shuffling closer to the opening, Uri moves as quietly as he can, although the sound of every move he makes in the tight space seems to be exaggerated. He can only hope that the noise of the stream will mask his approach. Now close to his exit, Uri reaches into his travel bag and takes hold of the Beretta handgun inside.

Now very close to the opening, Uri can smell his freedom and his body yearns to free itself from its constriction. He steadies himself, the Beretta at the ready, his heart racing. In a swift motion, Uri shoves the bag forward and out of the opening, the Beretta aimed ready to fire should anyone take his bait. Nothing moves. There is only the splash of his bag as it meets the stream. Uri waits a few seconds to be sure before he moves again. This time he doesn't stop moving until his head breaches the end of the drain, his Beretta searching for targets.

Only the stream is there to meet Uri and he pulls himself out into it with relief. His bag sits waiting in the shallow, slow-moving waters and, after he has stretched out his limbs and back, Uri takes hold of the handles. He moves cautiously down the stream; law enforcement could arrive at any moment. Just past the storm drain's outlet, the bank recedes in height and Uri approaches it, hiding behind the sparse foliage. He sees the blue flashing lights reflecting off the leaves, confirming that law enforcement has now arrived in numbers. It is a fact that doesn't surprise Uri after the 'surprise' they have just received.

Uri finds himself in line with the road that leads down to his building. Behind the gathering police units, the remnants of his workplace crown the scene. Smoke billows into the air from the destroyed building. The second floor has almost completely disappeared and the remaining section is being licked by flames. Shadowy figures move in front of the flashing blue lights and the flickering light of the flames. Uri knows that they won't stay in that vicinity for long. Officers will begin to fan out and look for evidence, and suspects. It's in their nature.

The distant sound of a helicopter approaching tells Uri that his sightseeing break is over and that it's time to make good on his escape. Stepping away from the stream's embankment and back into the water, Uri resumes following the stream. He doesn't need to follow it far to reach his destination, but the darkness means that he must tread carefully through the flowing water. The bed beneath his boots isn't that treacherous, he made sure of that when he planned his escape route, but when he'd walked this route previously it was daylight, however.

A beam of light reflects off the water as the helicopter flies overhead. Uri ducks down into the branches of an overhanging tree until it passes nearby. He hopes that the pilot hasn't started his search pattern yet and activated the aircraft's infrared camera, because hiding under branches won't fool it if they have. Thankfully, the helicopter doesn't slow overhead but flies straight for the burning building, freeing Uri to continue.

Shivering with cold and exhaustion, Uri is pleased when he sees the streetlight he is looking for on the opposite side of the stream to the one on which the authorities are massing near his building. He follows the light until he is almost level with it, at which time he heads for the stream's other embankment. Pausing to wash the slime and debris off his face and out of his hair means splashing cold water over those areas. More cold water is the last thing he wants running over him, but it is necessary before he climbs out.

A quiet residential estate spreads out on this side of the stream and Uri is thankful it is dark as he walks out of the foliage and onto its side streets. He can only imagine what a state he looks after his journey. Like a drowned rat covered in muck would be the answer if anyone saw him. The darkness hides his awful state though and there is nobody around to watch him make his way to the car he has positioned on the estate.

Uri ensured that the car was parked discreetly, away from prying eyes. He knew he would need five minutes if he was forced into using the car. After double-checking that no one is around, Uri quickly relieves himself of his soaking-wet clothes next to the open back door of the car. A bag in the footwell behind the driver's seat hides a bag of dry clothes and a welcome towel. Uri dries and dresses himself as fast as possible. His shivering hands hinder him, but he is soon stuffing his wet clothes into the empty bag.

The moment his butt hits the driver's seat, Uri starts the engine. Firstly, so that he can evacuate the area as fast as possible and, secondly, to get some warmth from the car's heater. Following the estate roads will bring him out into another part of the city entirely, well away from the authorities. By the time he leaves the housing estate behind, there is plenty of heat emanating from the car's heater, warming his cold bones.

Chapter 10

Uri meets deathly quiet roads as he leaves the housing estate. The much-delayed announcement of a city-wide curfew is finally having its desired effect of keeping the public off the streets. The empty roads might be good for progress, but they also make Uri stick out like a sore thumb. He could be pulled over at any moment and keeps checking his rear-view mirror, waiting for headlights to approach and then blue flashing lights.

Uri is concerned about attracting unwanted attention but is not panicked. He is now in a completely different part of the city to the explosion and, with any luck, the authorities will have more important things to concern themselves with other than a member of the public who is running late and not obeying the curfew. His isn't the only car on the road either but, if he is pulled over, he is well versed in sweet-talking police officers. It is a skill that seems to become easier to acquire the older he gets, which is certainly due to his ageing appearance rather than any improvement in his technique.

Just as Uri's confidence grows, his heart sinks when blue lights suddenly burst into action behind him. After waiting a moment to see if the police car passes him by, more in hope than expectation, he begins to indicate when it becomes clear that he is their target. A turning off the main road presents itself and Uri takes the opportunity to lead the police car off the main drag and onto a more secluded street. There, he will be able to converse with the occupants of the car more effectively and turn them to his way of thinking.

The police car rolls to a stop behind Uri. Its annoying lights persist in lighting up the dark street like a discotheque, attracting unwanted attention. Uri stays put behind the wheel and waits to be approached. A shadow cuts across the lights behind, Uri sees in the rear-view mirror, and he winds down his window ready to receive the police officer. He can't help but glance at the Beretta that is stowed under the dash just in front of him in a holster he fixed there just for this type of situation.

"Why aren't you observing the curfew, Sir?" the police officer asks, keeping a distance from the open window.

"I'm sorry, Officer. I am on my way home now. Unfortunately, I was travelling from out of town when the curfew was announced and I didn't have time to reach home before it came into effect," Uri answers, keeping his hand on the wheel in full view for the officer to see.

"The order clearly stated that if you couldn't reach your destination in time then you must find a place outside the city," the officer replies suspiciously.

"Really, Officer? I must have missed that part of the announcement," Uri offers. "My hearing isn't what it was either," Uri acts, rubbing his ear as he lies.

"You seem to be able to hear me well enough," the officer counters. "Driving licence."

The man isn't a young fool who can be easily manipulated, but an officer in his senior years who has been round the block more times than he cares to remember. *This could mean trouble*, Uri thinks.

"I'm sorry, Officer, I didn't hear it," Uri insists, handing over a driving licence. "What should I do now? My home is only five minutes or so away," Uri replies, trying to suggest that he should be allowed to continue on his way.

"Wait in the car," the officer orders and turns to return to his vehicle.

Watching the officer in his wing mirror, Uri knows the man has suspicions about him and his story. His cover isn't blown yet, or the officer would have ordered him out of the car at gunpoint, but it could go either way. Uri prepares himself to act.

His eyes switch from the wing to the rear-view mirror to try to determine if this policeman is on his own or if he has a partner riding shotgun in the car with him. The combination of the police car's headlights and its flashing blue ones makes it impossible to see if there is another officer behind the car's windscreen, no matter where Uri places his head to try to change his angle of sight. Quickly, Uri gives up on trying to see and relaxes in his seat. He doesn't want to appear to be twitching around nervously, although he does allow his hand a practice run towards the Beretta.

Eventually, there is movement in Uri's rear-view mirror and the officer approaches his open window again. Before he opens his mouth, Uri knows there is a problem. One, because he isn't handed his licence back and two, because the officer's hand is on his sidearm.

"Step out of the vehicle, Sir," the officer orders.

"Is there a problem, Officer?" Uri replies, now seeing movement in his rear-view mirror, confirming that there is a second police officer in attendance to slash his odds of escaping.

"Step out of the vehicle!" the officer repeats more forcefully. "And keep your hands where I can see them."

Uri holds his hands up innocently before moving one of them deliberately to the door handle. He tries to give off an air of vulnerability whilst steeling himself for battle. He has no choice now. The policemen might want nothing more than to confirm his story but, eventually, that story won't check out. Then he would be in handcuffs, sitting defenceless in the back seat of their patrol car. Uri is outnumbered and outgunned but he knows one thing for sure. One way or the other, he won't be wearing these officer's bracelets. Not tonight.

"I'm sorry I didn't make it home in time for the curfew, Officer," Uri says as a distraction, as he opens the car door and begins to get out.

"Keep your hands where I can see them," the officer repeats, his hand gripping his sidearm, preparing to pull it out.

Keeping his hand up, Uri rocks in his seat to try to exit the car without the help of his hands. He moans as he moves to suggest that his back and joints are protesting in his old age, which, after his recent ordeal, they really are. He struggles out of the car, as frail as an old man until it is time to act.

Uri turns his body, innocently, the motion helping his balance, but his body's positioning is quite deliberate. For a fleeting moment, his trailing hand moves out of the officer's sight and a moment is all his hand needs.

Before the officer at the side of the car realises what has happened, Uri has positioned himself again, this time with deadly consequences. The officer's realisation hits him like a thunderbolt. Panic and terror rip across his face as he sees the Beretta in Uri's hand and tries to react. The Beretta explodes in Uri's hand before the officer has any chance of reacting to defend himself. Two bullets slam into the officer before his sidearm has moved an inch. The first bullet smashes into the man's standard-police-issue bulletproof vest. The vest stops the bullet but not without a cost to the officer. Pain hits him instantly as he is knocked backwards by the force of the first bullet, a pain that is short-lived as Uri's second bullet slams into the officer's face, killing him instantly as it travels into his brain.

Uri's skill is impressive. He has dealt with the first police officer whilst concealing himself from the second behind his car. The other officer, to his credit, reacts quickly and two gunshots ring out from the rear of Uri's car. Glass erupts from the back of the car as the incoming gunfire crashes through its back window, aimed at the driver's seat. The bullets rip through the seat with ease, the seat's structure offering Uri no protection from the high-velocity bullets. Uri vacated the seat instantly when he fired his two rounds, predicting where the threat from the second officer would arrive. Uri had moved rapidly to outflank the second officer and gain an advantage.

Glass rains down onto the road beside Uri even as he rises just above the rear quarter of his car and begins to fire. The second policeman is exactly where Uri expected him to be, standing behind the open door on the passenger side of the patrol car. The officer's defensive position is totally inadequate. Perhaps if the powers that be had budgeted to fit police cars with bulletproof glass the officer might have stood a chance, but penny-pinching trumps an officer's protection.

Uri fires multiple rounds at the far front quarter of the police car. More glass erupts and steel punctures as Uri's bullets pass through the car's shell and hit the police officer multiple times. The officer spins away from his position under the deadly force of the bullets, disappearing down, behind the police car.

Moving quickly to seal his advantage, Uri rushes in between the two cars, behind his Beretta, toward the opposite side of the police car, where the officer fell. On arrival, Uri uses caution to find where the officer is. The man was hit but that doesn't mean he isn't prepared to defend himself from certain death.

On his back, next to the police car, the officer is motionless on the ground. His weapon lies next to him where it fell out of his hand. Uri wastes no time and takes no risks by checking the body for signs of life. He aims the Beretta and fires once, putting a bullet in the policeman's head to ensure he is dead.

Uri has no regrets as he turns to get back in his car, shooting another bullet into the first officer's head as he goes to be sure he's dead. He had no intention of shooting two police officers in the head tonight. He had no intention of blowing untold numbers of officers to smithereens either. Uri doesn't believe he should feel guilty for defending himself, it was the police who came hunting for him. How can it be his fault that they were underprepared and no match for him? He doesn't allow the reason they were hunting him to trouble his conscience.

Shadows lurk at the windows of the houses lining the street as residents wonder what is happening on their quiet street. *Don't worry*, Uri tells them in his head, *it's just the execution of two police officers, not the undead arriving.*

The residents could be counted as witnesses, but they are of no concern to Uri. They are all too far away to identify him in the darkness. He has just dealt with the only two witnesses who could do that. He suddenly remembers something, however, and turns quickly. *He must be getting old!* he thinks. He nearly left some evidence behind. His driving licence.

Uri finds the credit card-sized licence on the dashboard of the police car. Details contained on the card will already have been checked on police computers, so he isn't leaving the scene clean, without leaving any evidence behind. The details won't get them far, they are all fabricated, but at least he won't be leaving the physical evidence of the licence.

Speeding away from the crime scene, Uri guns the car straight down the residential street. He cannot risk joining the main trunk road again, certainly not now. The car's registration will be flagged and, besides, the shot-out back window and the bullet holes in the bodywork will attract attention like flies round a pile of shit.

Uri wasn't lying when he told the police officer that he lives five or so minutes away. Well not completely. His destination was about five minutes away, if he was travelling on the main road, not that he lives there. Calculating that it will be more like ten minutes using back roads, he decides to risk staying with the car and using it to get closer to his destination before he dumps it.

Under normal circumstances, after the execution of two police officers, Uri would expect the streets to be swarming with other police units in no time. These are not normal circumstances though. The police will be stretched to near breaking point with everything that is happening in the city tonight. He is riding his luck continuing in the car but it's a risk he is willing to take, at least for now.

Better progress is made than Uri expected on the back roads towards his destination. He shouldn't be surprised. There is absolutely no traffic to contend with and thankfully he isn't challenged by the police either before he pulls off the road.

The car mounts the kerb next to a piece of waste ground that Uri is familiar with. His destination is still about five minutes away on foot, but the car needs to be dumped before he nears it. Popular with local youths and fly-tippers, the waste ground is not unknown for having cars dumped on it, and very often in flames. One more won't raise too much suspicion, not immediately. Uri is in no doubt that the police will find the car and identify it as the one involved in the nearby shooting, and then link it with the explosion, but it won't matter by then. Uri will be in the wind again in no time and the police will be no closer to finding him.

Driving out of sight of the road and deeper onto the waste ground, where tree cover offers itself, Uri finds a nice spot to park. He is out of the car immediately, with his Beretta in one hand and his carry bag in the other. After throwing the bag to the side, Uri opens the car's fuel cap before opening its back door. In the opposite footwell to his bag of wet clothes is a fuel canister. Whipping off the top of the can, Uri throws fuel all over the interior of the car, making sure he leaves the can about half-full. He sets the can down on the back seat before taking a few steps back while searching his pocket for a book of matches he knows are there. Flipping open the book, he strikes one match and then uses it to set the whole book alight. As the matches burst into flames, Uri throws the erupting book through the car's open rear door.

A whoosh sounds the moment the fuel ignites and, almost instantly, the car's entire interior erupts into furious flames. Satisfied that it is properly alight, Uri grabs his bag off the ground and heads for the treeline as fast as he can. A muffled explosion erupts just as he reaches the cover of the trees. That explosion is the fuel can bursting as a result of its highly flammable contents, the force of the blast smashing all the car's windows out. A second, more violent explosion sounds as the car's fuel tank erupts just as Uri leaves the waste ground behind to join a narrow path that will take him into a shopping centre situated in this part of the city.

Now on foot, Uri doesn't delay. A police patrol car could appear at any moment and skid to a stop next to him. He is the only person around after all. There is no life in the shopping centre. Even all the late-night takeaways are closed and there's no traffic to hide his progress. As soon as he can, Uri leaves the streets and cuts through a church's graveyard that will take him away from the main shopping centre and back onto side roads.

His destination is on the very outskirts of the central shopping area. He is heading for a pokey flat above a barber's shop and he reaches its side door just as a car's engine sounds nearby. Uri's key is in the lock and turned in an instant.

Breathing a sigh of relief as the door closes behind him, Uri double locks it before heading up the stairs directly in front of him. He decides against switching any lights on when he arrives at the flat's one and only living area, besides the small bedroom and tiny bathroom. A streetlight shines straight through the front window and that will suffice until Uri has had a chance to regroup.

Dropping his bag on the floor, Uri goes to get a glass of water from the kitchenette, which is no more than a step away. He then plonks himself down on the two-seater sofa to drink his water and gather his thoughts.

His mind and body ache. The water refreshes his system, but he knows he will also need food to recharge his batteries… and sleep. Along the wall in front of him, behind a single swivel chair, is a bank of computer screens. He would dearly like to fire them up and begin researching how his main control centre was discovered by the authorities. He daren't plug in the computers or touch their power buttons though. Even in the traumatic excitement he has been through since he saw the three sets of headlights stop earlier, Uri has been debating. Nobody else knew where his base was. He was ultra-careful to conceal its position and took counter measures whenever he travelled to it. There can only be one explanation: that it was somehow traced through his online activity. Hence, he can't turn on his system until he knows for sure.

His immediate problems are that Janus is expecting Mr Easter to report in, and Mr Easter is meant to be issuing instructions at this very time to instigate the next phase of Foundation Day. Uri's head flops back. He knows that contingencies are in place for just this type of situation. Him going off-grid might delay the next phase of this momentous day, but it won't stop it. Janus will take appropriate action as soon as he realises that Uri is missing in action. Uri just hates letting Janus down, and possibly delaying the progress of Foundation Day.

Chapter 11

Cal's palms sweat in anticipation. He glances at Cassie beside him and can tell that her heart is racing too as the tactical team close in on the target. The entire room has fallen into silence as they watch the operation to raid the location of the suspect communication VPN node on the large screen.

Interference crackles across the screen and the footage is shaky as the team member wearing the bodycam rushes to a covering position behind the breach team. Cal squints to try to get a better view of what's happening but his squinting doesn't improve the feed from the black-and-white night-vision camera. Others around the desk lean forward to try to improve their view while Cal relaxes his eyes and decides to make the best of the picture without straining his eyes.

The bodycam catches a hand signal from a team member near the entry point and then all hell breaks loose. A bright flash whites out the bodycam for a moment and a bang sounds as an explosive charge is used on the entry door. As the picture returns it catches the last second of a battering ram hitting the door followed by a loud crash and then the team pile into the building.

Cries of "Armed police!" reverberate constantly as the bodycam follows the tactical team into the building. Through the darkness, shadows with rifles raised fan out into the ground floor of the building. Other shadows disappear into what can only be a stairwell. The ground floor looks devoid of anything and appears empty apart from rubbish on the floor and the odd discarded pallet.

"Take the stairs," a voice orders from inside the tactical room.

Cal doesn't see who gave the order from around the table, but the wearer of the bodycam follows his instructions immediately and turns for the stairs. Cal finds his head turning along with the bodycam, as if it will change his field of view. It won't. He will only see what is on the screen, he quickly realises, and so he tries to stop the reflex action of his head.

Up the dark stairs, the bodycam turns again onto another empty floor that already has other team members clearing it. All Cal sees on this floor is one stranded old desk, without even a chair to keep it company.

"Move up to the top floor." Another order is issued from the tactical room but still Cal doesn't see who spoke.

Turning for the stairs again, Cal feels his neck muscles go to move in the same direction as the bodycam. He stops himself turning his head as the team member wearing it rushes up the last flight of stairs.

Darkness is suddenly replaced by soft light as the bodycam moves out onto the top floor, which must have its lights switched on. Cal immediately sees that this floor contains equipment. His darting eyes see computer screens in the moment before the bodycam whites out again, this time completely. The screen on the wall bursts with white light, making the entire room recoil from the assault of blinding light. As quickly as the light burns onto the screen it is then thrown into darkness, leaving the room momentarily in confused silence.

"Have we lost the feed?" Khan demands.

"Comms are down," the voice that was issuing orders to the team confirms.

Interference replaces the total darkness on the viewing screen and it spreads like snow across its entire expanse. Cal stares at it in a trance, fearing the worst.

"Contact the tactical vehicle," Khan demands.

"Command, are you receiving? This is Agent Dwyer," a frantic voice suddenly bursts through the comms speaker.

"Report, Agent!" Khan demands, leaning forward. "Why have we lost the operational feed?"

"There's been an explosion on the top floor! Multiple casualties. We need urgent medical assistance. There are bodies everywhere!" comes the tragic reply.

The room around Cal falls into a shocked hush for a second, nobody seemingly knowing how to react to this devastating news.

"Commissioner Jackson, Sir. You need to order a major incident," Cassie insists, while others are still floundering.

"Cassie is right, Sir," Cal confirms.

"Help is on the way, Agent Dwyer," Jackson shouts in the direction of the comms receiver.

Jackson rushes out of his chair and out of the room without excusing himself. Two others, a man and a woman, both in police uniforms, follow Jackson out of the tactical room. All three of them have their phones in hand ready to make the necessary calls to instigate the major incident order.

"Another battle lost," Dunguard announces. "We seem to be one step behind at every turn."

"That's not what's happened here," Khan insists, still with a look of disbelief.

"Oh, really?" Dunguard replies. "What has happened then, Director? Because it seems that your tactical team has just walked into another trap. Surely this should have been foreseen?"

"We were close. This wasn't just a communications relay. It was an important part of their infrastructure," Khan surmises. "The explosion was a defence mechanism to prevent it from falling into our hands."

"Is that your evaluation?" Dunguard replies, unimpressed. "Or just a working theory?"

"Rewind the feed to just before it was cut off," Khan insists, ignoring Dunguard's taunts.

Cal immediately understands what Khan is getting at. He saw a fleeting glimpse of the set-up on the top floor in the moment just before the explosion. Cassie also understands and leans as far forward as the table in front of them will allow her to get a better look at the screen.

"There," Khan announces as the feed rewinds, "pause it there."

Everyone around the table waits with bated breath as the feed is moved frame by frame until it settles on the equipment in the room captured by the bodycam.

"You see," Khan says, as the feed comes to a stop focused on a workstation with three computer screens on top of it. "This was an active control site, not just a VPN node relay station. What is your assessment, Agent Sutton?"

"At a glance, I would have to agree, Sir," Cassie replies. "Somebody was actively using those computers."

"The destruction of the site when the team arrived would also corroborate that theory," Cal adds.

"Precisely," Khan insists. "We discovered more than we initially assumed."

"In that case, shouldn't more care and preparation have been taken?" Dunguard asks.

"In hindsight," Khan concedes.

"Who's to say that, whatever precautions were taken, the result wouldn't have been the same?" Cassie wonders.

"The site should have been put under observation before it was approached," Colonel Medlam insists.

"That's easy to say now, Colonel," Khan defends strongly. "We needed results and I don't recall you suggesting anything to the contrary when it was decided to send the team in."

"This was a civilian operation, Director. I assumed that you knew what you were doing," Medlam replies flatly.

"You piece of shit," Khan seethes, losing his temper. "Those were my men and I…"

"Director Khan," Dunguard interjects, cutting Khan off. "I'm sure the colonel forgot himself for a moment. Isn't that right, Colonel Medlam?"

Medlam is left with little choice as the Secretary of Defence stares him down, and he backtracks after a moment of silent tension.

"Where do we go from here?" Mayor Roberts asks, easing the tension somewhat after Khan and Medlam stand down from butting heads.

Lengthy discussions in the tactical room ensue to decide where the investigation now stands and what the current threat level in the city is as a result of the outbreak. Cal is pleased to hear General Peters report that his men have secured the Gas Street Basin area without further casualties. He wonders if Sergeant Locke is still at the basin raising hell.

Commissioner Jackson returns after issuing his orders to get help to the site of the explosion. He tells the room that initial reports suggest that there are eight dead and numerous casualties at the site. That medical teams are inbound and that he has also despatched a team of officers to investigate the explosion and the site for evidence. Cal insists that he and Cassie should travel with the investigation team, but he is overruled by Jackson. Jackson orders them to oversee the investigation from the safety of Mercury House, where he insists there is more than enough evidence for them to investigate.

After an inordinate amount of debate, Cal and Cassie are dismissed from the meeting to continue their investigations. Both get up wearily, ready to leave, and, as they do, Tilly, who has been sitting quietly, leaves her chair.

"Report any developments to me immediately, Detective. No matter what the time," Commissioner Jackson orders before they can leave the room.

"Yes, Sir," Cal replies, wondering what Jackson means, considering it is already the early hours of the morning.

"I'm running on empty," Cassie says, as they make their way out.

"I'm tired and hungry, and not necessarily in that order," Cal replies.

"Why don't you two take a break and visit the cafeteria? I will go and see if there are any new developments and, if there is anything urgent, I will contact you," Tilly offers.

Taking Tilly up on her offer, Cal and Cassie head to the cafeteria a few floors down. Cal finds himself eager to see what is on offer, thoughts of a hot meal causing his stomach to growl. On arrival, it is immediately apparent that his fantasy of a steaming plate of food is going to remain just that, a fantasy. The cafeteria is empty apart from one man who is pushing a mop around the floor. No smell of hot food greets Cal's nostrils, only that of detergent.

"This doesn't look very promising," Cal moans.

"It isn't. It's never good at this time of night, or should I say morning? And, from what I've heard, not many of the staff turned up today so the pickings have been slim all day," Cassie informs him.

"Great." Cal rolls his eyes.

"At least it will give us a chance to talk," Cassie offers.

Unfortunately for Cal, the pickings are very slim and he ends up with an uninviting sandwich wrapped in cardboard and cellophane, a small pipe of Pringles and a fizzy drink. The only hot items are offered by a drinks machine, which he will make use of once he's eaten.

"A shame we left those other sandwiches in your car," Cal says in disappointment. "They must have been better than this."

His reference to the bag of sandwiches that Cassie had bought from the upmarket sandwich shop yesterday evening makes him think of Chief Arnold. She had gone into the sandwich shop with Cassie and that is the last time Cal can remember her as she was. Everything after that was frantic until, finally, Arnold was attacked.

"They are the best from there. I can't remember the last time I was forced to use this place," Cassie replies, as she sits down at a table, away from the man with the mop.

"Isn't there an executive restaurant? Or haven't you made it to that level in your career yet?" Cal wonders.

"There isn't one. There are usually too many excellent local eateries to choose from to spend the tax dollar, so it isn't necessary," Cassie replies.

"That was then. We're all slumming it now," Cal observes, as he reluctantly splits open the packet of sandwiches.

"I'm going to send that message," Cassie announces, changing the direction of the conversation. "The destruction of that building might be a blow to the conspirators. Perhaps they need a new source of information."

"Something tells me that information isn't something these people are lacking," Cal says. "I can't look at anybody around here without suspicion any more. But it's worth a try."

"What have we got to lose?" Cassie states.

"I don't know. You tell me," Cal replies, digging.

"I will, my friend," Cassie promises. "Let me just send this message first."

"What are you saying?" Cal asks, after a minute and through a mouthful of bread.

"Just what we discussed earlier. I'm warning them about the evidence gathered from the arena," Cassie replies.

"Tell them about the tactical operation too and the explosion," Cal suggests.

"Are you sure?" Cassie replies, pausing her typing to look at Cal.

"What have we got to lose? Surely they will know about it anyway?" Cal insists.

"And if they don't, they soon will, but they might hear it from me first," Cassie agrees, and continues tapping the phone. "Writing a message on these burner phones is a nightmare," she adds.

"That's how we all used to do it before these new-fangled smartphones," Cal observes.

"Seems like another lifetime," Cassie replies, as she finishes up.

Cal doesn't answer her. Instead, he takes the last morsel of the sandwich, puts it in his mouth and remains silent. He decides that it's time Cassie tells him what leverage these people have over her and what she is being blackmailed with. He gives her time to finish her sandwich, which she looks totally unimpressed with. When finished, Cassie gets up and approaches the drinks machine.

"I guess it's that time," Cassie says nervously, putting a steaming black coffee on the table in front of Cal.

"I guess so," Cal agrees. "Don't be embarrassed to leave out any details. I need to know what we're up against and I've been around long enough to have seen just about everything. It's inevitable in my line of work."

"I'm afraid that if you are hoping for a tale of sexual debauchery you are going to be disappointed," Cassie says, through a forced smile.

"I don't know what to expect, if I'm honest," Cal replies.

"It's bad but PG-rated, I'm afraid. For the most part, anyway," Cassie says.

"Okay," Cal waits.

"I was a young new recruit, no more than a year or so out of training, and I didn't know my ass from my elbow," Cassie begins. "I'd never really had a proper boyfriend or been in love. I'd always been so focused on my grades and achieving my chosen career."

"What career did you have planned? I guess it wasn't becoming a spy," Cal states.

"It doesn't matter now. It was a schoolgirl's dream," Cassie replies. "But, needless to say, my grades were outstanding."

"And someone took notice?" Cal asks.

"They must have. I was recruited straight out of university by the intelligence services. They told me that I was just the type of person they needed and what they were offering was exciting. I can't deny it. But, anyway, I digress," Cassie replies.

"What happened to this new recruit?" Cal questions.

"She fell in love," Cassie answers, her face blushing deeply and her eyes dipping.

"I see," Cal offers.

"He swept me off my feet. I'd never felt anything remotely close to those feelings and haven't since. He moved in with me after only a month and we were even talking about marriage. I was blinded by love," Cassie admits, ashamed.

"That's nothing to be ashamed of," Cal consoles.

"No, but I was a lovesick fool. I didn't see what was happening right in front of my eyes. He knew what I did and that I'd have to report our relationship, but he begged me not to straight away. He told me his mother was in the country illegally and it would put her in jeopardy, so I held off. He promised me that her situation was only temporary.

"Weeks turned into months and nothing changed. It was forgotten about. If I tried to raise the subject, he became angry and defensive until I dropped it. It hung over my head, but I did nothing and didn't report it to my superiors. I was afraid of losing him. I was so stupid," Cassie admits.

"What happened then?" Cal presses.

"Apart from that, we were happy. Blissfully so. Then things began to change and it started when he told me he'd lost his job. He asked to borrow money from me, which I was happy to do. He needed my help and I gave it."

"I see," Cal says.

"Suffice to say, a small amount of money turned into a large amount over a short period and it was all lent to him in cash. I got into financial difficulty. I'd borrowed the money to lend to him and then he left, disappeared without a word. I came home one day and he was gone. All he left was a short note saying he was sorry and that he'd give me the money back," Cassie pauses, threatening to become upset.

"I'm sorry, Cassie. That's shocking," Cal offers.

"That's not even the worst of it," Cassie replies, steeling herself.

"Oh," Cal says.

"I went to pieces, completely. I was heartbroken and financially broken. I didn't know which way to turn. Then one day, a couple of months later, I received a message from him. He told me that he was sorry again, but that he'd paid me my money back. I checked my bank and there it was. All the money I'd lent him was in my account," Cassie announces.

"That was lucky," Cal surmises.

"That's what I thought. I was still in bits over losing him but at least I wasn't on the brink financially any more. I paid off my debts and wanted to try to get over him. To look to the future at last, but that is when the real shock happened," Cassie continues.

"Really? What on earth happened then?" Cal asks earnestly.

"That's when I became trapped," Cassie replies.

"Trapped?" Cal questions.

"It was a lovely summer's day. I was walking in the park, just passing the time on my day off, when a man approached me. At first, I thought he was just a pest who saw me and liked me. You know the type. But then he called me by my name. I went to turn to leave when he asked me how my job was going at Secret Intelligence.

"Oh, God," Cal says, thinking he has guessed where this sorry tale is going.

Yes, oh God," Cassie agrees in a state of shock. "I demanded to know who he was and what he wanted. He never answered the first part of my question, but he did answer the second part.

"He insisted that he worked for an interested party, without elaborating, and then he dropped the bombshell. I couldn't believe what I was hearing. He explained how it was his associates that had paid back the money I was owed and that it was all traceable. He said that one day my services would be called upon and that if I didn't comply my financial duplicity would be revealed to the intelligence services. That I would be arrested for counter-espionage and the evidence would be damning," Cassie says.

"I thought so. I presume you checked and what he said was true?" Cal asks.

"Yes, I checked. In hindsight, I should have checked the source of the money in the first place, but at the time I was just relieved to have it back. I don't know where the money came from. I still don't to this day. I couldn't do a forensic search without incriminating myself. I didn't know what to do," Cassie insists.

"What happened then?" Cal asks.

"That's just it. Nothing happened. The man didn't wait for my answer, he just gave me my warning and then left. I haven't heard a thing about it from that day to this, well not until my meeting in the park the other night. I thought... hoped that they had forgotten about me. It was years ago after all," Cassie replies.

"These things have a tendency to come back and bite you," Cal points out.

"Thanks, Cal. I realise that now," Cassie replies.

"Sorry, I didn't mean..."

"It's okay. I know you didn't," Cassie concedes. "What do you think?"

"I think you were young and that you got played. You're not the first person it's happened to and you won't be the last," Cal says. "In this instance, however, it might give us the advantage. They think they've got you in the palm of their hand and that message you've just sent will hopefully draw them in."

"They haven't answered yet," Cassie points out.

"They will. I feel it," Cal replies. "And, in the meantime, we can work on where the money came from. That might lead us somewhere."

"Yes, it might lead back to me," Cassie replies. "Or it might raise a red flag to the conspirators!"

"I can instigate the search on the bank details. I don't see how they would know we're doing it and if it leads back to you, then so be it. You've told me everything and I'll back you to the hilt. What have you got to lose? And anyway, nobody's going to pay attention to a search on some bank details, not now, not with everything that's going on right now. They have bigger fish to fry," Cal insists.

Cassie pauses for a moment in thought.

"You're right, Cal," she finally says. "I haven't got anything to lose. I'd rather be locked up with the key thrown away than help these motherfuckers. I'd rather die than be responsible for anyone's infection or death. We do anything to use this to our advantage and, if that means all this comes out and I'm arrested, then to hell with it. Slap on the cuffs!"

"It won't come to that, Cassie. But, if it does, then I'm 100 percent behind you!" Cal announces.

"Thanks, partner," Cassie says, looking Cal straight in the eye.

"There's no need to thank me. You'd do the same and, you never know, I might have some skeletons in my closet," Cal grins.

"I'm sure you have," Cassie smiles back, with a twinkle in her eye.

"Come on," Cal insists. "We've got work to do!"

Chapter 12

"Is there anyone you can trust to do the search on the bank transaction?" Cal asks Cassie, when they arrive in her office.

"Probably Agent Morgan. He's young and keen. He's been my kind of protégé recently," Cassie answers.

"You have no suspicions about him?" Cal presses.

"Nobody is beyond suspicion at this point," Cassie huffs, "but it's an educated guess," she adds.

"Apart from me, I hope!" Cal jokes, trying to brighten the mood.

"Yes, you're alright, I suppose," Cassie smiles.

"What are your thoughts on Tilly?" Cal wonders.

"That's your call, my friend," Cassie answers. "I'd never met her before yesterday, but she seems very capable."

"She is, and she really admired Chief Arnold. I can't imagine her having a part in what happened to the chief," Cal says.

"She might not have had a choice, as I know all too well," Cassie points out.

"It's a fucking nightmare, isn't it?" Cal responds.

"Let's get her in here to ask," Cassie insists.

Before Cal can object, Cassie is heading out of her office to find Tilly. He goes to say something but stops himself. What other way is there to try and find out if Tilly can be trusted?

Moments later, Cassie arrives back, with Tilly following her. She asks Tilly to take a chair in front of her desk while Cassie goes around the desk to her chair. Cal decides not to come between the two women and stands to the side. He lets Cassie carry out the questioning. It was her idea after all.

"How long did you work with Chief Arnold?" Cassie asks Tilly, innocently enough.

"Just over two years," Tilly replies sadly.

"What were you doing before that?" Cassie continues.

"I was just a regular beat officer. Why?" Tilly replies.

"How long did you do that for?" Cassie asks, ignoring Tilly's question.

"Over four years. What's this about?" Tilly asks again.

"I'm just interested. What do you know about the attacks?" Cassie asks out of the blue.

"Only the same as you," Tilly responds. "Why? What are you suggesting? Are you suggesting that I'm involved in some way?"

"Are you?" Cassie demands.

"No, I am not, Agent," Tilly insists.

"It seems a bit strange to me that one day you're walking the beat and the next you're assisting the chief of police," Cassie says accusingly.

"I wouldn't call it strange. I'd call it hard work, Agent Sutton. Like spending two years at night school, along with walking the beat. Then applying for different positions within the force, where I could make more of a difference and further my career," Tilly reveals.

"So, how come you ended up assisting Chief Arnold?" Cassie presses.

"Ended up!" Tilly proclaims. "I didn't end up working for Chief Arnold. I worked hard and applied for the job, like everyone else. We clicked and she offered me the position."

"I see," Cassie replies.

"It's all above board and on record, Agent Sutton, but that isn't what this is all about, is it?" Tilly insists.

"Why don't you tell me what this is about then?" Cassie replies.

"You believe that the people behind these attacks have infiltrated law enforcement agencies and you want to know if I'm one of those people. You want to know if you can trust me," Tilly says.

"And if that is true?" Cassie wonders.

"I think it would be almost impossible for me to prove that I'm not one of those people," Tilly replies.

"So, you understand our predicament," Cassie asks.

"Of course I do. I have been asking the same questions about almost everyone involved in the investigation. Including you, Agent Sutton," Tilly answers.

"I see, and what about Detective Chambers? Can you trust him?" Cassie asks.

"Yes," Tilly answers simply.

"At least that's something we can agree on," Cassie says.

"Sorry we had to ask you those questions, Tilly," Cal says. "We just needed to be sure."

"No need to apologise. I understand," Tilly replies. "I will do anything in my power to bring the people who are responsible for Chief Arnold's death to justice. Including answering a few uncomfortable questions."

"Are you satisfied?" Cal asks Cassie.

"As I'll ever be. Thank you, Tilly."

"Shall we ask Agent Morgan to join us?" Cal suggests.

Moments later a smartly dressed young agent lets himself into Cassie's office. Cassie makes the introductions while the young man almost stands to attention in the middle of her office.

"Good to meet you, Agent," Cal says to break the ice, whilst offering his hand to shake.

"Sir," Morgan says, shaking Cal's hand.

"Thank you for joining us, Morgan," Cassie continues. "Detective Chambers and I have asked the two of you here because we have work to do that needs to be done by people we can trust.

"Whatever we discuss between us goes no further, not even to the hierarchy of both S.I. and the police force. We don't know who we can trust. So, if you're not comfortable with that then please feel free to leave us," Cassie insists.

Neither Tilly nor Agent Morgan move a muscle.

"Good. Then let's get started," Cassie says.

"There will be things that Argent Sutton and I are working on that you will be unaware of," Cal interjects. "But we need you to trust us until we are in a position to bring you up to date and we're ready to act."

"You're in charge, Detective Chambers," Tilly says. "I am here to help in whatever capacity you see fit."

"As am I," Agent Morgan confirms. "We are under your direction."

With that acknowledgement, Cassie hands Morgan a piece of paper detailing the bank transaction for the payment that appeared in her account. She mentions that the transaction was from years ago, but she doesn't divulge any further detail. She doesn't need to at this stage. The information on the piece of paper should be all Morgan needs to carry out the search.

"What have you got for me?" Tilly asks.

"We need you to be our eyes and ears in the office, Tilly," Cal says. "Bring us anything you think needs our attention and might move the investigation forward."

"The same goes for you, Agent Morgan," Cassie adds.

"Agent Sutton and I are working on other leads that we will need to concentrate on and more evidence is about to arrive from the site of the explosion," Cal states.

"I have something that I've just discovered," Agent Morgan says.

"Oh," Cal replies. "What have you got?"

"After the dramatic events at the industrial unit, I did some digging into the property," Morgan reveals.

"Yes, and you found something?" Cal encourages.

"Possibly, Sir. The property is owned by a multinational umbrella company called International Property Partners, abbreviated to IPP. IPP have numerous industrial sites on its books across the globe. The company leases out all the sites. They are basically a landlord for businesses. The company was leasing out the property where the explosion happened to another company, named Bricknell Resources. Bricknell Resources is a phantom company. It isn't registered anywhere and is probably untraceable. I haven't been able to trace any other information on it. There isn't even a website for the company, which I think you will agree is very strange in this day and age."

"Strange, but not unheard of," Cal offers.

"But why would a reputable company like IPP accept a phantom company onto its books to lease one of its properties? All their other properties, as far as I can see, are leased by medium to big businesses, all of them above board. It looks shady to me, Sir, as if they were in collusion together," Morgan surmises.

"Who owns IPP?" Cassie asks.

"It's a publicly traded company. I was just beginning to research who the major stockholders are when you called me in here," Morgan replies.

"Keep on it, Agent," Cal says enthusiastically. "This could be a major breakthrough."

"I will, Sir. But there's something else," Morgan reveals.

"Yes?" Cal pushes.

"As I said, IPP hold property across the globe. Property worth billions of dollars but they only have two properties on their books in this city, which I've seen from my initial research: the site of the explosion and a small retail property on the outskirts of the city centre," Morgan says.

"And your point is?" Cassie asks.

"The property where the explosion happened is small fry for a company like IPP. They own entire industrial estates, office blocks and skyscrapers. That property is odd enough, but the small retail property makes no sense whatsoever. Could the second property be linked to the destroyed property?" Morgan explains.

Cal and Cassie look at each other, as the penny drops for both of them.

"Give me the address," Cassie tells Morgan.

"I have it here," Morgan says, pulling a piece of paper from his pocket.

Cal snatches the paper from Morgan's hand to look at the address.

"I know this area," he says. "It's not more than ten minutes away."

Silence falls over Cassie's office as the four of them consider the implications of Morgan's revelation.

"Are you thinking what I'm thinking?" Cassie breaks the silence, looking at Cal.

"If you're thinking we need to check out this address then yes, I am," Cal replies.

"You should send a surveillance team to the address," Tilly suggests.

"You're probably right," Cal replies. "Can you get me some information, Tilly?"

"Of course, Sir," Tilly smiles.

"See if you can find me the name of the firearms sergeant who led the team that got us out when the arena was overrun, please," Cal requests.

"You are referring to Sergeant Neal," Tilly replies without delay.

"Am I?" Cal replies, surprised at Tilly's knowledge.

"I believe so, Sir," Tilly confirms.

"Okay. Can you find out where he is?" Cal asks.

"Certainly, Sir," Tilly agrees. "Do you want me to put him on alert?"

"Yes, Tilly. Thanks. Tell him to be ready if we need him," Cal replies.

"Okay. What are you planning to do?" Tilly asks.

"We're going to have a look at this address," Cal insists.

"I see," Tilly says, looking decidedly dubious at Cal's decision.

"Thank you, Tilly. You and Agent Morgan carry on with your tasks. I'll let you know what Agent Sutton and I decide to do," Cal instructs.

"She's right," Cassie says after they leave. "We should send a surveillance team to the address."

"Probably, but I've got a feeling this could be important. Putting a surveillance team in place is going to create noise and possibly alert whoever is watching the investigation. Plus, it will take time to get a team in place," Cal argues. "Where's the harm in us taking a look?"

"Do I need to remind you about what's happened since we teamed up?" Cassie smiles.

"Fair point. But I'm sure this time will be different," Cal grins back.

"Come on then," Cassie submits, rising from her chair.

After informing Tilly that they are going to check out the property, Cassie takes them down to the car park. She tells Cal to remain near the exit while she goes off to commandeer another car. Cal checks his phone while he waits, but there is nothing of interest to click on. Nothing from Tom or Kim, not that he's surprised considering the lateness of the hour. He hopes that Kim is not totally consumed by her loss and is managing to get some sleep. Deciding not to risk disturbing her, Cal puts off trying to contact her until the morning. *Well, later in the morning*, he tells himself, glancing at the clock on his phone.

Admitting to himself that he's exhausted, Cal wonders to himself if he will get any rest before the sun comes up. He doubts it. Not that he isn't used to pulling an all-nighter in the name of justice. Another one of Kim's gripes. Cal reminds himself that he always saw to it that he had a good meal when it didn't look like as if clocking off was going to happen, and not a flimsy sandwich. Plus, he had very little sleep the night before. *Stick with it*, he tells himself, as the sound of a car engine approaches.

"You should have been a racing-car driver," Cal teases, when Cassie accelerates hard again, after skidding to a stop next to him.

"I just like to get where I'm going," Cassie replies, as she tugs on the steering wheel.

"So do I, preferably in one piece," Cal insists.

"Don't worry. I'll get you there in one piece, Detective, and in half the time," Cassie giggles.

"Do you know where it is?" Cal asks.

Cassie replies with a sideways glance of disdain in response to Cal's question, so he shuts his mouth and lets her drive.

"We will be closer to the Arena District," Cassie says, breaking the silence.

"Yes, we will. I don't think the undead could possibly be approaching that far out yet though," Cal replies.

"You really are an optimist, aren't you?" Cassie insists.

"You're the first person who's ever accused me of that, to be honest," Cal replies.

"Perhaps it's me that brings it out of you then," Cassie smiles.

"You must do," Cal mumbles, wondering how to take Cassie's words.

"Don't be shy about it," Cassie says.

"I'm not," Cal stumbles.

"Don't worry. You're not my type, Detective," Cassie sniggers and slaps Cal on the leg.

"Very funny," Cal defends, as he realises that it is Cassie's turn to do the teasing.

Cal looks out of his side window as the car climbs to see if he can see the Arena District. His mind wonders back to Cassie as he searches, wondering what type she does go for, feeling his leg smarting from her slap.

"Sorry, what did you say?" Cal blurts, realising that Cassie is talking to him.

"I said, have you heard how your wife is?" Cassie repeats, as if she had heard where Cal's thoughts might have been heading.

"Er, not since earlier. She was asleep and I don't want to risk disturbing her until later," Cal replies.

"No. That's probably for the best," Cassie says.

"So, what about you? Is there anyone special in your life?" Cal risks.

"That's a bit of a personal question, don't you think?" Cassie answers, but this time Cal catches the glimmer in her eye, as she tries to have him on again.

"You don't have to answer if you're embarrassed," Cal fences.

"Touché." Cassie looks at Cal and smiles. "No, there isn't. Since what happened to me, I concentrate on my job and keep things very casual in the romance department."

Cal realises what Cassie means and he doesn't ask any further questions, owing to his own embarrassment, much as he'd like to hear more detail. *Men, eh?* he tells himself, as he decides to change the subject.

"How long have you and your wife been separated?" Cassie asks, before Cal can change the subject.

"Too long," Cal answers.

"It must be tough, in more ways than one," Cassie says.

"That's for sure," Cal replies, again wondering what Cassie is referring to.

"Do you think you'll reconcile?" Cassie persists.

"If I'm honest, I really don't know. Sometimes I think there's a chance for us but then other times it looks impossible," Cal admits.

"What do you want?" Cassie asks.

"That keeps changing too. I remember how Kim and I used to be but, recently, and before she became pregnant, nothing I did was good enough for her," Cal admits, both to Cassie and himself.

"And now all this. Sometimes life can be a bitch," Cassie says.

"And then some," Cal agrees.

"Well, that conversation became very depressing very quickly," Cassie jokes.

"Sorry about that," Cal replies.

"Don't worry. I think we're both as bad as each other," Cassie smiles. "Anyway, we're almost there. Where shall we park up?"

"I think I know a spot," Cal responds.

Chapter 13

With the headlights off, Cassie crawls the car into position. She has to hand it to Cal: he knows the area better than she does. The small three-storey car park across from the row of shops is only reachable down a narrow side road and is all but hidden by surrounding trees on the lower level.

"That's it," Cal encourages, as Cassie comes to a stop on the second level. "The property should be opposite."

"Which one is it?" Cassie asks, as she applies the handbrake.

"That one. The barber's shop," Cal replies.

"Agent Morgan was right. The property does look low-ball for such a big property company," Cassie observes.

"It looks deserted though," Cal says, putting a pair of binoculars to his face. "Lucky these were in the car," he adds.

"Not luck. This is a tactical car. I made sure of it. You should see the toys hidden away in the back," Cassie announces.

"My mistake," Cal replies. "I should have known better."

"You'll get used to me," Cassie jokes. "Here, let me have a look."

Cal hands Cassie the binoculars but continues to stare at the target property. It isn't the only one in total darkness and all the others have shut-up stores below. Shadows move inside the residences with lights on. There is nothing particularly out of the ordinary about the target property Cal is looking at, but he definitely has a feeling in his gut. There is something sinister about the property and Cal learnt long ago to trust his gut instinct.

"What do you think? It looks empty, but I've got a feeling about it," Cal asks.

"Looks can be deceiving, as I'm sure you know. Let's wait and watch," Cassie suggests.

While Cassie zooms in on the target with the binoculars, Cal decides to have a closer look at the local terrain using his phone. He knows that the main shopping centre is close by and that a tree-lined park is situated beyond the row of buildings they are watching. He zooms in on the map that he has opened to familiarise himself with exactly where the park is in relation to the target building. Unfortunately, as he suspected, the row of buildings backs directly onto the park, offering the perfect escape route for anyone inside the building. On the other hand, the park would provide a favourable approach to the building should they decide to go in.

"We're going to need some help," Cassie says.

"Why? What's happening? What have you seen?" Cal asks eagerly, diverting his field of view back to the property.

"There is movement inside, on the top floor. There is definitely someone in there with the lights off. I can see their silhouette moving like a shadow," Cassie confirms.

"Let me see," Cal demands, holding his hand up to take the binoculars.

"Just inside the main window," Cassie explains, handing them over.

"I don't see any movement," Cal says, after a moment looking.

"There is someone inside, I'm telling you," Cassie insists.

"I believe you; they're just not showing themselves now," Cal replies. "Maybe they've just sat down or something."

"Do we go in?" Cassie questions excitedly.

"It's risky. It could be booby-trapped as well," Cal replies. "I see them," he adds, as a shadow moves behind the window.

"We can't refuse this opportunity," Cassie insists. "There can only be two ways out of that property: front and back. If we stay out of sight, we have the element of surprise."

"That doesn't mean the property isn't booby-trapped," Cal points out.

"They aren't going to blow the place up if they're still inside," Cassie argues.

"I wouldn't put anything past these fuckers," Cal counters.

"It's a risk I'm willing to take. That could be the person responsible for all this in there," Cassie insists.

Cal thinks for a moment. Cassie is right: this could be the breakthrough they've been working towards. A chance to bring the horror to an end, but are they willing to take the risk? Cassie is. She's made that clear.

"Have you had a reply to your message?" Cal asks.

"What do you think?" Cassie answers in frustration. "I'd have said, wouldn't I? This is our best opportunity!"

"Okay, I'll speak to Tilly," Cal concedes.

"Hello," Tilly answers almost immediately.

"Did you speak to Sergeant Neal?" Cal asks bluntly.

"Yes, he's standing by. Why? What's happening?" Tilly asks.

"We have a suspect inside the property," Cal replies. "Tell Sergeant Neal to meet us. I'll send you our location. We are on the second floor of a car park overlooking the target."

"It could be another trap!" Tilly insists.

"We are aware of that, thank you, Tilly, but we can't miss this opportunity," Cal replies. "Tell Sergeant Neal to bring a small team and to approach quietly."

"As you wish, Sir," Tilly answers. "But please take every precaution."

"We will. Any new developments there?" Cal asks.

"Nothing solid. Agent Morgan is still digging, but it's turning into a big spider's web," Tilly answers.

"Why am I not surprised?" Cal replies.

"Indeed, Sir. I'll speak to Sergeant Neal and then inform you of his ETA, okay?" Tilly says.

"Thank you. Let me know if anything new is uncovered," Cal finishes.

"She's worried," Cassie says, after Cal hangs up and goes to send Tilly their location.

"Can you blame her after what happened at the other site?" Cal replies.

"No, but we've got to speak to whoever is in there," Cassie insists.

"Maybe he'd speak to us if we knocked nicely on the front door?" Cal replies jokingly.

"Yes, and invite us in for a cup of tea." Cassie rolls her eyes.

"Sorry, bad joke," Cal admits. "Let's get a plan of action together for when the firearms team arrive, shall we?"

"Yes, although they'll probably rip it to shreds when they hear it," Cassie observes.

"Probably, but it'll give us a starting point at least," Cal argues.

"Okay, what are you thinking?" Cassie asks.

Tilly messages quickly to inform them that the firearms team's ETA is 15 minutes. Cal and Cassie spend that time debating their entry plan and watching the property. Cal constantly checks the time, impatiently waiting for the backup to arrive.

Approximately 15 minutes later, and without warning, Cal sees a glimpse of movement in the car's wing mirror. The sudden movement shocks him and he turns in his seat to see what is happening. There is no sign of the firearms team's transportation and he panics that maybe they have become the target.

A tap on a back door window turns Cal's head to see a pair of eyes under a combat helmet. The eyes belong to Sergeant Neal, he realises with relief.

"A lovely morning for it!" Sergeant Neal announces as Cassie opens the car to let him in and he slides onto the back seat.

"Where's the rest of your team?" Cassie asks, confused.

"Parked up at the rear of the car park. Driving the tactical van into a confined space like this car park would make too much noise. It would be like a lion's roar echoing out and would give away our presence. The engine on that thing is loud enough without amplifying it," Neal replies.

"I see," Cassie says.

"What have we got?" Neal asks.

"We have identified that property, the barber's shop," Cal says, pointing, "as being potentially linked to the property destroyed earlier. The lights are off but there is a potential suspect inside."

"Just the one suspect?" Neal interrupts.

"Undetermined. It's hard to see in the darkness but we have seen movement," Cal replies.

"May I?" Neal asks, holding up his hand to take the binoculars from Cassie.

"Be my guest," Cassie says, handing them over.

"Do you know what's to the rear of the building?" Neal asks, as he peers into the property.

"There is a park. It should provide good cover to approach," Cal replies. "We thought if your team go in the front, we'll take the rear," he offers.

"Negative," Neal states. "My team will take both. Tilly will have my guts for garters if anything happens to you,

Detective. She made that very clear. You can follow us in once the target is secured."

"But…" Cal begins to argue, even though he feels relief that Neal and his team will be facing the danger.

"Sorry, Detective. I'm in tactical command and I don't want you getting in our way," Neal insists. "No offence," he adds.

"Okay," Cal concedes. "We are worried about booby traps though."

"It's a risk, but they're inside and if we surprise them, it might mitigate the risk," Neal replies.

"I'm sure the other team thought the same earlier on," Cassie points out.

"That was an S.I. team and, from what I've heard, they bowled in without surveying the target," Neal counters. "We have eyes on a suspect. We'll hit them out of the blue and at this time they'll probably be asleep. There are no guarantees but there never are in this line of work."

"When do you want to go?" Cal asks.

"I'll brief my team and then we'll move out," Neal replies, turning for the car door. "Are you coming?"

Cal and Cassie get out of the car with Neal. They follow his lead by softly closing the car doors behind them and by staying low until they are well out of the line of sight of the property. Neal then leads them down through the car park and out to his team.

The large boxy van could easily be confused with a commercial vehicle, especially considering that there are no police markings on its outside. Neal, out of habit, checks his back before pulling the back door of the vehicle open.

"Move along," Neal orders his men, who fill the back of the van.

Cal counts five other heavily armed men waiting inside, who are forced to squeeze together to allow three more bodies in. An immediate hush falls over the confined space the moment the back door is closed. Neal's men are eager to hear the briefing, and to get on with the task at hand, and they are not made to wait.

Neal briefs his men and hands out his orders clearly and efficiently. He plans to split his team into two, with three of his men approaching through the park to secure the rear while three storm the front door. Cal and Cassie will cover the front team as they work but remain outside until the property is secured.

"I trust you followed Tilly's request and kept this operation off-book," Cal asks, when Sergeant Neal asks if there are any questions.

"Yes, Detective, and we will be using short-range radios for the operation. I won't ask why this is necessary. I'll trust your judgement... for now," Neal replies.

"Thank you, Sergeant," Cal says, without elaborating in front of the men.

"We need the suspects alive," Cassie adds. "We have to hope they hold vital information."

"Understood, Agent," Neal replies. "Now, if there is nothing else, let's synchronise watches."

The team make sure their watches are correct and Neal tells the second team to be in position in ten minutes and to wait for his command. Three of the team let themselves out of the van to begin their journey to the park. They have been ordered to move through the back roads to the park to make sure they can't be seen from the property as they make their way around.

Nervous tension rises in the back of the van as they wait five minutes to give the other three men time to get to the park. Neal issues Cal and Cassie with rifles. This time, he doesn't make any fuss regarding the protocol, as he did at the arena after rescuing Cal and Cassie. Weapons are checked and, finally, black scarfs are pulled over faces when Neal moves for the door.

Neal hits the ground first, followed by his two men, one of whom carries a battering ram with him. Cal follows Cassie out and quickly turns to quietly shut the door before heading off in pursuit of the others. Neal also uses a back road to move past the property unseen before he turns for the target road.

The team scurry across the road to arrive on the side of the target property, but they are a good distance away. Now, they make their approach, staying tight to the buildings on their left to remain out of sight should the suspect be looking out of the property's window. Neal leads them closer, stepping carefully and deliberately down the dark road and staying as close to the buildings as he can to remain in the shadows. Cal is confident that they are out of sight, short of the suspect leaning out of a window and looking down the street, which is unlikely.

Just short of the charity shop and its side door into the residence above, Neal signals for Cal and Cassie to halt. They obey his order and take up covering positions as Neal leads his men into position.

Converging on the target door, the three men pause while Neal communicates with the second team at the rear of the building. After a second, Neal nods and the battering ram is swung into the air.

Smashing into the door with an almighty crash that rings out across the entire road, the battering ram bounces hopelessly off the sturdy door. *Shit*, Cal panics, *if the suspect didn't know they were coming, they do now.* The ram is swung again, with the same hopeless result. Almost instantly, Neal decides to act and aims his rifle at the area of the door's hinges.

A massive crash bellows up the stairs and into the tiny flat, where Uri has fallen asleep after changing his wet clothes. He is sitting on the small sofa with his head hanging over the back, his mouth gaping open, catching flies.

He jumps with shock on the sofa as if 20,000 volts of electricity have been applied to his testicles. Uri's neck cricks, shooting with a pain that darts into his brain. Confusion consumes him. He has lost all knowledge of where he is and what he was doing. *Was I dreaming? Was the crashing sound in my dreams?* he panics, as he realises where he is. Slobber dribbles down his chin and more pain shoots into his neck as he tries to rise from the sofa.

Uri jumps again as terror washes through him as another almighty crash hammers against the front door at the bottom of the stairs. *This is no dream*, he scolds himself, as he manages to rise from the sofa, trying to ignore the pain shooting through his neck.

He grabs the Beretta out of the top of his bag, realising that he's been found and that the authorities are trying to bash in the front door. Uri's escape plan from this location is far more mundane that the one he had formed at the industrial park. He had never envisaged that the authorities would find that location, but he meticulously made his escape plans from that site, just in case. Asking questions about how they have discovered this back-alley bolt-hole so quickly is for another time. All he needs to concentrate on now is trying to escape. At least the reinforced door is delaying his pursuers, but that won't last.

Uri heads for the plastic door on his right at the back of the building, beyond which is a flight of metal steps down onto a path next to the park. He realises that it might already be too late, that officers could be positioned out back. All he can do is hope that this team are as unprofessional as the last one that tried to catch him and he regrets that he didn't form a proper escape plan.

He rips open the door but pauses at the top of the steps. Luckily his eyes are already accustomed to the dark and he scans the park beyond the path. Uri doesn't see any movement and so he goes for it. Gunfire blasts as he turns to shut the door behind him and he realises that the front door hinges are being targeted. With the Beretta out in front of him, Uri descends the metal stairs as quickly as possible, hoping he can at least get into the treeline before his pursuers smash open the front door and realise where he has gone.

The steel steps reverberate with every step Uri takes as he descends, but he cannot afford to slow down. Uri feels a glimmer of hope that he might escape, as his boots hit the gravel at the bottom of the stairs. The treeline is close and, once inside its cover, he can disappear.

Ignoring his tired, aching body and the pain in his neck, Uri presses forward towards the trees, just as a loud crash sounds in the building behind. The front door has given way and it won't take them long to realise where he has gone.

"Armed police! Drop your weapon!"

Uri hears the words a second before he sees the three figures appear from the darkness of the treeline. The black-clad police officers blend into the dark surroundings almost perfectly and each has an automatic rifle trained on him. Blood rushes to Uri's head and panic sets in. Decades in the field tell him that he is cornered, that he has no chance of escape. The only question for Uri now is whether he surrenders or whether he fights and dies.

In the blink of an eye, Uri makes his decision. He isn't ready to fall on his sword and into eternal oblivion. Living to fight another day is far more preferential than fading into nothingness, which he decided long ago, after studying his victims, is all that awaits the dead.

"Drop it on the ground," Uri is ordered as he lowers his Beretta.

Two of the officers move in on Uri the moment the gun clatters into the gravel. The other officer keeps his weapon aimed at Uri, even as his hands are zip-tied behind his back.

"One suspect secured," one of the officers reports into his radio.

Plastic cuts into Uri's wrists, but he is too tired to protest. Not that it would do him any good anyway. Noise sounds from the top of the stairs as more police officers appear from inside.

"Bring him up here," one of them orders from above.

Each of Uri's arms is grabbed and he is frogmarched back the way he came before being pushed towards the stairs. He climbs them under his own steam. There is no point in being difficult: all that would get him is a jab to the ribs or his arms twisted up his back.

Uri steps back through the door, where another armed officer stands, together with two people in plain clothes. Uri recognises both of them immediately. It is his job to know key players after all and one of them he's met previously.

"Sit down," one of the armed officers orders and shoves him towards the sofa.

Uri debates his best course of action and does as he's told and turns to sit. Should he play dumb or toy with his captors? Maybe he can aid Foundation Day in a different, unforeseen way. He sees Agent Sutton staring at him, her recollection of their clandestine meeting a few nights ago flooding back to her.

"Nice to see you again, Agent Sutton," Uri says, looking directly at Cassie.

"I wish I could say the same," Cassie manages to reply through her shock.

"And it's nice to meet you finally, Detective Chambers," Uri says, switching his focus.

"You have me at a disadvantage, Mr...?" Cal replies calmly.

"Mr Easter, Detective," Uri reveals.

"A pseudonym, no doubt," Cal accuses.

"I couldn't possibly say," Uri smiles.

"So that's how you want to play it, is it?" Cassie growls. "No comment and games."

"You are here uninvited after all, Agent Sutton. I was just resting," Uri smiles.

"I'm sorry if we disturbed you, Mr Easter. Can you tell us why you think we did?" Cal attempts.

"I couldn't possibly say," Uri replies.

"What accent is that?" Cal questions.

"Mine," Uri replies.

"You're wasting your time, Detective," Cassie says in frustration, reaching for her phone. "He's a martyr to the cause, no matter how demented the cause may be. My guess is that he's an Israeli with a sad story."

"I knew there was a reason we chose you to help," Uri says, genuinely impressed by Cassie's assumption. "Would you like me to smile?" he says, as Cassie points her phone at his face.

"It makes no difference nowadays," Cassie says, as she focuses her phone's camera.

Cassie's camera takes a perfectly acceptable picture, even in the dim light, and she wastes no time in sending it to Agent Morgan. With any luck, facial recognition will put an actual name to Mr Easter by the time they return to Mercury House with him in custody.

"How long have you been part of the cause?" Cal asks.

"A while now," Uri replies, vaguely.

"How can you live with yourself, causing such horror and suffering?" Cal pleads.

"You wouldn't understand," Uri replies.

"Try me!" Cal demands.

"You're wasting your breath, Detective," Cassie interrupts. "This type of person has no consideration for anyone but themselves. He's suffered, so everyone else must suffer too."

"Isn't that the way of the world, Agent Sutton?" Uri counters.

"Your world, Mr Easter. Not mine," Cassie replies angrily. "All you see is hatred."

"Perhaps you are correct, Agent Sutton. But aren't I a product of my surroundings?" Uri argues.

"That depends," Cassie replies.

"On what exactly?" Uri asks.

"On how weak you are and if you are strong enough to rise above your own misfortune to make a positive impact in the world. Instead of projecting your fear over everyone you encounter," Cassie seethes, taking a step towards Uri.

"You think I'm weak?" Uri snaps. Cassie has obviously hit a nerve.

Uri leans forward on the sofa in anger, his legs pushing him up to meet Cassie. Cal moves forward to protect Cassie from the attack he is sure is coming from their suspect. Sergeant Neal also acts, his rifle rising, ready to shoot.

"SIT DOWN!" Cassie shouts, her right arm shooting forward.

Uri buckles under Cassie's punch to his gut, which accompanies her shout. He crumples straight back down onto the sofa, groaning in pain and struggling for breath. Cal stops his forward motion and Neal lowers his rifle and takes a step back.

Under normal circumstances, Cal would strongly object to violence being used on a suspect in his custody. In this instance, however, all he objects to is that Cassie got her punch in before he could.

"Is it you who receives my communications?" Cassie demands, standing over their captive.

"Sometimes," Uri coughs.

"I see," Cassie says. "You were at the location that exploded and somehow managed to escape. Was it you who triggered the explosion?"

Uri glances up at Cassie with a sinister look, telling her all she needs to know.

"So, you murdered all of those people to cover your tracks and destroy the evidence," Cassie continues. "Now you're afraid your communications might be compromised and have remained dark since the explosion. That's why you haven't answered my message."

"What message?" Uri splutters, still bent over.

"It is of no consequence to you now. You're out of the game, permanently. You were right to be suspicious of your communications because, ultimately, they led us here and now any delusions of grandeur you had are in tatters," Cassie announces.

"We will see," Uri counters.

"No, we won't. You're done as far as your co-conspirators will be concerned," Cassie insists. "We know that you have moles inside the police force and inside Mercury House. They will be reporting the capture of Mr Easter soon enough and do you think you'll be allowed back into the fold once that information gets back?

"Even if you do manage to escape you would be a liability. I wouldn't be surprised if plans aren't already being drawn up to assassinate you, even as we speak."

"My work was almost complete in any event," Uri replies, unconvincingly.

"And this is how you planned it to all end? Stuck here with us or having your throat slit in a cell? You must have had other plans for your future. I bet promises were made to you," Cassie guesses.

"I knew the risks and they were risks I was willing to take for a higher good," Uri replies.

"A higher good! Don't make me laugh," Cassie insists. "You aren't fooling me. You weren't doing this for a higher good. You were doing it to satisfy your own twisted insecurities."

"Even so." Uri struggles to reply to Cassie's barrage of home truths.

"I don't think you even cared much for this cause, whatever it is. You just wanted to feel useful again in your old age. How old are you? Seventy? Eighty? A sad state of affairs. I hope your life's work brings you solace when the end nears, which, by the look of you, isn't far away." Cassie doesn't hold back.

"You could still be useful," Cal says, as Uri flounders somewhat to reply. "We know you're just another patsy, like Merle Abital. Why don't you help us bring this madness to an end? It's only a matter of time until your accomplices are found and stopped and the whole operation is brought down. Help us stop the suffering of innocent people now. Do something good for once in your life."

"You have no idea what you're up against," Uri replies. "This is just the beginning. You can't stop it, and neither can I."

"Are you too afraid to try?" Cal demands.

Chapter 14

A muffled crack of gunfire sounds from outside before Uri can answer Cal's question. Neal's rifle is up instantly, ready for action, as are the other officers who have remained with him. Cal realises the sound came from the street out front and not from the rear of the property. He turns urgently to the window next to him, which looks out over the road below.

A deathly scream vibrates through the window's glass as Cal peers out. Another gunshot sounds. The shot comes from low down, by the smashed-in front door, and then, fearfully, Cal sees ominous shadows on the other side of the road.

"They're here," Cal says grimly.

"How many?" Cassie asks, urgently joining him at the window.

"It's too dark to say," Cal replies, "but there are dozens at least."

Boots crash on the stairs up from the front door before one of Neal's men bursts into the room in a state of panic.

"We need to get out of here," the man blurts. "We're going to be overrun and the front door is compromised."

"Out the back?" Cal asks urgently, looking at Sergeant Neal.

"I don't like it," Neal admits nervously. "It's dark and the trees will give them cover. We wouldn't see them coming. We'd be sitting ducks."

Gunfire blasts out from inside the property, coming from the top of the stairs, where another of Neal's men must be positioned, covering the front door.

"How long can we hold out here, Sergeant? We need to go before we become surrounded and it would take a full-frontal attack by the army to free us!" Cassie protests.

"And so it begins," a menacing voice comes from the sofa.

"Shut the fuck up before I shut you up, permanently," Cassie growls at Uri, her eyes like daggers.

Cal ignores the remonstration as he scrolls through his phone. They need an emergency evac and Cal just might have a new acquaintance who might be able to assist.

More furious gunfire erupts from the top of the stairs, threatening to drown out the sound of Cal's phone as it rings. *Pick up*, Cal thinks desperately, as he tries to call the pilot of the helicopter who rescued them from the arena only to then take them to the basin, and then on to Mercury House. The only other option is to go through official channels to get help but that would take time.

"We need to go, Cal!" Cassie barks.

"Hold on a second," Cal pleads. "I'm trying to get us a lift out of here."

"Hello," a voice finally answers.

"Is that Pilot Monks?" Cal asks, repeating the name he saved to his phone.

"Yes," Monks replies, confused.

"It's Detective Chambers here from earlier," Cal shouts above the din. "We need an emergency evac. Where are you?"

"I've just landed back at base to refuel," Monks replies.

"Can you come? We're in a desperate situation here. We need you now," Cal begs.

"I need to get clearance. I can't just take off without clearance," Monks insists.

"Get clearance on the way, man," Cal pleads, "or there will be no one to pick up! Tell them I ordered you."

The line goes quiet for a moment, even as Cassie pulls at Cal's arm to move him towards the back door. Neal and his men are already preparing to evacuate the building.

"Where are you, Detective?" Monks finally says.

"We'll be in Craven Park. We'll signal you when you arrive," Cal replies urgently.

"I'll be there as soon as possible," Monks confirms.

"Thank you. Please hurry," Cal finishes.

Neal's men are already descending the metal staircase at the back of the building when Cal stuffs his phone away.

"A helicopter is coming for us," Cal shouts to everyone.

"It had better be quick," Neal replies, as he orders three of his men down the steps with a quick hand signal.

"It will be," Cal says, in hope more than expectation.

Cassie swiftly follows the three men down, her automatic rifle up and ready to fire.

"Here, take hold of this," Neal tells Cal, offering Uri's zip-tied hands for Cal to take control of.

Cal reluctantly does as he's asked, taking a firm grip on the plastic in between the hands, which are tied behind Uri's back. He'd much rather be able to take hold of his rifle than the prisoner. Instead, Cal pulls out his sidearm with his free hand and leaves the rifle slung over his shoulder to dangle at his back.

Neal waves Cal on to follow Cassie down the steps, with Uri in front of him. Thankfully, the prisoner seems to be cooperating and eagerly descends the steps just in front of Cal. Cal is forced to bend slightly to keep hold of Uri as he goes down. He daren't release him for one second. The prisoner might be just as eager as anyone to escape the threat of the undead but that doesn't mean he wouldn't bolt to escape at the first opportunity.

When Cal arrives at the bottom, Neal gives the order for the men remaining inside, covering the retreat, to move. The gunfire stops immediately as the men move and, within seconds, they are out of the door and onto the metal steps. The last one out pulls the plastic-and-glass door closed behind them. Nobody is under any illusions that the door is going to stop the zombies for long, it's too flimsy for that, but it might buy a few vital minutes.

"Which way?" one of Neal's men asks.

"Mercury House is close to that tall tower," Cassie insists, pointing to the right, above the park's treeline.

Nobody challenges Cassie's suggestion; the direction is as good as any. The three men upfront move out towards the cover of the trees, their rifles swiping in every direction nervously. The trees might offer cover, but they also loom ominously, threatening to spew out undead starving beasts, ready to feed, at any moment.

A loud bang from behind spurs everyone forward. The park appears perilous, but it is nothing compared to the threat of the apocalyptic creatures that will soon burst through the door behind them.

"Watch your flanks," Neal orders, as they close in on the trees.

Uri stumbles, almost falling forward, almost losing his footing. Cal's hand grips the plastic tie more tightly, despite it cutting into his hand. He wonders if the stumble was manufactured by his prisoner to try to escape his grip so that he can make a run for it as they enter the darkness of the treeline.

"If you run, I will shoot," Cal promises.

"I have no doubt about that, Detective," Uri replies. "But that would be foolish of me in these circumstances."

"Just be warned. I will shoot," Cal repeats.

Progress through the trees is quick and they emerge into the open expanse of the park on the other side. The darkness recedes as they thankfully move out into the open. Footpaths criss-cross the park, which is lit by occasional lights hovering above them. There is also a brick structure on the other side of the modestly sized park that also has lights around it. The structure is in the direction they are heading and becomes a beacon for them to aim at. Cal hopes the exit out of the park won't be that far past the structure and beyond more trees that tower just after it.

As they move out into the open, the pace is increased but Neal keeps control of his men. For all they know, there may be zombified creatures ahead as well as behind after all. Rifles point in every direction as they move, covering as much ground as possible.

In the distance, a loud crash echoes through the trees. The door has given way, but it is what follows that fills each of them with terror. The scream of a banshee pierces the night sky, stopping them in their tracks. One atrocious scream follows another, until a chorus of evil noise seems to envelop their surroundings. Each scream brings its own threat but it is also a signal, promising death from every shadow.

"Run." Cassie is the one to snap them out of their terrified paralysis.

Uri pulls at his bindings, desperate to flee. Cal keeps a tight rein on them though, needing no encouragement to follow his prisoner. His hand also tightens around the grip of his Glock, sure it will soon be called into action.

Almost any caution is thrown to the wind; *fear tends to do that*, Cal thinks. The entire team want to get out of the menacing park as quickly as possible. Neal and his men take up the baton, sprinting ahead, aiming for the brick structure. Cal and Uri are more cumbersome, running in tandem, and fall behind, with Cassie keeping a watching brief.

Screams of death come again, but this time they sound closer. Cal risks a glance over his shoulder. However, the darkness of the treeline behind him conceals the beasts he knows must be emerging. His mind sees their shadows looming to attack them at speed, even if his eyes fail to see the danger. How he wishes their evacuation transport would suddenly appear in the sky, buzzing over their heads but there is no sign of Monks' helicopter. They are on their own and must either evade the infected creatures or find somewhere to hold up until Monks arrives.

Neal and his men have drawn the same conclusion and have decided to take the second option, to find somewhere to hole up. The only refuge on offer is the structure across the park that they are closing in on. Another round of chilling screams is heard, this time even closer, making Cal wonder if he will make it to the structure in time. The men ahead seem to have abandoned the stragglers behind them as they run for their lives. Cal begins to doubt whether they will remember the vital suspect, if not him, before they are cut down by the undead.

"Run faster," Cassie shouts. "They're coming!"

Cal cannot stop himself from glancing behind again, even though he knows he should be concentrating on catching up with the men ahead. Dark figures fill Cal's vision, the shocking sight horrifying. Fearsome beasts baying for blood have rapidly closed in behind, the ferocious creatures almost in position to strike.

"Run!" Cal shouts as his hand releases the bindings of his prisoner who, freed, doesn't deviate from reaching their only chance of survival.

Neal and his men have reached the structure, well ahead of Cal and Cassie, leaving them in no-man's-land. Cal's mind reels. Should he turn and use the machine gun on his back to fight? That act has every chance of being suicidal but at least it may give Cassie valuable time to escape. She would see to it that their prisoner would be secured and broken, to divulge what he knows. His life might be worth that much if it helps stop the city's torment and results in safety for Kim and his unborn child.

Gunfire erupts from in front of Cal. Neal hasn't forsaken them after all: he and his men are laying down covering fire to give them a chance. Bullets whizz past Cal's head to take out the closest threat at their backs and, amazingly, the structure draws closer. Now Cal doesn't glance back, all of his concentration is consumed by reaching Neal's line of men.

"Get inside!" Neal bellows, as the three stragglers career past him.

They don't need his encouragement. Even the prisoner with his hands bound shoots straight for the small brick building that has finally presented itself. Only now can Cal see that the building is a shuttered-up confectionary outlet that only recently would have been selling ice creams, coffees and cold drinks to the park's visitors.

Heading for the movement at the side of the building, Cal sees one of Neal's men shouting and waving them in closer. A chilling scream in amongst the rapid gunfire from behind forces Cal to turn. Beneath the feeble man-made light that is cast across the scene, the carnage is unfolding. The zombie attack has cut into the line of officers covering the escape. More screams bellow out as the gunfire diminishes due to officers being taken down by vicious beasts that have escaped the onslaught of bullets. Men on the grass fight for their lives as creatures brutally tear into them, baying to ravage their flesh.

Cal has grabbed the rifle from his back before he knows it and opens fire in a desperate attempt to break the undead assault and to give any of the men a chance of escape. The officer at the door grabs Uri to throw him inside the building, which is no more than a small brick hut. Cassie stands beside Cal, her rifle ricocheting into her shoulder as bullets blast out of her weapon.

The armed officers only a short distance away find that their weapons are no match for the overwhelming numbers of creatures joining in the feeding frenzy. Neal stands with his men, piling bullets into quivering undead bodies until his magazine empties. Cal concentrates his fire on trying to cover the police sergeant as he stands his ground to try to save his men. The sergeant even resorts to pulling out his sidearm to enable him to continue to fire.

"Retreat, Neal!" Cal shouts at the top of his voice, but the sergeant won't abandon his men, even in the face of the terrifying odds.

Eventually, Neal's sidearm clicks empty and his fight is done. Cal sees the realisation on the sergeant's profiled face but redoubles his efforts to cover him. Cassie also concentrates her fire on Neal's position and Cal shouts 'Retreat!' once more.

This time Neal takes heed of Cal's desperate shouts and turns. The sergeant tried valiantly to save his men, but now it is time to try to save himself. Just as the attempt to cover Neal appears to be lost, the officer at the door, just behind Cal, opens fire. Those few extra bullets give Neal the precious seconds he needs to escape the onslaught and, miraculously, he sprints past Cal and through the open door.

Cal expends his last few bullets as Cassie disappears inside before he pulls his rifle in to follow her. Neal's final remaining man is the last through the door, which is slammed shut after him.

Cassie, who slammed the door shut, wedges her shoulder against it. The lock had been broken to gain entry to the refuge and Cal immediately crashes against the door next to Cassie to add his weight. Neal and his empty rifle crumple to the floor in dismay, the spotlight attached to the rifle's barrel wobbling as the rifle settles on the ground.

Within seconds a body smashes into the door from outside, forcing it inwards an inch or two before the weight of Cal and Cassie slams it shut again. Cal pushes harder against the door while looking around at the same time to try to find something to block it with. He sees nothing inside the cramped space that can be used. The area is empty apart from bare shelves and a serving counter.

"We won't hold them off for long," Cassie insists, just as there is a tremendous crash on the door.

This time, the door is forced inwards more than a foot and both Cal and Cassie use all their might to repel the attack. Before the door shuts again, another assault hits, forcing it wider. A few more blows at the most and the door will be breached and the undead horde will be victorious. Tortuous screams accompany the attack and, just as Cal begins to fear the worst, he hears another sound.

"The helicopter is here!" Neal's last surviving officer exclaims.

"Fantastic," Uri counters. "How are we going to reach it?"

"Shut the fuck up, asshole," Cassie barks at Uri.

Cal agrees with Cassie's sentiment but is forced to acknowledge the suspect's valid point. How the hell are they going to reach the helicopter with a horde of zombified creatures surrounding the building, frantic for fresh meat? While he contemplates that conundrum, Cal's phone begins to ring. Perhaps Monks has an idea, Cal hopes, as he answers the pilot's call.

"Where are you? I can't see your signal," Monks demands.

"We're trapped in the building on the city side of the park. We're surrounded. Have you any suggestions?" Cal shouts desperately.

"I see the building. Hold on and I'll get closer," Monks replies.

Cal waits with his phone clamped to his ear as the barrage against the door escalates. Neal remains forlorn on the floor whilst his last man has joined Cal and Cassie in adding his weight against the door.

"What's happening?" Cassie demands breathlessly.

"He's coming closer," Cal replies, even as the sound of a helicopter increases.

Cal's eyes rise to the ceiling of the building as the powerful noise of the helicopter increases. Vibrations flow through the building's structure as it suffers the force of the helicopter's buffeting downdraft. Almost inconspicuously as Cal feels the helicopter move overhead, the barrage against the door dissipates to nothing and the door finally shuts completely closed. Their attackers have been distracted by the flying hulk above, a distraction that might give them an opening to escape.

"Let me take a look," Cal demands.

Pressure against the door is eased by Cal's colleagues to allow him to carefully ease the door open, all of them ready to rejoin the fight if another attack hits.

Through the crack, the wind blows like a hurricane as a spotlight from the helicopter throws down light. Surrounding foliage and long grass fight against the wind, whilst pieces of litter swirl into the air. Rabid creatures caught in the spotlight's glare rush around like headless chickens, some of them blown over by the awesome power of the downdraft. The ferocious beasts pack into the light, fighting to gain an advantage and to get closer to the hovering object that has appeared.

Although the assault on the door has ceased, Cal sees no opportunity for escape. More creatures are constantly appearing from out of the darkness and, if Cal and the others move out of the building, they will surely be seen and attacked.

Just as Cal's despair begins to rise again, and without warning, gunfire erupts from out of the blackness behind the spotlight. Bullets and red tracer fire surge down to rip into the pack of creatures. The fire is concentrated on the main pack, which has been drawn into the light. Heads explode, ejecting blood and brain matter into the air and the beam of the spotlight. Together with the red flashes of tracer fire, the light turns a grizzly shade of red. Zombified bodies are cut into by the unrelenting killing power of the barrage from above, ripping them limb from limb. Bodies of mutilated creatures, torn to shreds, fall and begin to pile up. For a moment, Cal thinks that the entire horde might be exterminated right before his eyes, but his optimism doesn't last.

"What's happening?" Cassie shouts from behind Cal.

"They're firing on the pack," Cal shouts back, knowing he needs to make a decision… a life-or-death decision.

Under the onslaught, the pack have begun to scatter away from the unforgiving carnage of the raking bullets. Beasts scatter in every direction to escape the threat, their eyes glowing red from the bright tracer fire. Cal realises that the beasts' survival instinct hasn't entirely deserted them. The horde won't be exterminated before his eyes and so their escape to safety won't be that easy.

"The helicopter's here, but we're gonna have to fight our way to it!" Cal shouts above the din.

"How many are there?" Neal replies from the floor, regaining some of his composure.

"It's hard to say, but the helicopter has eliminated a large number," Cal replies. "We're going to have to go for it. Now is as good as it's going to get!"

"How far away is it?" Cassie demands.

"Not far," Cal tells her.

"Let's do it then. We have no other choice," Cassie says.

"You must be crazy if you think I'm going out there," Uri announces from across the room. "We need to sit tight here and let them wander off. Tell the pilot to leave."

Uri's words are like a shot of adrenaline to Neal. The sergeant scowls at Uri as he rises from the floor with his rifle in both hands.

"Shut your fucking mouth, cunt," Neal seethes, pointing his weapon at the prisoner. "You're responsible for this terror and you're going out the door first. If I were you, I'd get to that helicopter as fast as you can. Either that or be eaten by your buddies."

With that, Neal approaches Uri angrily, his rifle aimed directly at Uri's head. Uri has been around long enough to know when someone is bluffing. He instinctively knows that the police officer would be quite happy to shoot him where he stands, or indeed let him be ripped apart, just as his men were.

"I understand," Uri concedes.

Uri holds his hands up in submission and stands up straight, showing he is ready to move. Even leaving the refuge to face the zombie pack gives him a chance to survive, whereas a bullet to the head doesn't. *Live to fight another day*, Uri tells himself, an old saying he has lived by for many years.

"Tell the pilot we're coming out!" Neal orders Cal.

Cal barks exactly that into his phone, praying that Monks is still on the line. When he hears "Received" shouted back at him, however, Cal is suddenly fearful about leaving the safety of the shelter.

"He's ready," Cal announces with trepidation.

Neal pulls his prisoner away from the wall on the opposite side of the room and towards the door. Uri reluctantly allows himself to be manhandled, deciding to sprint for the helicopter no matter what happens behind him. No one else here is his concern.

"Ready?" Cal asks nervously, his hand moving to open the door.

Neal nods, moving behind Uri, ready to go, and Cal yanks open the door.

Wind blasts in through the door but nobody flinches away from it, or from the overpowering sound of gunfire. Neal pushes his prisoner forward and out of the door, into the melee of beasts scattered around the area outside.

Cal glances at Cassie to make sure she is beside him as they follow Neal and his man out of the door. Gunfire rains down, annihilating anything in its path, the stream of bullets obliterating torsos and exploding heads. Shadows of creatures flee in every direction. The chaos is almost overwhelming.

Pulling his trigger, Cal fires the moment he is out of the door, the mindless creature inadvertently stumbling in his direction. Chaos surrounds them as they move forward. Gunfire is unrelenting from the helicopter as it fights to create a landing zone. The downdraft increases as the aircraft descends, closing in on the ground.

The total chaos brings the bonus of cover. The creatures are in a state of panic and either haven't realised that humans are in amongst them or are too concerned with their own survival to care. The team press forward towards the promised safety of the helicopter's rotors.

Some creatures are not fooled by the ensuing carnage and attack, their ferocious faces baying for only one thing... blood. Their sporadic attacks are fired upon by the first person who sees them coming. Cal fires again as a large male beast bursts towards them. Cassie sees it coming too and opens up with her weapon. The creature is filled with bullets and drops in a heap onto the swirling grass.

Everything changes when Monks touches down, still a distance away from them. The constant gunfire from the helicopter is forced to give way to measured bursts of fire in the opposite direction to the team's approach. This gives the pack of creatures a chance to regroup and to realise what they have within their midst... fresh meat.

Uri, seeing the new threat, takes his chance and scurries towards the aircraft, even before it has touched down. This isn't his battle after all and he has no weapon to fight with.

The four remaining members of the team don't break ranks but continue their progress towards safety. They move steadily and deliberately. Losing their shape now could be disastrous. Every direction must be covered and their rate of fire increases as the enemy's panic subsides and they rush to attack.

Figures appear from out of the shadows and from the darkness beyond the lights of the helicopter. Vicious, bloodthirsty creatures no longer held back by the awesome power of gunfire threaten to overwhelm the four before they can reach their means of escape.

Fearsome ghouls with twisted and demented features rush at the tight formation that Cal finds himself at the rear of. Cassie is on his right and Neal on his left and each of them is forced to defend their perimeter with all the bullets they have and gradually they close in on their goal.

Cal feels the helicopter's rotors directly above him, and knows that the safety of its hold is close. He expends more bullets as a creature flies directly at him, the small beast difficult to hit. Bullets whizz past his head from behind and slam into the creature's head, moments before it crashes into Cal.

"Move! Get on-board!" a voice bellows.

Cal recognises the voice before he risks turning around to look inside the helicopter's hold, which is now at his back. Sergeant Locke stands tall above Cal on the hold's platform, his rifle pointed over Cal's head as bullets explode out of its muzzle. Just the sight of the Special Forces operative instils confidence in Cal and he moves to board the evac transport. Cassie goes to climb into the hold in front of Cal and he pushes her backside to help her up.

"You next!" Neal, who doesn't stop firing, orders Cal.

Cal's hands reach for the floor of the hold in front of him, his rifle dangling across his midriff on its strap. Suddenly Cal's backside is forced up, his weight leaves the ground and he is pushed into the hold. The moment Cal is in, he turns to see that Neal's last surviving man is the one who helped him up. *I really must get his name*, Cal tells himself, as he offers his hand to the man to help pull him up.

Only Neal remains on the ground and Cal shouts to the sergeant to move. Locke is laying down constant covering fire and another flank of covering fire has opened up on the other side of the hold's doorway. Neal turns, takes Cal's hand and pulls himself up.

"Lift off!" Locke bellows at the top of his voice the second Neal's feet leave the ground.

With everyone on-board, Cal shuffles back further into the hold to give the other men space and, in all honesty, to move further away from the danger. Locke doesn't cower back, however. He remains at the door's threshold, continuing to fire as the helicopter's engines power and it lifts off to a safe height. Even as they gain altitude, Locke doesn't relent, and neither does Atkins, who is the man on the other side of the doorway. Their rifles remain locked into their shoulders as they continue to take potshots at the enemy below.

Chapter 15

Eventually, as the ground falls away and Monks manoeuvres the helicopter around, Locke and Atkins finally relent. Locke turns away from the hold door as Atkins pulls the door across and slams it shut. Suddenly the atmosphere inside the hold calms considerably and Airman Harris points Cal to a seat and a headset.

"Where are we heading?" Monks' voice sounds through the headset.

"Back to Mercury House, please, and thanks for coming to get us," Cal replies.

"I think I'm going to regret giving you my number, Detective," Monks replies in jest.

"You might be right about that," Cal says.

"I see you've got yourself into another tight spot, Detective," Locke says into his headset, after he has claimed a seat.

"You could say that. Thanks for coming to our aid," says Cal, thanking the entire rescue team.

"That's what we're here for," Locke grins.

"I'm surprised to see you again," Cal says.

"We were getting a lift back to base to await further orders when your call came through," Locke replies

"What the fuck were you doing out there?" Atkins interjects.

"Following up on a lead," Cal responds.

"I hope it was fucking worth it," Locke growls.

"So do I, Sergeant. It came with a heavy cost," Cal replies, his eyes falling on the prisoner, the loathsome Mr Easter.

Locke's eyes follow Cal's to Uri, who is sitting against the side of the helicopter's fuselage, all but pinned up by Sergeant Neal, who is in the seat next to his prisoner.

"Who's that?" Locke asks.

"One of the conspirators behind this carnage," Cal answers.

"Really? Are you sure?" Locke asks.

"We're sure, Sergeant," Cal replies.

"Then it was definitely worth it," Locke says.

"I hope so. We've lost good men down there," Cal replies, sadly.

"Many more will be lost if we don't stop these fuckers," Locke points out.

"Yes, but the prisoner isn't being very cooperative so far," Cal replies.

"Give him to me and I'll have him singing like a canary," Locke offers sternly.

"What would you do?" Cal asks, not discounting Locke's offer.

"Do you really want to know? It wouldn't be a nice chat over tea and cake, I can tell you that much," Locke replies, easing back in his seat, unfazed.

"I see," Cal replies, looking over at Mr Easter again, who is oblivious to the conversation. "I will try standard procedure to start with, Sergeant. But I will keep your offer in mind."

"Do we really have time for standard procedure? This man is probably trained in interrogation resistance and, with all due respect, anyone can hide behind "No comment" in a police interview. The sooner I get to work, the sooner he will break," Locke replies, with a menacing expression.

"He's right," Cassie interrupts. "Let's get the fucker squealing like the pig he is!"

"Cassie!" Cal protests, taken aback by her outburst as Locke grins.

"This isn't the time for pussyfooting around, Cal. He isn't going to just roll over if we tickle his tummy. People like him only understand one thing: fear," Cassie argues.

"You might both be right, but I'm going to try before we start pulling out fingernails," Cal insists.

"I love a good fingernail-pulling session," Locke announces.

"It sounds delightful," Cal replies.

Cal glances at the prisoner, who looks back at him, straight in the eye. The look sends a chill down Cal's spine. *Perhaps Mr Easter isn't as oblivious to the conversation being carried on about him as I thought*, Cal thinks uneasily.

"Get him in cuffs," Cal tells Neal, who has not relieved the pressure on his prisoner.

Neal doesn't need asking twice and takes great delight in manhandling Uri to get the handcuffs on him. He pulls Uri around and forces his face into the side of the fuselage to get to his hands. Neal isn't shy of twisting an arm muscle or two to get the metal bracelets in place. Cal notices that Mr Easter doesn't fight or protest about his handling but wears a look of resignation. Deep down, Cal knows that Locke and Cassie are right: it is going to take more than some stern questioning under caution to get any meaningful information out of the prisoner.

The flight is quickly over and Monks brings them into land on the roof of Mercury House. Cal thanks the pilot and Airman Harris profusely after the wheels touch down and the noise of the engines dissipates. Monks tells Cal not to mention it before telling him, tongue in cheek, not to phone him again and to delete his number. Cal replies that he can't promise anything, before thanking him again.

"Thanks again, Sergeant, and good luck," Cal says, offering his hand to Locke before they disembark the helicopter.

"I've decided to tag along with you for a while, Detective," Locke informs Cal. "Just in case you need to call on my skills," he winks.

"I see," Cal replies, unsure if this is a good idea. "Won't you be wanted elsewhere?"

"Probably, but this is where the game is and I'm all in to bring this nightmare to an end," Locke insists forcefully.

"There isn't much action around here," Cal replies.

"Who are you trying to kid? Action follows you around like a bad smell," Locke grins.

"You're not wrong there, Sergeant," Cassie agrees.

"I'm just doing my job," Cal argues.

"So am I," Locke retorts. "I have a feeling I'm needed here and I'm sure Agent Sutton would agree."

"I get the feeling I'm being ganged up on," Cal replies.

"Look," Locke says seriously. "You're at the heart of trying to bring these fuckers down and, right now, that's my sole purpose in life too. I have family in this city. I have family all over this country. If your interrogation of the prisoner goes well and I'm not needed, then brilliant. But even if it does, you're still going to have to follow up on that intelligence and you'll be off on the next mission. You need us to watch your back. We're the best at what we do. Isn't that right, Atkins?"

"Fucking A!" Atkins responds, holding up his rifle whilst sporting a wide grin.

"We need all the help we can get. Things aren't going to get any easier," Cassie encourages.

"Okay," Cal says. "But I can't let you get in the way of the investigation. You need to do what I ask. Are you prepared to do that?"

"You're the boss, Detective. Until the bullets start flying and the shit hits the fan, that is," Locke agrees.

"Well, then, I suppose you're right. Having my own Special Ops team can't do any harm," Cal concedes.

"You know it makes sense, Detective. I will need Agent Sutton to make a few phone calls to smooth over our secondment. If that's okay?" Locke asks, looking at Cassie.

"I might not need to make any calls. General Peters and Colonel Medlam might still be in the building," Cassie replies.

"Medlam? Happy days," Locke says, rolling his eyes.

"Is that a problem?" Cassie asks.

193

"Not at all. Me and Medlam get on like a house on fire. Don't we, Atkins?"

"Er, yes Sarge," Atkins replies, but this time with considerably less bravado.

"Colonel Medlam told us he'd put his best man on the job at the arena," Cal points out.

"Well, he wasn't fucking wrong there, was he?" Locke smiles. "Even if he is a bit of a tosser."

Above their heads, engines begin to whine, telling them all that it is time to exit the helicopter. Monks glances back to confirm that point: his services have obviously been called upon elsewhere.

Sergeant Neal and his men have already pulled the prisoner off the helicopter. They wait just off the helipad, with Neal taking a tight grip of Mr Easter's cuffed hands, which are behind his back. Something tells Cal that Neal would be more than willing to help Locke 'soften up' the prisoner if Cal's interrogation doesn't bear fruit. Neal is already holding Mr Easter's arms in an awkward position.

Cassie leads the way into the building. Neal frogmarches his prisoner behind Cassie, one hand gripping his bound hands and the other gripping his shoulder.

"What's your name?" Cal asks Neal's last remaining officer.

"Stack, Sir," the man replies, his rifle trained on Mr Easter, just in case the prisoner becomes unruly.

"Where do you want the prisoner?" Neal asks on the way down the building.

"Where do you suggest, Agent Sutton?" Cal asks Cassie, being unfamiliar with the facilities.

"Don't worry. I have an interrogation room lined up for him," Cassie replies.

I should have known Cassie would be prepared, Cal tells himself, as they arrive back in the main office on Cassie's floor of Mercury House. A hush falls over the office, as their motley crew walk in. The office is still busy despite the early hour. Cal immediately looks around for Tilly, but she isn't in sight. He does see Agent Morgan at his workstation. The bleary-eyed young agent is still hard at it.

"Follow me," Cassie tells Sergeant Neal, and they stride off to secure the prisoner.

Cal leaves Cassie to it. He wants to see where Tilly is and if there have been any developments with Agent Morgan's leads.

"Why don't you two get something to eat and get some rest? There is a cafeteria in the building, although the selection left a lot to be desired when I was there earlier," Cal suggests to Locke and Atkins, who are standing like spare wheels.

"We'll eat anything as long as it's not a ration pack," Locke replies.

"It's not quite that bad," Cal says. "There's basically sandwiches and drinks."

"Good enough for me," Locke insists.

"Great. It's a few floors down. The button is labelled," Cal replies.

"We clocked it on the way down. Don't worry about that," Atkins grins.

"Of course you did," Cal replies.

"You know where we are if you decide to go on another jaunt," Locke says.

"Don't worry, Sergeant. I'm not planning on going anywhere without you. I've had enough scares lately to teach me that lesson," Cal confesses.

"And if you need any tactical advice or planning for an operation, you know where to come," Locke adds seriously.

"Absolutely, and thanks for volunteering," Cal replies.

"No thanks required, Detective. It's all part of the service," Locke insists.

"Okay. Feel free to come back up when you're finished eating," Cal says, and the two men turn to leave.

Cal still isn't sure where Tilly is and he doesn't know where Cassie has taken Mr Easter. The agents in the office, on the whole, have turned away to continue with their work. By all rights, Cal should report in with Commissioner Jackson immediately, update him with the latest development in the case and inform him about the apprehension of the suspect. That is not his plan, however. He wants to keep the apprehension of Mr Easter off the record for the time being and keep him out of the system, for two reasons. Firstly, because Cal doesn't want anyone else getting to the suspect before they have had the chance to question him and, secondly, in case that questioning needs to go the way Locke and Cassie have suggested it will.

Agent Morgan hasn't turned back to his computer screen to return to his work, as his colleagues have. The agent remains looking at Cal with interest.

"Where is Tilly?" Cal asks, as he approaches Morgan.

"I'm not sure, Sir. I haven't seen her in a while," Morgan replies.

"How is your work progressing?" Cal asks.

"I have found out some interesting information, Sir," Morgan replies quietly, his eyes discreetly checking that none of his colleagues are eavesdropping on their conversation. "I see you have also been productive, Sir."

"Yes. Let me find Tilly and then, once Agent Sutton is finished, we'll have our own briefing. Okay?" Cal says.

"Yes, Sir. As soon you're ready," Morgan agrees.

With that, Cal turns and pulls his phone out of his pocket to see if Tilly has phoned or messaged him. There is nothing new on his phone and so he calls Tilly to see where she is. By the time Tilly's phone rings out and goes to voicemail, Cassie has appeared back in the office from an adjoining corridor.

"Have you seen Tilly on your travels?" Cal asks Cassie.

"No. Isn't she around here?" Cassie replies.

"I can't see her and Agent Morgan hasn't seen her in a while either," Cal says.

"If she has any sense, she is getting some rest," Cassie insists, looking tired herself.

"She could be. Where is Sergeant Neal?" Cal asks.

"They're guarding the prisoner. I told him the room is secure, but he insisted," Cassie replies.

"Neal's right. The room might be secure, but we don't want him got to while our backs are turned," Cal points out.

"No, we don't," Cassie agrees, turning for her office.

"Locke has gone to get something to eat and Agent Morgan says he has new information," Cal says, following Cassie. "We need to find Tilly."

"She'll turn up. Have you rung her?" Cassie asks.

197

"She's not answering," Cal replies.

"Strange," Cassie says, as she goes into her office.

Cassie is positive that she left the office lights on when they left and wonders who has been inside. *Has someone been snooping at my desk?* she thinks as she reaches for the light switch. She gasps when the lights flash on.

Lying on the floor under the light switch and along the wall is Tilly, with what looks like a coat under her head. The sudden burst of light does nothing to stir Tilly from her slumber, which Cassie looks down upon with some jealousy.

"It looks like we have our answer," Cassie tells Cal, who hasn't spotted Tilly yet.

"Oh, God, yes," Cal whispers upon seeing Tilly. "Well, you can't blame her. Could do with some shut-eye myself."

"No rest for the wicked I'm afraid, Detective," Cassie says flatly, now lowering her voice.

"No," Cal agrees.

Cassie turns away from Tilly, not attempting to rouse her. *Let her sleep while she can,* she thinks, as she moves to her desk.

"What did Agent Morgan say?" Cassie asks, slumping into her chair.

"Nothing specific," Cal replies, easing himself wearily into a chair in front of Cassie's desk. "I said we'd have a private briefing once you came back and we found Tilly."

"You'd better wake Sleeping Beauty up then," Cassie suggests.

"I will, in a moment," Cal agrees. "But first, I want to know how far you are willing to go with the suspect?"

"As far as it takes, Detective. I've got no qualms if we start pulling fingernails, as you say," Cassie replies. "That fucker is to talk, one way or the other. There's a bigger picture and he made his own bed. No pun intended."

"I agree. I'm just not familiar with those kinds of methods. Are you?" Cal asks.

"That's classified information, I'm afraid," Cassie replies, looking at Cal, knowing full well her answer will tell him all he needs to know.

"I see. If I'm honest, I don't think me questioning him is going to get us anywhere. I'd normally let him stew for a few hours, or overnight if time allowed," Cal says. "I'll give him the opportunity to cooperate, though, before we release Locke to do his business."

"Fair enough," Cassie concedes. "But he won't talk willingly. I've dealt with his sort before and they never do. Not without some persuasion and what have we got to offer him other than fear?"

"Immunity. We could offer him a deal?" Cal suggests.

"You can try, but something tells me this is part of one last crusade for that old man. He isn't going to care about your offers. He might string you along for as long as he possibly can or feed you false information. Anything to delay us and help the cause, I'm sorry to say," Cassie explains.

"How do we know the other method will produce any viable intelligence?" Cal asks. "He could still feed us a load of bullshit to try to throw us off track."

"He could if he's that well trained and determined. Nothing is guaranteed," Cassie concedes.

"It's difficult, but we need answers," Cal insists.

"Okay, I admit I've witnessed detainees in the field subjected to, let's say, strong interrogation methods. Some of them held out for a time but, believe me, all of them broke eventually. The screw just needs to be tightened until they do," Cassie confesses.

"How long does that take? We haven't got time to waste on a prolonged process," Cal insists.

"It varies. As I said, there are no guarantees," Cassie replies.

"You're back. What's going on?" Tilly's voice sounds from the back of the room.

Cal turns, wondering how much of the conversation Tilly has listened to as she surfaced from her nap. What they're considering doing to the suspect in custody will be divisive. Personally, Cal is uneasy to even be considering it. Others, including Tilly, might object to the use of torture out of hand and seek to protect the suspect by whatever means at their disposal. The fewer people who know about it, the better.

"We're just discussing options," Cassie replies, as Tilly sits up. "We have a suspect in custody."

"Really?" Tilly says excitedly. "Were they at the property Agent Morgan uncovered?"

"Yes," Cassie replies. "We have him in a holding room."

"I'm sorry I was sleeping in your office, Agent Sutton. I just came in for a rest while I waited for news and must have fallen off. I had my phone with me!" Tilly insists.

"We wondered where you were and I tried to phone you," Cal informs her.

"Oh, God. I must have slept through your call. I'm so sorry," Tilly replies, mortified.

"Don't worry about it. No harm done. We can't blame you for taking the opportunity," Cal says.

"What has the suspect said?" Tilly asks, getting to her feet.

"Nothing yet. That's what we were just discussing," Cal admits.

"What do you need me to do?" Tilly asks, with an air of embarrassment for having fallen asleep.

"Can you ask Agent Morgan to join us, please?" Cassie asks. "He has some new intelligence he wants to brief us on."

"Yes, of course," the young police officer replies, overenthusiastically.

"Do you think she heard all that?" Cal asks, as Tilly leaves the office.

"Does it matter?" Cassie shrugs.

"It does if she takes offence to torturing a prisoner!" Cal insists.

"She'll be okay as long as we keep her at a distance from it," Cassie replies confidently.

"I hope you're right," Cal replies.

"You'll be surprised what people become accustomed to. I'm a bit surprised you're questioning it so hard," Cassie admits. "Just think what this man has been involved in, what he's responsible for!"

"I know. You are right. We must do whatever is necessary," Cal concedes.

"Even if that means doing things that we would normally find abhorrent for the greater good?" Cassie asks.

"Yes," Cal answers simply.

A knock on the door brings Tilly and Morgan in to disturb the conversation, which had come to a natural conclusion anyway. Both stand behind Cal, waiting for instruction.

"Tilly, you sit there, while Agent Morgan goes to get himself a chair," Cassie says, pointing at the spare seat next to Cal.

"Did you run into trouble when you detained the suspect?" Tilly asks, while they wait for Morgan to return.

"Let's wait for Agent Morgan before we get into it," Cal replies.

"Of course," Tilly agrees, playing with her hands in her lap.

Soon enough, Morgan returns with a chair and both Cal and Tilly shift around to make space for him to sit on the other side of Tilly after he has shut the office door.

"While you were fetching your chair, Tilly asked if we ran into trouble," Cassie says, looking at Morgan. "We did. Men from the firearms team were slaughtered when we tried to evacuate the suspect who we discovered at the property. I think it's fair to say we were all lucky to escape with our lives."

"We were," Cal agrees.

"The new prime suspect," Agent Morgan says.

"He refers to himself as Mr Easter. Has facial recognition found him on the system, Agent Morgan?" Cassie asks.

"Yes, Ma'am. His name is Uri Levy, an Israeli national. He has ties to the Israeli military and, indeed, Aman, the Israeli military intelligence service. His file is long and goes back decades. Our information will be incomplete, but he has operated in multiple war zones all over the Middle East and Eastern Europe and he spent time in Russia. We can assume that he is a highly trained Israeli military spy. There is no information regarding any ties to the outbreak we are currently experiencing, Ma'am," Morgan informs them.

"Uri Levy, eh?" Cal repeats.

"I don't believe that his involvement with this plot will have anything to do with Israeli intelligence. He left the service more than 15 years ago," Morgan adds.

"I agree," Cassie says. "This is a personal project for him."

"What do you intend to do with him?" Tilly asks.

"We keep his capture between us for now. Understood?" Cal insists, and both Tilly and Morgan nod their agreement.

"We must break him and quickly," Cal continues, "if we have any hope of bringing this horror to an end. I'll ask you to leave his interrogation to us. Things could get nasty and we don't want either of you involved."

"That's right. There's no need for you to be involved," Cassie agrees.

"We are under your direction," Tilly confirms.

"Thank you," Cal says. "Now what have you got for us, Agent Morgan?"

"Sir, I've been delving into the web of companies related to IPP, its real-estate holdings and its shareholdings," Morgan replies.

"Have you found anything solid to go on?" Cassie asks.

"It's a tangled web, Ma'am. Shell companies, offshore companies, worldwide trusts and even government accounts. You name it. The shareholders of IPP are well hidden," Morgan replies.

"Doesn't sound very promising," Cal interjects.

"At first it didn't look very promising," Morgan continues. "But if you know where to dig and you dig deep enough, sometimes you find a gold nugget."

"Oh, yes," Cassie presses.

"IPP does have one majority shareholder," Morgan reveals. "A company registered in the Cayman Islands named FA Holdings, which I've discovered is a wholly owned subsidiary of Arnoult Pharma."

"Francis Arnoult's company, the multinational pharmaceutical corporation?" Cassie asks urgently.

"Yes, Ma'am, that's correct. Francis Arnoult is the Chairman, CEO and majority shareholder. He effectively owns Arnoult Pharma and therefore FA Holdings," Morgan confirms.

"Does the FA stand for Francis Arnoult?" Cal asks.

"I assume so, Sir," Morgan replies.

"This can't be a coincidence!" Cassie insists, her eyes wide. "One of the world's largest pharmaceutical companies just happens to be the owner of the company that owns the property where the outbreak was launched from."

"You're right. It can't be," Cal agrees. "But the link is tenuous. We need more evidence before we can take this any further. You can bet your life that whoever at Arnoult Pharma is behind this has covered their tracks. We need more."

"Whoever's behind it?" Cassie proclaims. "My money is on Francis Arnoult. He made some very bold claims about climate change and overpopulation a few years ago. For a time, he was constantly banging on about it on TV and social media. Then he disappeared from the public eye. He became a recluse five or six years ago. I bet he decided to do something about it!"

"You may be right, Cassie. A theory isn't good enough though. We need hard evidence. Arnoult is a powerful man, with friends in high places. He will be protected and, if we are going after him, we'd better have all our bases covered," Cal insists.

"Let's see what Uri Levy has to say about it then," Cassie announces, rising from her chair.

Chapter 16

Cassie strides out of her office, without saying another word. Cal pauses for a moment before chasing after her to tell Morgan to keep digging and to tell Tilly to give him all the help he needs. Cassie is disappearing into a corridor on the other side of the main office by the time Cal leaves Tilly and is forced to break into a jog to catch her up. He gets some strange looks from the staff sitting at their workstations as he goes.

"Cassie! Hold on," Cal shouts, before he loses her completely.

He has no idea where Uri is being held and thankfully Cassie does stop to let him catch up.

"Calm down, Cassie. We need to talk before we question the suspect," Cal insists.

"I am calm, Detective," Cassie replies, but her expression begs to differ.

"I'm serious. We can't afford to blow this," Cal states.

"What do you want to say then?" Cassie asks, frustratedly.

"I've told you I want to give the suspect a chance to cooperate before we go down the other road. So, give me that chance!" Cal insists.

"Okay. You play good cop and I'll play bad. How does that sound?" Cassie asks.

"That's fine, as long as you let me take the lead and question him properly," Cal replies.

"Okay. Yes, do your thing, but it's not going to get you anywhere. You do know that, don't you?" Cassie repeats.

"That's what I intend to find out before we go all mediaeval on his ass, Cassie. At least I'll have tried," Cal says.

"If it puts your mind at rest, then be my guest," Cassie concedes.

"Thank you," Cal replies, feeling a bit foolish for being so by the book.

Cassie seems to calm down slightly as they continue on to the holding room. Outside the room, Sergeant Neal and Stack are sat in chairs dozing right outside the door. Both men force themselves upright when they hear Cal and Cassie approach.

"How's the suspect?" Cal asks.

"Quiet. He keeps trying to go to sleep against the table, but I keep banging the door or going in to pull him off the table," Neal replies, although, to Cal, he looked like he was all but asleep himself. "I didn't want him rested for when you arrived."

"Thanks," Cal replies dubiously.

"Is there recording equipment available inside?" Cal asks.

"Yes," Cassie replies. "It's a standard set-up, but do you need to record this?"

"Nothing will be submittable as evidence without proper procedure," Cal replies. "In any event, recording the interview will give us the chance to review his answers if we need to."

"What if he asks for a lawyer?" Cassie asks.

"Let me deal with that eventuality," Cal replies.

"Okay. Shall we then?" Cassie asks impatiently.

The suspect is slumped across the table in front of his chair when they enter the room. He hardly stirs with their presence, that is until Cassie goes around and pulls him upright in his chair by the scruff of his neck. Cal immediately sees fresh blood pooling on the suspect's lip and a bruise around his left cheek. *Neal must have given the suspect a welcoming gift*, Cal thinks, deciding to ignore the injury.

"I was wondering where you two were," Uri yawns.

"Missing us, were you?" Cassie growls in return.

"Not particularly. I'll just be pleased to get this over with so I can be taken to a holding cell and can get some rest," Uri smiles.

"Good luck with that!" Cassie retorts.

"I don't need luck, Agent Sutton. I know my rights," Uri replies.

"Thank you," Cal interjects, before Cassie loses her temper. "Mr Easter, we have some questions we would like to ask you and we shall be recording the interview. Can we get you any refreshments before we begin?"

"No, thanks. But what if I asked for legal representation?" Uri grins.

"Then we wouldn't be able to proceed until it arrived and I'd have to leave you in my colleagues' hands. I'm sure they'll take care of you. They've been doing a good job of it so far, by the looks of it," says Cal, subtly veiling his threat.

"Let's just get it over with," Uri says. "I don't need a lawyer anyway."

"As you wish," Cal replies, setting up the recording equipment.

Once ready, Cal begins the interview by stating the date and time and who is present at the interview and by restating the suspect's rights, including the fact he has declined legal representation.

"Mr Easter," Cal begins. "Can you tell us how you came to be at the address where you were arrested tonight?"

"A friend said I could use it for a couple of nights," Uri replies.

"What friend?" Cal asks, knowing that the suspect has changed tack from when he was taken into custody, when he tried to antagonise them.

"His name is Mike. I met him at a bar last night and he offered," Uri states.

"An answer which is obviously not true," Cal replies, but the suspect just shrugs. "You gave your name as Mr Easter. Is that your actual name?" Cal asks, getting down to business.

"That's my name," Uri answers simply.

"Another lie," Cal states. "Isn't it true that your actual name is Uri Levy?"

"No comment," Uri replies.

"You're an Israeli national who was in the Israeli military and subsequently in the military intelligence unit known as Aman. Isn't that right?" Cal continues.

"No comment," Uri repeats.

"We have contacted Agent Sutton's counterparts in Israeli intelligence to confirm this information," Cal bluffs. "Why don't you save us all time and simply confirm what we already know?"

"No comment," Uri says again.

"Okay." Cal readies the line of questions he hopes will catch the suspect out. "Can you tell us what your relationship is with Arnoult Pharma and Doctor Francis Arnoult?"

"No comment," Uri persists, after a slight pause, but Cal sees at that moment that he is rattled by the question.

"What about International Property Partners, known as IPP? The company that owns the address where you were arrested. What can you tell us about that company?"

"No comment," Uri says again. "I don't know anything about these questions. You are wasting my time," he adds.

"But I can see that you do know, Mr Levy. I have been doing this for a long time and I'm good at it. I saw your tell when I asked about Doctor Francis Arnoult. So why don't you tell me the truth? Why prolong this? Too many people have died already because of your crackpot conspiracy, but you can help us put an end to it. Surely you know it's a fantasy? This plot will never work. All it will do is cause misery for untold numbers of people until we put a stop to it. As you can see, the net is already closing in," Cal pleads, looking the subject straight in the eye.

Cal sees Uri pause in consideration for a moment before he repeats his standard response and replies "No comment".

"I'm trying my best for you here, to help you, Mr Levy. If you cooperate, maybe I can help you even more and get you a favourable deal. We know for a fact that you're involved, so why don't you do yourself a favour and get the best outcome you can from this? Help us and I'll help you. What do you say?" Cal begs, hoping he is getting through.

"No comment," the suspect replies flatly.

"So that's the way you want to play it, is it? Have you been brainwashed to that extent? Radicalised beyond the point of return?" Cal wonders, but the suspect doesn't rise to Cal's insinuation and remains silent.

"Did you know that my colleagues said I'd be wasting my time with you?" Cal continues. "They wanted to go another way from the off, other than me asking you reasonable questions, as I'm sure you can imagine. They gave me the chance to try to be reasonable but, if it gets us nowhere, then I am afraid I will have to defer to them and their alternative methods.

"I'm not familiar with these methods, you understand, as a police officer," Cal says honestly. "I admit that I have roughed up the odd suspect in the past when necessary. Nothing serious, just twisting an arm more than needed and I did once stamp on a suspect's foot to get him to talk. I didn't enjoy it. In fact, I felt guilty afterwards and promised myself I wouldn't use those methods again. You probably think that's soft, but that is why I'm trying to do this the right way. With the situation as it is, there are people who can't wait to get their hands on you, if you know what I mean.

"I don't want it to go that way, as I'm sure you don't. So why don't we talk sensibly between us and come to an agreement?" Cal asks genuinely.

Cal can see that it might be dawning on Uri Levy that he may not have as many rights in this instance as he first thought. A glint of fear might have twinkled in the suspect's eye as Cal laid out the alternative to his questioning under caution. Nevertheless, Uri Levy remains tight-lipped and stony-faced.

"I told Detective Chambers this was a waste of time," says Cassie, breaking her silence. "That you were too far gone to reason with. Yet he insisted that he wanted to try to do it by the book and give you a chance to cooperate. I find that admirable in him, if I'm honest. He has his principles. Wouldn't you agree?"

Uri shrugs his shoulders, unconcerned.

"I, on the other hand, as you already know, have a different outlook and my principles are not so admirable. I have an understanding of how people like you operate, which Detective Chambers may not. I've seen people like you, so forthright and proud of your fanatical beliefs at the beginning, broken into slobbering wrecks. Some break quicker than others but, in the end, they all do. It just depends on how much pain and trauma they can withstand.

"But I'm not telling you anything you don't already know. Am I, Uri? This is not new information to you. In fact, this is something you've participated in on numerous occasions yourself. Isn't it? You've probably been the person responsible for inflicting the damage on your prisoners and I bet you were good at it and took pride in your work. I wonder if you have ever been on the other side. Have you been the one sat in the chair, being broken?" Cassie asks.

Uri shifts uncomfortably in his chair, Agent Sutton's voice grating on him. She is not wrong; in the past, he has taken great pride in breaking people in his care. No method was off the table for him: sleep deprivation, mental torture or administration of chemicals, but his preferred method was inflicting physical pain, whether that be doling out a beating or using a more sophisticated method. He once revelled in the feeling of power he felt when he made someone suffer and inflicting physical pain gave instant gratification.

Uri tries to remain calm and not to let Agent Sutton get to him. He has never been the one "sat in the chair", as she put it. On occasion he came close to it but, somehow, he always managed to avoid that horrific trauma, a trauma he was more than willing to dish out but one that fills him with terror. He has seen the results, after all. The unimaginable pain and suffering as bones are cracked and flesh is sliced. The strongest of men turned into crying babies and then becoming shadows of their former selves, if they recovered at all.

He tries to determine whether Sutton is bluffing. Uri is an expert at playing mind games too. His eyes glance at the recording device. Surely, they wouldn't be recording this and making threats at the same time if it wasn't a bluff. Nobody would be so stupid as to record that evidence. Would they?

He decides that Sutton is bluffing. They would never torture a prisoner. This isn't some lawless backwater country without rules and, if she isn't bluffing, then so be it. They might rough him up a bit but there is no chance they would inflict any prolonged pain. Uri can handle a quick beating; he is sure of that. *I will not let down Janus or put his plans in jeopardy. The cause is too important!* Uri decides.

"I see you are looking at the recording device," Cassie says. "Don't think that will save you. We are recording this for our reference only, not to submit it as evidence. Nobody but a select few people even know that you're here. Not even your accomplices in this building, who we know are here. They won't come to your aid.

"Are you sure you wouldn't like to start this over?" Cassie finishes.

"So be it," Cal announces, as he gets up when Uri stays silent. "This is your choice, Mr Levy."

"Did he say anything?" Sergeant Neal asks, when Cal and Cassie leave the interrogation room.

"What do you think?" Cassie quips.

"So, what now?" Neal asks.

"We have no alternative," Cal says solemnly. "We can't afford to play his games."

"Locke?" Neal asks, and Cal just looks at him.

"Are you sure about this?" Cal asks Cassie, as they walk back towards her office.

"Yes, we have no alternative. There is too much at stake. Surely you can see that?" Cassie questions.

"I can see that, but that doesn't make it any more palatable," Cal replies.

"I don't like it either, if that makes you feel any better," Cassie admits.

"Not really," Cal responds.

"We've got to accept it, Cal. Now, I suggest that we go and speak to Locke down in the cafeteria. Away from prying eyes," Cassie says.

They stop to tell Tilly and Morgan where they will be on their way through the main office, where they are sitting at computer stations, continuing to research Morgan's line of enquiry.

Thankfully, there are only two people in the cafeteria when they arrive. Locke and Atkins have made themselves at home at one of the tables, which is now littered with empty food packaging and paper cups. Both men turn to look at Cal and Cassie as they approach, with knowing looks.

"He's decided on door number two then, I take it?" Locke says seriously, as they sit at the table.

"Are you surprised?" Cassie asks.

"Not surprised, but he might have seen reason. I'm sure you tried your best, Detective," Locke consoles.

"I tried, at least," Cal replies.

"You did. So don't feel bad about what must happen next. This is his choice. He has put himself in this position," Locke states.

"He has shown no concern for the turmoil he's helped inflict. He deserves whatever is coming to him," Cassie adds.

"How will this work then?" Cal asks.

"Where is he now?" Locke asks.

"Being held in an interrogation room," Cassie replies.

"Is it soundproof?" Locke asks.

"More or less, I think," Cassie answers.

"No. I mean totally soundproof. We don't want his screams heard," Locke insists.

"I see," Cassie thinks. "Then we need to find somewhere else to take him. There are too many people on that floor that might hear if the volume is too high."

"Which it will be," Atkins grins.

"We need a discrete location," Locke insists.

"How many times have you done this before?" Cal asks nervously.

"Only once before," Locke answers honestly. "But don't worry. I know what to do," he adds chillingly.

"I think I know a location," Cassie offers.

"Oh, yes," Locke replies. "Where?"

"I've heard this building has a basement. Apparently, there is storage and a maintenance room down there," Cassie reveals.

"A maintenance room, eh? With tools, I presume?" Locke asks, with a sinister expression.

"I assume so," Cassie confirms.

"It sounds perfect!" Locke announces. "Can you get access?"

"I'm sure we can find a way," Cassie replies.

"Let's move the prisoner then," Locke announces, downing his coffee and getting up.

Tilly asks what is happening as she eyes Cal's rifle when the suspect is taken back through the office. Cal says he'll update her when he can as he helps escort the prisoner out. Locke and Atkins have waited in the corridor outside the office in an attempt to keep the questions to a minimum. The ploy makes little difference, however. Everyone turns to watch as Sergeant Neal frogmarches the prisoner back out. The only consolation is that nobody in authority seems to have got wind that there is a suspect in custody. Should Commissioner Jackson or Director Khan have turned up to see what is going on they would not have been so easily fobbed off. Perhaps the early hour of the morning has covered their tracks, but Cal knows that advantage won't last. He needs to get his story straight for when the questions begin to be asked.

Chapter 17

Atkins makes easy work of gaining access to the basement, which they find is behind a locked door when they exit the lift. Another locked door is prised open to get into the maintenance room, which turns out to be a large room with work benches and an array of hand tools.

"It's like Aladdin's cave in here. Plenty to play with, eh Uri?" Locke taunts the prisoner. "Let's get you settled in," he adds, picking up a chair.

And so it begins, Cal thinks, as Neal and Stack manhandle Uri into the chair, which has been placed in the middle of the room. Cal's stomach is flipping somersaults in anguish about what is about to happen. Locke's fearsome presence is enough to instil fear, without the threat of violence. He can't imagine how the suspect must be feeling. He must be beyond petrified.

"It doesn't have to be like this," Cal steps forward, desperately hoping the prisoner will see sense. "All we are asking is for you to cooperate to help bring this horror to an end. Will you cooperate?" Cal pleads.

"You don't want this on your conscience, Detective. Put a stop to it now." Uri looks at Cal, his eyes filled with terror.

"You're goddamn right I don't. I don't want anything to do with this!" Cal exclaims. "But what other choice have you left us? We know that you are deeply involved in the horrific things that are happening. Hundreds, thousands of people are being slaughtered and where will it end if we don't put a stop to it? I've tried to reason with you but if you don't cooperate now that's your choice!"

"You are supposed to uphold the law, Detective. I have my righ..."

The punch comes from nowhere. Uri's head is slammed to the side, the crunching sound echoing off the walls. The terrific force of Locke's blow makes Cal step backwards in fright.

"There's your rights, motherfucker!" Locke seethes, standing in front of Uri.

Suddenly, the old man in the chair appears ancient as blood splatters onto the concrete floor and, for a moment, he doesn't move. Cal thinks he has been knocked out with a single punch, or possibly killed. The prisoner's chest suddenly heaves in air and then a deep spluttering cough escapes as more blood, mixed with saliva, drools from his mouth down onto the floor.

Everyone in the room remains silent, eyes wide with astonishment. Everyone apart from Locke, that is. Locke bends down to look into Uri's face. He wants his quarry to see him, even though his head hangs down to the side. Locke's arm moves and his hand cups under Uri's chin to pull his head up and straighten him back up in his chair.

"Are you having second thoughts, my friend?" Locke asks, looking directly at Uri. "One way or the other you will tell us what we need to know. You do know that, don't you? You've been around long enough to know that everyone breaks, sooner or later. Do yourself a favour and give it up.

This is just the start. I'm happy to do whatever it takes to make you talk.

"Look into my eyes and you'll see that I'm deadly serious. LOOK AT ME!" Locke bellows, his spittle showering Uri's bewildered face. "Who are your accomplices? TELL ME!"

Cal's stomach churns and bile seeps into the side of his mouth as Uri remains silent and Locke rises, straightening his back. Cal's heart races and his stomach flips when Locke's arm retracts ready for the next assault. Uri's eyes widen as he sees Locke's fist rise in the moment before it is released.

This time Locke jabs his arm out straight, a controlled but devastating blow. The fist crunches into Uri's nose with a snapping motion. Uri's head whips back as bone and cartilage crack in the instant before blood explodes from his nose. The cracking sound sends a chill down Cal's spine as blood gushes from Uri's nostrils. Thick red liquid flows down to soak into the material covering his upper body.

Uri groans in agony as his head flops back forward, sending more blood pumping from his nose. More groans follow as Locke steps forward and takes a handful of hair on the top of Uri's head. Without ceremony, Locke pulls Uri's hair sharply back to raise his head. Uri's eyes roll back in their sockets as blood streams from his badly broken nose, which is set at a strange angle and is beginning to swell badly.

"Are you ready to talk now, my Israeli friend, or shall I continue? I'd prefer you to keep quiet, as I'm just getting warmed up. What will it be?" Locke demands.

Only heavy breathing and more groans answer Locke's question and Cal sees a wide grin spread across Locke's face.

"As you wish," Locke says, releasing Uri's hair to let his head flop back down.

Locke's fist swings into Uri's stomach. The heavy blow winds Uri instantly and he buckles over in the chair. All his breath bursts from his lungs in a heavy groaning heave and more red drool slips out onto the floor. Uri coughs uncontrollably, struggling to draw breath again, unable to lift himself up or is he trying to hide from the next attack?

Locke straightens from his wide stance, appearing to have ended his brutal assault on the prisoner. The feeling of relief Cal feels at seeing Locke move away from his quarry is short-lived. Locke goes over to the nearby workbench to search for something. At first, he doesn't seem to see what he is looking for but, as tools clatter together on top of the bench, he stops and selects something. When Locke turns again to approach Uri, he holds a hefty pair of pliers in his hand.

Cal almost protests and goes to call Locke off, his belly flaring again. He stops himself though, reminding himself of what is at stake. They need the information the prisoner has. He cannot interfere with Locke's process, not until Uri breaks. Cal looks around the room as Locke moves in. Cassie has a tormented expression, similar to how Cal must look, whilst the two police officers look prepared for the next phase. Atkins' expression is eager. He wants proceedings to resume and Cal recognises he wouldn't be averse to an invitation to assist Locke... hands on.

In the chair, the suspect has managed to find his breath, but he hasn't risen from his bent-over position. To rise would be to invite another attack. Little does he know what is coming and what his assailant holds in his hand.

"Come on now," Locke says menacingly, grabbing Uri's hair again. "Don't be rude. Look at me while I'm talking to you."

Uri is pulled up by his scalp again, blood still pouring from his mangled nose and swollen mouth. Locke ensures that his prey sees the pliers he holds as he lifts him back upright. Uri's eyes widen in fear as the pliers register in his mind and he goes limp in the chair, almost sliding off it.

"Atkins, get that strap," Locke orders, pointing.

Atkins doesn't need to be asked twice. He immediately turns to do as he's ordered. He grabs a green nylon strap that is hanging on the wall nearby and then helps Locke tie the prisoner to the chair to keep him upright.

"There. That's better, isn't it? I don't want you to miss anything," Locke says, tormenting Uri.

Locke then grabs Uri's left hand, bringing the pliers to bear. Uri fights to release his hand from Locke's grip but the Special Forces officer is too strong for him to resist. Slowly, Locke positions the widened nose of the pliers around Uri's little finger, in between his knuckles. Once the knuckle is gripped in the pliers, Uri's struggle is over.

"Have you reconsidered your position?" Locke demands, standing over Uri, his hand poised on the plier's handle. "Talk now and the pain will all come to an end."

The tension surrounding Locke and Uri is palpable. Uri's finger is locked between the pliers and everyone watches on to see if he will relent and begin to talk. A moment passes before Uri finally raises his watery bloodshot eyes to look at Locke. All listen intently for what Uri will say, but no words come. His battered and bruised face just looks at Locke.

Locke's body tenses and, without further warning, he begins to apply pressure to the pliers. This time, Uri doesn't groan. Instead, his mouth juts open to release a high-pitched scream. The scream is hideous and it continues as Locke continues to squeeze the pliers. The sickening noise only stops when all of the air has been expelled from Uri's lungs.

"This is your last chance," Locke bellows. "Talk!"

Panting for breath is the only sound that comes from Uri's mouth and, to be fair to Locke, he waits a moment to give him time to catch his breath. Only then, when no words come from the suspect, does Locke reapply the pressure on the pliers.

Another bloodcurdling scream echoes out of Uri's mouth as Locke gradually increases the pressure on his knuckle. Blood appears from around the metal sides of the pliers as Uri runs out of breath again, but this time Locke doesn't stop until, with one swift motion, he increases the force on the pliers. The sound of cracking bone is even more disturbing than the screams that proceeded it. With a snap, the nose of the pliers shut completely and the snap is followed by a whimper of intense pain.

"That is just your little finger," Locke taunts. "I will keep going from one finger to the next until I arrive at your thumb. The thumb is the most important digit, isn't it? Don't let that happen. Tell us what we need to know!"

Below Locke, Uri's head has dropped again and only the green strap around his chest keeps his body in the chair. Locke's hand pulls the pliers apart and blood drips from the mutilated finger, the release of pressure causing pain in itself.

Uri's drooped shoulders vibrate as if he were sobbing, his head joining in the motion. A snivelling sound escapes from Uri's hidden mouth as Locke's hand moves back to his hair to pull his head back up. Blood and water glisten on Uri's face as light hits it, but still no words come from him.

"You've got some balls. I'll give you that," Locke says, as he positions the pliers around Uri's ring finger and begins to apply pressure.

A garbled sound comes from below Locke, the word inaudible.

"What did you say?" Locke asks calmly, not releasing the pressure on the ring finger.

This time Cal hears what is said. The word forced from the suspect under cruel duress is familiar to him, but he must rack his memory to try to remember why he knows it.

"What does that mean?" Locke demands, unsure if he has heard correctly.

Slowly, Uri raises his head and battered face to look at Locke. "Janus," he repeats. "Janus is my handler."

"Is he really? Or are you playing games?" Locke replies, unconvinced, as he pinches the pliers slightly.

Suddenly it dawns on Cal why the word Janus is familiar to him and he whips out his phone to confirm his revelation. The picture in his phone's gallery is the last one the phone has taken and he zooms in.

"He is telling the truth," Cal announces, before Locke breaks another finger. "Look," he says, holding his phone up towards Cassie.

Cassie's eyes widen as she too remembers the evidence that they discovered alongside the dead body of Merle Abital. The bright piece of paper that was stuck to the side of Abital's destroyed computer tower had what appeared to be a username and password scribbled on it. One of those phrases read JANUS18.

"Yes, I think he is," Cal confirms to Locke.

Locke's shoulders slump slightly. His hand opens the pliers and he releases his quarry's finger. An air of disappointment now that his fun is over follows Locke as he removes himself from his position hanging over Uri Levy, whose head drops again with a groan.

After a moment, silence falls over the room. Cal realises that it is his turn to approach the suspect to question him. He steps forward nervously, debating how he should approach his line of questioning.

"I'm sorry it came to this, Mr Levy. It was not how I wanted things to go, but you left us no other option," Cal begins, in a consolatory manner, but Uri's head doesn't move from its forlorn position.

"Who is Janus? What is his real name?" Cal asks.

As Uri is still unresponsive, Cal asks the question again, but no answer comes. Locke then moves behind the chair and once again grabs hold of Uri's scalp, pulling his head back to look at Cal. Close up, the suspect's face is a rainbow of bruised colours beneath the blood, which is starting to congeal in places. His nose is badly broken, forcing breath to be taken in through his mouth, which is also in a bad way, and Cal wouldn't be surprised if his jaw was broken.

"There are no names," Uri finally slurs through his injured mouth, his eyes struggling to focus.

"What do you mean?" Cal presses.

"He called himself Janus. That's all I know," Uri answers.

"Are you sure? Because I can pick up those pliers again," Locke snarls from behind.

"Everything is need to know. I'm Mr Easter, he is Janus," Uri mumbles.

"So, a stranger calling himself Janus approached you, and you decided to sign up for genocide on the strength of that?" Cal questions.

"No, it was a long process. We talked for weeks and what he said rang true. The planet is dying and we must do something to stop overpopulation killing it. He proved to me that they had the resources to make a difference and it gave me a chance of redemption," Uri reveals.

"Murder and slaughter are redemption for you?" Cal asks in amazement.

"In the bigger picture? To rescue the planet? Then yes," Uri replies.

"Do you have any idea how twisted your logic is? How inhumane the misery you have caused is?" Cal asks, flabbergasted, but Uri doesn't reply.

"Tell me about Arnoult Pharma and Francis Arnoult," Cal insists.

"All I know is that I suspect Arnoult Pharma is the company that developed the virus," Uri answers.

"Is the company responsible for the entire plot?" Cal demands, finally getting somewhere with his questioning.

"I don't know for sure," Uri replies. "I only found out by chance that they developed the virus. There was a misplaced label on a delivery I received. Perhaps the virus was stolen from the company or it might have been supplied to a third party for another reason."

"It can't be a coincidence," Cal states.

"I don't know. I am just a small piece of the jigsaw. There are many factions involved. Many powerful people hold an interest, as I'm sure you have become aware," Uri confesses.

"Is there a cure or an antidote for the virus?" Cal asks.

Just as Cal asks this vital question, the lights in the room suddenly switch off, plunging it into complete darkness.

Chapter 18

Cal presses the button on his phone, which he is still holding, to illuminate the screen. The light is the first to pierce the unexplained darkness that has enveloped them without warning.

"What the fucking hell has happened?" a male's voice asks from the darkness.

"Keep calm," Cassie replies, as more phone screens throw out light before Cal presses the button for his phone's torch.

A second later, more beams of light flash on as the well-prepared professionals switch on the flashlights attached to their rifles or retrieve their close-to-hand proper torches. Cal quickly kills the light on his phone to save its battery.

"You can't stop it. It's too late. Soon there will be other outbreaks, across the entire planet," Uri's impaired and haunting voice sounds from the darkness.

Uri's chilling revelation makes Cal turn towards him once more. He is greeted again by the suspect's grizzly, wounded face, which has taken on the disturbing features of an infected person in the gloomy light. Cal goes to ask him again about a possible cure, but he is stopped when his phone begins to ring.

"What's happening, Tilly?" Cal answers, putting the call on speakerphone so that everyone can hear.

"Haven't you seen or heard it?" Tilly replies in a panicked voice. "The building is under attack by the infected."

"What? How?" Cal demands.

Cal knows the answer even as he asks the question. The infected are spreading out into the rest of the city. *Why didn't they account for it?* he curses himself. They were attacked in Craven Park. Why wouldn't the creatures keep spreading out?

"How far into the building are they?" Cal asks, before Tilly answers his redundant question.

"We can't be sure. We know they have broken into the ground floor and are in the stairwells," Tilly answers urgently.

"Why has the power gone off?" Cal asks.

"We still have power here. Isn't it on where you are?" Tilly asks.

"No, it's just gone off. We're in darkness," Cal replies.

"Where are you?" Tilly asks.

"In the building's basement," Cal replies sheepishly.

"Hold on," Tilly says, not asking why they are in the basement.

Cal hears her having a heated discussion in the background, trying to find out what's happening. Around him, the others watch on, waiting for information.

"We don't know why the power is off there, but I've been told that there are power fluctuations in the city. Maybe you're on a different part of the grid?" Tilly guesses.

"Okay. What's the plan? Is the building being evacuated?" Cal asks.

"That hasn't been determined yet. We are trying to find out, but there's a problem. The lifts aren't working either, so we have no way of getting off this floor at the moment, not with the infected in the stairwell," Tilly replies fearfully.

"Shit," Cal responds. "So we're all trapped?"

"It looks like we are stuck up here. At least for now. They are starting to barricade the doors," Tilly says.

"Has anyone in authority come down to you?" Cal asks.

"No. Apparently Director Khan was on the phone a short time ago, but we haven't seen him," Tilly replies.

"Nice of him to call," Cal says sarcastically.

"What are you going to do?" Tilly asks.

"I don't know yet. We'll decide now and I'll let you know," Cal replies.

"Thanks. Agent Morgan and I are continuing our research and I'll inform you of any developments," Tilly says.

"Listen, if there's a chance for you to evacuate, don't hesitate to go," Cal insists.

"Don't worry. We will," Tilly assures. "Speak soon."

Tilly hangs up and Cal looks around at the faces watching him.

"Looks like we're fucked." Officer Stack breaks the silence.

"I'll have less of that talk," Locke barks. "I don't want to hear it!"

"What are our options then?" Cal asks. "The ground floor of this building is compromised, as are the stairs, and the lifts aren't working, even if going up was an option."

"Where is the emergency exit from the basement and where does it lead? Does anybody know?" Locke demands.

"I don't know. This is the first time I've been down here," Cassie says, as everyone looks at her, expecting an answer.

"Atkins, you're with me," Locke orders without delay. "The rest of you, wait here."

Locke and Atkins move out of the maintenance room in formation, with their weapons raised. Cal lets them proceed without interfering. This is their territory after all and Cal agreed that he would let Locke take the lead in such instances.

"I know you didn't like it," Cassie says to Cal, "but we got good intelligence from him, which could make all the difference."

"I know. I should have updated Tilly and Agent Morgan, but I didn't like to with the current danger. They're stuck in the middle of this building, with God knows how many others," Cal laments. "At least we're on solid ground with heavy weapons."

"I think you should update them. They deserve to know and it will give them something else to concentrate on," Cassie suggests.

Cal decides Cassie is right and phones Tilly back. Needless to say, Tilly's head is elsewhere and she doesn't fully absorb what Cal is telling her. She takes down the information, like the professional she is, and asks if Cal needs anything else. Cal just asks Tilly for an update, but there isn't anything new she can tell him.

"What are you planning on doing?" Tilly asks, before the call is ended.

"We are looking if there is any way out of here," Cal replies, with a feeling of guilt.

"Agent Morgan says that the building connects to the metro. Can you escape through there?" Tilly asks.

"I don't know. We're checking out options, but we need to evacuate everyone, including you two," Cal replies.

"You can't help us up here, Sir. If you find an escape route, then use it. I'm sure someone will come for us as soon as they can put a rescue mission together," Tilly says, but sounding unconvinced.

"Let me know if that or anything else happens," Cal says.

Tilly assures Cal that they will keep in touch and the call ends. The feeling of guilt deepens within Cal. If Locke does find an escape route, how can they just go and leave their colleagues behind?

"Don't beat yourself up. This isn't your doing," Cassie says, seeing Cal's turmoil.

"No, it isn't, Detective. We know whose fault it is, don't we?" Sergeant Neal interjects, turning towards the man tied to a chair.

"Leave him be," Cal says solemnly, before Neal loses his composure.

A gunshot sounds from beyond the door of the maintenance room, causing them all to turn before Neal can argue. The single shot is followed by an eerie silence, making each of them wonder what is going on outside in the darkness. Neal begins fidgeting with his weapon as an almighty bang follows the shot, but this sound comes from a different direction.

"That came from the direction of the stairs," Cassie says fearfully. "Tilly said they were in the stairwell."

"Don't worry, the door is locked," Cal assures. "I checked it when we got out of the lift."

"How long do you think a locked door is going to stop them? We need to move," Neal insists.

"We wait for Locke and Atkins to return," Cal says.

"Where are they then? They could be in trouble," Neal questions.

"Or gone without us," Stack adds.

"Not a chance that Locke has gone without us," Cal hopes.

Neal covers the door whilst Cal goes to take a look outside to see if he can determine what's happening. Another crash sounds just as Cal pulls the door open. He flinches in fright and waits for a second in case the noise escalates. Silence is restored and Cal risks sticking his head out into the corridor.

A movement to his left, in the opposite direction to the stairs, makes Cal turn his head nervously. Shadows move out of the gloom and, to Cal's relief, both of them are carrying rifles.

"There's only one way out," Locke says, after he has ushered Cal back inside the maintenance room. "And it's risky."

"Not the stairs?" Stack interrupts.

"Shut it," Neal snaps at the young officer.

"The emergency exit at the back of the basement leads up to the building's ground floor. A few metres away, on the ground floor, is an entrance to the metro. The gate is closed, but I'm suggesting we use the metro's tunnels to escape the area," Locke says.

"Aren't the infected on the ground floor?" Cassie asks.

"Yes, but not in great numbers, and they're mostly over near the reception area. The run to the gate was clear," Locke replies.

"The locked gate?" Cassie protests.

"We'll get through the gate," Locke promises. "We're trapped here and we can't rely on anyone else to come for us. I said it was risky, but if anyone has a better suggestion?"

Nobody offers an alternative and so Locke tells them to prepare to move.

"What'll we do with him?" Neal asks, referring to Uri, who is still bleeding and tied to the chair.

"Leave the fucker here, where he belongs," Locke growls.

"No. He comes with us," Cal demands. "There are still questions we need answering."

"What do you mean? I bet he can hardly stand and we can't afford to carry passengers," Locke insists.

"He's right, Cal. We will have to move fast. We can't take him," Cassie says.

"I'm not just leaving him here to be slaughtered or to rot," Cal replies.

"It's all he deserves, Cal!" Cassie argues.

"Maybe. I've let this go far enough though. He's in my custody and I'm not leaving him. You go ahead if you wish," Cal replies stubbornly.

"I can run," a mumbled voice sounds from the chair.

"For fuck's sake!" Neal says angrily and approaches the prisoner.

Neal unties the strap from around Uri's chest to release him from the chair and stands back.

"Let's see you get up then, if you reckon you can run, and we haven't got all day," Neal challenges.

Wobbly at first, Uri pushes himself upright. His head goes dizzy as he stands but stand he does.

"He can hardly stand!" Neal announces. "He ain't going to be able to keep up. He'll get us killed!"

"It was just blood rushing to my head. I'm ready!" Uri insists out of his badly swollen mouth, as blood drips from his little finger.

"Let's move then. If he can't keep up that's his problem," Locke says, already turning for the door.

Cal has given Uri Levy a chance; the rest is up to him. Cal doesn't plan on putting his own life at risk to help the godawful man. Cal has other priorities, like stopping Uri's accomplices and returning to his wife and unborn child.

Locke takes them straight out into the corridor, the light mounted on his rifle showing them the way. Atkins is on Locke's shoulder and, under Locke's orders, Neal and Stack bring up the rear. Uri takes up a position near to Cal and Cassie. His position won't buy him any favours. Cal can promise him that.

A heavy crash against the stairwell door behind them makes Cal turn but not stop moving. Locke ignores the threatening sound completely as he rushes down the corridor in the opposite direction. Next to Cal, Uri struggles to breath. His smashed nose isn't working and his swollen mouth isn't helping matters. That said, he is managing to keep up, for the time being at least.

Past other doors on either side of the corridor, Locke slows their pace as he nears a fire door, which has a green emergency exit sign mounted above it. Beams of light cut through the darkness as Locke gently presses the bar of the opening mechanism, so as not to cause unwanted noise. He slides through the opening, before disappearing right.

Cal follows Cassie through, following her as she turns right and begins to climb the stairs, which are on the other side of the door, behind Atkins. Just as Neal moves to close the door another almighty crash sounds and, this time, it is accompanied by the unmistakeable noise of splintering wood.

Nobody comments on the disturbing new sound. Everyone is just grateful that it wasn't followed by the screech of zombified creatures, but it won't be long until they're through and their chase can begin. More dreaded bangs are muffled by the fire door as they climb the stairs, turning four times as they go.

Light breaks into the darkness of the stairwell when Locke pushes another mechanism to open the door. This one opens out into the building's extensive ground floor, where the entrance and reception area are. *At least the power is still illuminating the lights out there*, Cal thinks. Moving out into the darkness with the infected undead on the hunt would be terrifying.

"The run to the gate is still clear," Locke turns and whispers.

"How are we going to get it open?" Cassie questions quietly, her head turning to look around Locke.

"It's only padlocked," Locke replies. "The problem is the padlock is on the other side."

"Here," Neal says after a moment, passing something to Locke.

"Ah, perfect," Locke says, as he takes the twelve-inch long by about one-inch diameter bar off Neal. The bar is rounded to a point at one end and has a flattened blade at the other.

"Where did you magic that up from?" Atkins asks.

"It's a vital tool when you have to break into as many places as you do in my line of work," Neal replies.

"Okay, listen up," Locke says, as loudly as he dares. "We go together before they even realise we're there. Everyone cover the rear while I break the padlock. Any questions?"

"How many are there out there?" Cassie asks.

"Too many, but it won't matter. As soon as we're through the gate, we'll secure it behind us," Locke says confidently.

Locke's confidence is short-lived as another muffled crash sounds from the bottom of the stairwell and, this time, following the crash, a deathly screech vibrates up to them.

"Move!" Locke orders and immediately pushes his way through the door and into the light.

Within seconds of Locke appearing and just as Cal emerges, a horrifying scream pierces the otherwise quiet space. Cal sees the closed gate and the clear path to it for a moment as he runs, following Locke in its direction. The chilling scream draws his attention to the right though, towards the threatening sound. Numerous horrific beasts watch them emerge from the stairwell, their bodies tensing immediately, ready to attack.

From the stairwell behind, another loud crash sounds just as the door at the top swings shut. The enemy will burst from the stairwell at any moment to add to the numbers already coming for them. If Locke doesn't break the padlock and get the gate open as soon as he reaches it, they will be swamped by a bloodthirsty horde of zombies.

With Locke focused on his vital task, it is Atkins who takes action to try to buy them some time. His arm swings rapidly through the air and he releases a small round object. It arcs across the inner space as he shouts "Grenade".

Locke slams into the gate just as the explosion erupts. Cal dives to the floor, skidding closer to the gate as the violence of the grenade engulfs the entire area. The explosion is massive in the confines of the building. Fire, shrapnel and searing hot gas blast out from the epicentre, vaporising multiple creatures instantly. The explosion spreads to scorch more beasts, whilst super-hot metal fragments rip into other bodies.

Cal realises that Cassie is on the ground next to him as the force of the blast dissipates. Her eyes blink, confirming she is stunned but still conscious, and, behind her, Cal can see Sergeant Neal trying to move. Gunfire breaks out above Cal's head, even as he flounders. The overwhelming noise crashes into his head before he has recovered from the blast of the grenade. Without having to look, he knows that it is Atkins, already laying down covering fire.

"Fight!" a voice cries out into Cal's ringing ears.

The cry energises Cal, pulling him out of his trauma. The battle is happening now and, if they don't fight, they will die. Cal's arms push against the floor as he forces his head to clear after the blast and to concentrate on survival.

His right hand is still curled around his rifle and he brings it up with him. He sees Locke using the metal lattice of the gate to pull himself back up, the rod of steel clutched between his fingers. Gunfire rattles constantly from beside Cal as he fights his fear and prepares to turn and face the enemy.

Remaining on one knee, Cal swivels around, dreading what will greet him. His finger is already hovering over the rifle's trigger as the horror of the building's ground floor presents itself to him.

With his heart racing and his head still ringing, at first Cal only sees carnage and smoke. Many of the lights in the ceiling have been destroyed by the explosion and those that haven't are dulled by the billowing smoke haze that rises. Cal wonders if Tilly felt the explosion numerous floors above as the moving shadows intertwined in the smoke become prevalent.

Cal focuses in on the closest shadow and pulls the trigger. The rifle ricochets back into his shoulder and bullets slam into the body of the shadow, with little effect. Cal re-aims, cursing himself for wasting bullets as the beast breaks through the smoke haze. He aims for the vicious eyes of the terrifying creature, the twisted malevolent features of which crave only one thing… human flesh with blood pulsing through it.

Behind Cal, at the gate, Locke's hands shake as he tries to push the steel rod through the gate and to nestle its pointed end between the body of the padlock and its shackle. Smoke begins to sting his eyes as adrenaline pulses through his body, making him rush his task. He sees the sharp end of the steel poke into the space he was aiming for on the padlock and wrenches the steel bar up, using the metal gate as a fulcrum.

The bar snaps up but, hopelessly, it has popped out of the padlock instead of snapping its locking mechanism. Still in place, the padlock falls back into position with the gate still secured tightly shut. *Fucking hell!* Locke shouts in his head as the gunfire escalates behind him and he goes to try again.

This time, Locke steadies himself, calling on all his training and extensive experience to find his inner calm. He blocks out the chaos behind him, trusting Atkins and the others to hold off the enemy and cover him. Carefully, Locke nudges the steel back into position above the padlock's body and, this time, he ensures it is pushed in tightly. Only when he is satisfied that the steel has gone through the padlock as far as it can go does Locke jerk the other end of the steel bar up with all his might.

Pivoting up against the gate, the bar comes to a sudden stop. Locke doesn't relent; his well-trained muscles strain until finally the bar snaps up again and the padlock pops open. Without a moment to lose, Locke's hand reaches through the gate to push the padlock free.

Cal's second volley slams into the creature's forehead and it falls to the ground, dead. He fires again almost instantly at another shadow as Cassie also opens fire beside Cal. Neal and Stack have joined in the battle too and, for a moment, the threatening shadows are driven back.

That moment is only fleeting and is extinguished when, to Cal's horror, the stairwell door bursts open on their right flank. The first beast that tumbles into the open is riddled with bullets in an instant, but its body is trampled by the pack of undead creatures that pile out behind it.

Automatic gunfire escalates again as they desperately try to defend against the new wave of death attacking from the right. Cal switches rapidly from shooting at the threat that is still ahead to releasing bullets to the right before switching back again.

"The gate is open!" Locke shouts urgently and not a moment too soon.

Uri moves first to go through the gap; his attention is not taken up with trying to hold back the enemy. Neal sees him move and immediately goes to follow him, afraid that he might disappear into the metro tunnels beyond the gate. Stack is next as Locke opens up his weapon from the other side of the gate.

"Go, Cassie!" Cal shouts, as he stands ready to follow her.

Cal and Atkins keep firing as they back towards the safety of the metal gate that Cassie has already reached. She joins Locke in firing from the other side, covering Cal and Atkins' retreat. Cal slips through first, only pausing his fire until he has found a position on the other side and then finally Atkins crosses the threshold.

Locke pushes the gate closed the moment Atkins is through and threads the padlock back through its housing. The padlock no longer locks down, but its shackle will secure it.

"Let's get out of here!" Locke shouts as he releases another volley through the gate and into the pack.

Cal fires one more shot as the horde of creatures is finally released to close in on the gate. He turns in unison with Cassie and, before they have even gone the short distance to a flight of stairs that leads down, bodies slam against the metal barrier behind them. Neither of them turns to look as they all pile down the stairs and out of sight of their attackers.

Chapter 19

There is no light at the bottom of the stairs apart from that is provided by the flashlights fixed to rifles. Cal assumes that this part of the metro is on the same power circuit as the basement they have just escaped from. He looks beyond their current position into the metro station but sees nothing but ominous pitch-black darkness. *Are we really going to venture deeper into the darkness?* he wonders. Who's to say that the infected haven't spread into the underground tunnels already? There must be numerous places along the line that would give them access.

"Will that gate hold them back?" Neal asks, as they pause at the bottom of the stairs.

"I wouldn't count on it," Locke replies. "There were a lot of them. The padlock was broken and wouldn't close. The shackle will break if enough pressure is applied. I fear it's just a matter of time."

"What's the plan now?" Cal asks, looking fearfully into the darkness again.

"We need to find a safe part of the city to go up into," Cassie responds.

"Are there any safe areas left?" Stack questions.

"We need some intel," Locke suggests, as his phone lights up. "Has anyone got a signal?" he asks, worried that he hasn't.

One phone illuminates after another but nobody has any good news.

"We must be in a blind spot," Atkins says. "We might find a signal as we move."

"Move where?" Cassie asks.

"Maybe this motherfucker can tell us where might be safe," Neal suggests from next to Uri.

"I don't know where is safe any more," Uri mumbles in admission.

"We need to evacuate this area. That gate could give way at any moment," Locke insists. "Does anyone know this station?"

"I do, vaguely," Cassie offers. "There is a ticket area ahead, then another flight of steps down to the platforms."

"Okay, follow me. Let's get down to the platform and get some distance away from that gate. We can decide on our next move when we're down there."

"What if the infected are already in the metro system?" Cal asks, before Locke can move. "We could be walking straight into their clutches."

"We don't know," Locke replies. "But we do know what's up there, so we're going to have to risk it."

Locke is right, but that doesn't stop Cal's feeling of dread when he looks into the ominous darkness that they are just about launch into. He sees that Cassie is also trying to put a brave face on the situation as Locke and Atkins turn.

The lights on their rifles pierce the darkness to show the ticketing machines, just as Cassie had said. Beyond the machines are the waist-high access barriers that will have to be climbed over. Shadows crawl across the floor and up the walls as rifles move in hands to cover them as they move into the gloom.

Before they have even managed to take a few steps, a loud metallic creaking sound echoes down the flight of steps behind them. The sound is of bending or cracking metal, and probably both. The gate or the padlock is giving way under the horde's pressure. At any moment the undead will be piling down the stairs, with a burning hunger to feed.

"The gate is giving way," Neal shouts under his breath. "We need to get out of here now!"

Locke stays calm but picks up his pace towards the access barriers that stand beyond the ticket machines. Atkins climbs straight over the barrier and takes up a covering position next to an even darker black hole, which must be the opening for the stairs down to the platforms. Locke doesn't climb over, instead he covers the rear with Stack whilst everyone else gets over the barrier. Neal is forced to help Uri climb over, his broken finger hampering him. As Cal climbs, he wonders how long the barrier will delay their pursuers once they break through the gate, if at all.

"This looks inviting," Cassie comments, as she stands next to the black abyss in front of them.

"We could always turn back," Cal offers.

"I didn't know you did jokes too," Cassie retorts.

"Just trying to lighten the mood," Cal grins, pleased with his pun.

"Oh dear," Cassie laments. "I'd stick to police work if I were you."

"Come on, that wasn't bad," Cal protests.

"Get us out of here, Sergeant," Cassie pleads as Locke arrives over the barrier, "before I have to listen to any more of his jokes."

"Lovely that is, you'd rather descend into the bowels of hell, would you?" Cal protests peering down into the black abyss, as Locke completely ignores them and takes up a position next to Atkins.

"We're just about to find out," Cassie replies.

Locke and Atkins peer into the abyss, to investigate the way forward as best they can. The lights on their rifles shine into the darkness but their power only penetrates so far. The rest will only be revealed as they descend.

"Me and Atkins will take us down," Locke decides. "You cover the rear, Sergeant."

Neal and Stack nod their agreement without question. The two firearms officers may be the cream of the crop of the police force, but they understand Locke is different gravy. Both men are prepared to defer to him, especially if it means he is the first to descend into the threatening black hole.

His orders issued, Locke begins to descend with Atkins without hesitation, the beams of light coming from their rifles leading the way. The two men step down deliberately and in unison, prepared to open fire at any moment. Cassie holds Cal back for a second when he goes to follow. He realises that she is giving the two men ahead some breathing room. He waits, and then follows when she decides to go.

Another creaking noise echoes down to them as Cal steps out. Nobody mentions it or panics though; they keep walking ahead at Locke's pace. Cal's heart rate increases with every step he descends into the darkness. He can only follow the light being thrown by other people. How he wishes his rifle had a torch attached to it.

The stairs down go deeper than Cal had imagined and, with every step Locke takes, Cal prays it will be the last before they reach the bottom. He tries to calculate how far down they have travelled but he gives up. All he knows is that they are deep under the city, where the rats reside. *Let's hope that rats are the only creatures haunting the nooks and crevices of the tunnels*, Cal thinks to himself.

Locke finally comes to a stop just ahead, but Cal quickly sees that he still isn't on the platform. He has only come to a turn in the stairwell. After gradually scoping around the corner, Locke decides that the way is clear and continues, with Atkins on his shoulder. Deeper they go until at last Locke stops again. This time Cal can see that they have arrived at the platform level. A glint of light reflecting off the steel tracks below confirms it.

The two Special Forces men take their time to check that the area is clear. Locke's rifle points left out of the stairwell while Atkins' weapon points right. There are no guarantees when Locke takes his first step onto the platform. The beams of light emanating from their rifles are almost insignificant, becoming lost in the cavernous space of the platform. Anything could be lurking in the darkness beyond the light, but Locke calculates that anything waiting to attack would have seen the light and done so.

The sound of the empty platform seems to echo on itself. Any slight noise is amplified by the shape of the curve-walled tube. Cal feels a breeze against his face as he goes to step onto the platform after Locke has given the signal. The breeze is welcome, even though the air cannot be described as fresh.

"What time's our train?" Stack jokes, as he arrives on the platform with Neal.

"Keep your concentration, Officer, and cover the stairs," Locke demands impatiently.

"Wouldn't that be nice? A train coming to whisk us away," Cassie dreams.

"Electricity and light would do at the moment," Cal answers.

"Is electricity and light part of your plan, after world domination?" Cassie growls at Uri. "Or are survivors expected to return to living in mud huts? That's if there are any survivors."

Uri doesn't answer as he cradles his painful hand in the other. His battered face is hard to read but Cassie thinks she may see a tinge of regret behind the blood and bruising. Perhaps now that the reality of the horror he has helped bring to fruition has begun to sink in he is having doubts, or maybe it's just that his hand is hurting and his face is aching.

"What now?" Cal asks. "The gate is going to give way at any time. Those creaking sounds won't last forever," he adds, referring to the continuing ominous sounds echoing down to them.

"Are there other exits from this platform?" Atkins asks.

"Only ones that lead up to street level," Cassie replies. "And I wouldn't recommend going onto the streets above us in the current situation."

"We go through the tunnel," Locke states.

"Great," Cal says. "But which way?"

Locke reaches to his side and proceeds to pull out his frighteningly large combat knife. Within a second, he has twisted a covering cap from its butt to reveal a built-in compass.

"We need to head east, away from the Arena District. That's where these creatures must be spreading from," Locke decides, looking in each direction.

"Which tunnel do we take then?" Cassie asks.

"That's a good question," Locke replies. "This tunnel is heading north and south."

"It's the south tunnel," Atkins announces. "The north one bends around to the west after leaving this station."

Locke immediately moves to join Atkins, who has found a map of the metro system mounted nearby in the darkness.

"Yes, the south tunnel. It will take us south-east and hopefully out of harm's way," Locke agrees.

"How long is the tunnel?" Cassie asks.

"Fuck knows. These maps aren't to scale," Locke replies.

"Great. So the next station could be a few hundred metres or a few miles," Cassie sighs.

"It doesn't matter where the next station is. We need to put some distance between us and this part of the city so we will pass a few stations as we go," Locke replies.

"Where are you planning on taking us?" Cal asks.

"I reckon Newtown should be far enough," Locke answers.

"Newtown!" Cal exclaims. "That's got to be one or two miles from here."

"Closer to two, I would say. So let's get moving," Locke insists.

"Fuck me!" Cassie spits.

"No problem. We march two miles before breakfast," Atkins encourages.

"Whoopee do for you," Cassie says, unimpressed. "I bet you don't do it through metro tunnels, after the day from hell and whilst being hunted by zombies!"

"Er, no," Atkins grins, as he follows Locke to the edge of the platform, "this will be a first."

Cal is just about to console Cassie when a crashing sound hits them from the stairwell where Neal and Stack are still positioned. Everyone freezes for a moment, looking at each other in terror.

"We need to get outa here!" Stack shouts foolishly.

"That's it, give away our position, you fucking idiot," Neal curses Stack under his breath.

Locke doesn't hang around to berate the young police officer himself. Stack's face already shows that he is mortified. Instead, he jumps straight down from the edge of the platform, taking care not to land on a steel rail track or anything else that might risk injury.

"Watch where you land," Locke orders in a loud whisper.

One after the other they make it onto the tracks without injury, some deciding to ease themselves down rather than risking a jump. Cal, Cassie and Uri take extra care. They can only rely on other people's lights to show them where they'll land. Locke and Atkins are already at the mouth of the south tunnel when the last of them, Sergeant Neal, makes it onto the tracks. Locke holds his position with Atkins whilst everyone else catches them up.

"Sergeant, you take the lead," Locke orders Neal. "We'll cover the rear. There could be infected ahead also, so be careful."

Neal moves immediately into the mouth of the tunnel to take them inside, just as a chilling screech echoes closer. Cal gives Locke and Atkins an encouraging nod as he passes them. His admiration for the two men's courage rises as they volunteer to be the first line of defence against the oncoming threat.

Cassie is the first to sacrifice her grip on her weapon to switch the torch of her phone on and Cal quickly follows suit. Railway sleepers, cables and rail tracks underfoot are the biggest threat right now. Untold injuries await anyone who takes a trip and falls over. A broken ankle or concussion now would be disastrous.

Neal and Stack traverse the obstacles of the tunnel with seeming ease, the beams of light from their rifles showing them the way. Cal and Cassie do their best to keep pace but the light from their phones is not as powerful, plus they aren't as finely trained. Uri fares even worse. He has no light of his own and his head aches, which causes him to fall behind as he stumbles along, trying not to go down.

All of them are pushed along by the chilling screeching sounds of zombified beasts somewhere behind them. Are the tunnel's acoustics amplifying the threat? Cal doubts it. Bloodthirsty creatures are closing and there's no point in trying to deny it.

Cal begins to lose his bearings as his lungs gasp for breath and his legs strain. How far have they travelled and when will the next station arrive? He doesn't know the answer to either question. The darkness has swallowed them whole.

Something shoots across the tracks down low in front of Cal, his phone's light only just catching a glimpse of it. *A rat*, he thinks. Their presence will be disturbing the local rodent population, which is more used to underground trains careering past threatening to cut off their tails... or worse.

His foot kicks something soft as he runs, another rat, the resulting squeal of protest confirming it.

"I hate rats," Cal hears Cassie moan from beside him.

So does Cal, but he'd rather run across a few rats than the undead. A thought suddenly hits him as he pants for breath. Is it their presence that is disturbing the rat population or is the rats' sixth sense alarming them, warning them that a malevolent force is fast approaching?

"Here they come!" Locke shouts in the second before the sound of gunfire crashes off the walls of the tunnel.

Fear grips Cal, the darkness threatening to consume him. A beast could be running next to him, its mouth salivating, and he wouldn't see it in the pitch-black tunnel. *What does Locke want them to do? Turn and fight or keep running?* Cal questions, unsure what to do. Flashes of light erupt again as more bullets are fired back down the tunnel. Cal glances back to try to see what he should do, to gauge how close the threat is. All he sees are flashes of light, blackness and the shadows of Locke and Atkins. Their shadows are still moving and Neal ahead keeps going and so Cal keeps running, following on to God knows where.

"Find cover," Locke bellows in a panic from behind them, and in between bursts of gunfire.

Just as Locke shouts, the tunnel's atmosphere changes. Even in the darkness, Cal feels the adjustment. He shines his light to the right and sees the tunnel's wall expand out and the shadow of a platform appear.

Ahead, Sergeant Neal is already heading for the haunting concrete platform. The higher ground is their only chance of finding cover. Using their hands, Neal and Stack bounce up onto the platform in an instant. They immediately turn, crouched on one knee, ready to lay down covering fire.

Two beams of light shine from their rifles, helping the others see their way up.

Cassie doesn't hang around. She climbs up quickly, whereas Cal forces himself to turn and wait for his prisoner, who finally appears out of the gloom. Uri looks in a bad way as he grunts towards the platform, totally exhausted.

"Move it," Cal demands urgently.

Locke and Atkins appear from the tunnel in reverse with their guns blazing. Cal wonders how many creatures they are fighting as he picks up Uri's legs to heave him up onto the platform. Cal follows Uri up, who stays flat on his back, exhausted, and looks for Cassie as he does. She is nowhere to be seen, however, and for a moment he begins to worry. A light shining across the platform puts his mind at rest as he realises that she must be looking for a defensive position or the chance of escape.

Gunfire erupts from close by, taking Cal's attention. Neal and Stack have opened up with their weapons to cover Locke and Atkins as they retreat towards the platform. Both men run with their heads pulled into their shoulders, shouting something that Cal cannot hear over the rattle of gunfire.

A flash of blinding light pulses out of the tunnel like a camera flash, illuminating Locke and Atkins in their feverish retreat. The sonic boom follows the explosion an instant after, blasting out of the tunnel in a wave that shocks Cal to his core, forcing him to duck his head in reflex. Locke and Atkins don't let the awesome explosion delay their progress. They bound up onto the platform before the smoke has started to billow from the tunnel's mouth.

Cal wonders what everyone is aiming at as the smoke billows and the aftermath of the explosion dies down. Surely anything in that tunnel will have been obliterated by the massive blast? The force was fierce on the relatively open platform. Inside the completely enclosed tunnel it must have been calamitous.

"We need to find an exit," Neal demands.

"Hold position, Sergeant," Locke orders. "Let's see if anything comes out. We're still below the dangerous part of the city."

"We don't know that. We don't know where they have spread to," Neal protests. "I'd rather be out in the open than suffocating down here."

"You can bet they're above us," Locke insists. "Our best option is to continue down the tunnel if the grenades have taken care of the ones following us."

Neal curses under his breath but holds his position.

Cal keeps out of the heated debate. His eyes are fixed on the tunnel's mouth and on the beams of light that are criss-crossing through the smoke drifting out. The swirling smoke is hypnotic, especially with the lights cutting through it. Shadows form out of thin air as clouds of smoke drift on the breeze. Cal's eyes dart from one point to another as his vision plays tricks on him, forming silhouettes of figures that disappear just as mysteriously. He blinks as another silhouette appears, his mind unable to decide what he is seeing for a second. This time the formation doesn't vaporise on the breeze. Instead, it solidifies.

Cal blinks once more to ensure he isn't mistaken. The mutilated beast is severely injured to the point where it is almost unrecognisable. It consists of a torso perched on two legs. The left side of its body and the arm that was attached to it are missing. In a daze, it steps further out of the smoke, its balance askew as a result of its catastrophic injuries. Not seeing the train track at its feet, it doesn't lift its foot and trips on the solid metal rail. A badly burnt right arm that is in tatters swings feebly out to try to stop its fall, but the left arm that it was expecting to help save it is non-existent.

Nobody wastes bullets on the sorry creature. Instead, they let nature take its course. Gravity pulls the beast down over the rail, its remaining mutilated right arm floundering to break its fall. With a sickening crack of bone on steel, its head whacks into the second rail. After a small bounce back into the air, the head hits the rail again and the creature lies motionless across the two tracks.

"It's fucking grim, isn't it?" Cal hears from someone beside him.

Whoever said that isn't wrong, Cal thinks, in the second before another shadow appears through the smoke haze. This shadow is caught in a light beam almost immediately and light reflects back off the charred skin that oozes a revolting bloody slime out of the cracks between the pores of its burnt skin. This creature shows no concern for its trauma. It fixes its eyes in the direction of the light and snarls.

"I've got it," Locke announces, as a single bullet explodes from his rifle's muzzle.

The bullet smashes straight into the forehead of the charred, snarling creature. Blood and brain matter erupt into the air as the creature's head whips back, taking its body with it. Before the beast has hit the ground, another wanders out into the light.

"Find us another way out, Detective," Locke orders urgently and then fires again.

Chapter 20

Cal doesn't delay. Locke's order was crystal clear. They need another exit strategy, one that doesn't include venturing back into the pitch-black tunnels. Cal can't say he's sorry about that but, as the gunfire escalates when he turns, he knows that they are in dire straits. The smoke from the tunnel may be thinning but the infected creatures emerging out of its mouth are increasing in numbers and their wounds from the explosion are diminishing after the explosion.

Where is Cassie? Cal asks himself desperately as he looks across the platform in the same direction in which he saw her a few moments ago. *Has she found an escape route for them already?* Cal thinks, his heart lifting. If she has though, where the hell is she?

Bullets fly from behind Cal's back as he shines his phone's light over the platform, looking for any movement from Cassie. The darkness is stifling and the light isn't strong enough to penetrate it to any great distance. He rushes up the platform, searching for any break in the side wall that might the offer hope of escape and/or reveal the whereabouts of Cassie.

A horrific, bloodcurdling scream bellows across the platform. The sound rises even above the blasts of gunfire.

Cal spins in fright, believing a beast might be right behind him. He finds nothing but darkness next to him. Beyond, at the tunnel's mouth, he sees multiple figures bursting into the station and escaping the barrage of gunfire.

"Cal! This way," Cassie shouts.

Turning again, Cal sees Cassie's worried face through the gloom, her body hidden inside a doorway. He runs over to her as her head disappears back behind the doorway. Aiming for where she vanished, Cal turns away from the platform and finds himself next to Cassie in a small alcove with a heavy metal sliding door that is folded in on itself.

"I've tried to get it open, but I can't budge it," Cassie says.

"Is it locked from the other side?" Cal asks.

"It must be," Cassie replies. "There's no other way out. I've looked."

Another screech reverberates from close by, threatening their position. Cal turns, his rifle coming up ready to defend them as he steps forward. Bodies of the undead litter the tracks below the platform, the creatures slaughtered by the incessant gunfire. Locke glances back in Cal's direction, his face praying for a solution.

Cassie's rifle releases a burst of fire as Cal urgently signals Locke to move. *Is this the right call?* Cal wonders as Locke answers his call.

The four professionals rise and begin to shuffle back in an orderly retreat towards the supposed evacuation point. They continue to fire as they attack the never-ending stream of creatures emerging out of the tunnel. Cal and Cassie lay down fire to try to take some of the burden, but they only have a finite number of bullets.

Tagging along with the retreat is Uri Levy, who has managed to get himself back onto his feet. The prisoner is still in a daze and, without realising, stumbles into Cal's line of fire, forcing him to pause his fire until the man stumbles past and into the alcove.

"What have we got?" Locke demands, taking a knee beside Cal.

"A way out but the door is locked solid," Cal shouts in reply.

"Cover me!" Locke bellows, as he moves to see.

Just as Locke moves, Cal fires another round of bullets as another group of ferocious beasts bursts out of the tunnel, moving at a frightening speed. All of Cal's bullets miss their targets and he aims again, but this time the rifle clicks empty.

"I'm out of fucking ammo," he shouts to anyone who cares.

Nobody acknowledges him; they are all too worried about defending the position and about the amount of ammo they have remaining. Cal turns to see if he can help Locke get the door open. If it doesn't slide across soon, they will all be doomed. The undead creatures are getting closer to the edge of the platform with every bullet that is fired.

"Get it open!" Cal begins to panic, shouting at Locke.

Uri is holding himself up against the edge of the alcove as Locke pulls at the door, which doesn't budge.

"Watch out!" Neal shouts, appearing from nowhere.

Locke does as he's told immediately and Neal aims his rifle at the edge of the door, moving its light up and down the small gap between the door and the wall it is locked against. Cal sees the glint of metal about a quarter of the way down the edge of the doorframe, just as Neal fires a short burst of bullets up at the anchor. Sparks erupt and metal shards fly as Neal trains his rifle down at a second, lower anchor holding the door shut.

"Have you any grenades left?" Cassie shouts in terror at Locke.

He and Cal spin around to witness a pack of beasts surging towards the platform. The diminishing number of bullets being spent is proving fatal. The horde are just about to breach the side of the platform.

"I'm out," Locke replies horribly, just as a beast leaps up to their position.

Locke steps forward, his rifle up in an instant, and fills the creature with bullets. The beast topples back off the platform and into the oncoming horde.

"We need a diversion!" Atkins shouts, as his rifle clicks empty and he searches for another magazine.

Locke looks back at Neal, who is firing again at the door's anchors. Locke then looks at Cal with a sorry expression in the instant before he turns, his expression changing. Locke grabs one of Uri's arms without warning, pulling him away from the wall that he is cowering against. Before Uri can process what is happening, Locke spins ferociously, pulling on Uri's arm with all his might.

Locke releases Uri, his aim true. Uri's feet dance frantically to try to bring himself under control, his face delirious with fear, and Cal watches on in disbelief. Locke has found their diversion and a different kind of grenade to throw. The horde of undead seem to be just as astounded. All the eyes in the entire confined space watch as Uri Levy pirouettes uncontrollably towards his doom. A cry of panic escapes Uri's mouth when his feet reach the white-painted edge of the platform, his fate sealed.

The arms of the undead reach into the air, waiting to welcome their gift. Uri's arms wave one last time to try to rebalance his weight but the motion is futile. His feet leave the side of the platform and he falls, into the clutches of the horror he helped bring to reality. Cal catches one last glimpse of Uri's battered and petrified face as he is pulled into the throng of beasts, their teeth already bearing down on his flesh.

In shock and disgust, Cal turns angrily towards Locke, but the soldier has disappeared. Cal turns again to watch Locke and Neal strain every sinew in their bodies as they try to wrench the door across. The folding steel door judders as gunfire sounds again from behind. Locke, who has taken the handle, pulls again through gritted teeth, his face reddening from the strain. With a crack, the door pops away from its anchors and slides open.

"Not now," Locke pants at Cal, knowing he will have something to say about Uri's sacrifice. "Get inside!" he orders.

Cal and Cassie follow Neal through the gap that has thankfully opened up. Cal struggles with the fact that Locke has just saved his life after committing such a barbaric atrocity right in front of him. He can't help the relief he feels, telling himself that *it is nothing but a natural feeling after such a close shave with a hideous death.*

Stack squeezes through the gap to the other side, which appears even darker than the metro line, if that is possible. Atkins comes through next as gunfire continues and then, finally, Locke comes through sideways, breathing in as he does.

"Help me shut it," Neal demands, standing next to the door, ready to heave it closed.

Needless to say, Locke puts his toned body against the door to help Neal move it. When the door finally meets back up with the wall, Atkins catches Lock in his light beam to check he's okay.

"Awesome job, Sarge," Atkins tells his superior enthusiastically. "Without that play we'd have all been chop suey for them fuckers."

"Yes, well done, Sergeant," Neal adds. "That vile cunt deserved it. Probably the only useful thing he's ever done in his miserable life."

Stack nods his agreement and Cassie even steps forward to pat Locke on the shoulder.

"Thank you, Sergeant," Cal offers. "Not that I can agree with your method."

"I know, Detective, but needs must when the devil drives," Locke counters. "You can read me my rights later. We still aren't out of the woods and I haven't the energy right now."

Locke doesn't wait for a response. He pushes himself off the door just as a heavy bang hits the other side. Ducking in reflex and turning, his weapon at the ready, Locke prepares to take up the fight again.

"Easy, Sergeant," Neal calms. "We're safe, at least for now. There's no way they are getting through that any time soon."

"You have more confidence than me," Locke replies, as another body slams into the door, rattling it in its runners.

"It will hold," Cassie assures. "And they will lose interest as soon as they realise it's not budging."

"What have we got then?" Locke asks, Cassie's words seeming to relax the tough Special Forces man.

"Looks like more tunnels and stairwells I'm afraid, Sarge," Atkins answers.

"I'm never using the metro again," Locke sighs.

"You won't get the chance if we don't stop this," Cassie points out.

Locke grunts as he adds his beam of light to those shining down the tunnel in front of them.

"Did anyone notice what station this is?" Locke asks.

"Crosskeys," Cassie confirms.

"We haven't got far then," Locke bemoans.

"At least we're still breathing," Neal points out.

"Always a bonus, I suppose," Locke comments. "Anyone familiar with it?

"Has anyone got a signal?" Locke asks when no one answers his first question.

Again, nobody gives a positive answer and so, without saying another word, Locke moves to begin stalking the tunnel ahead. Everyone falls into the formation that is now becoming familiar. Locke and Atkins lead, with Cal and Cassie in the centre, and then Neal and Stack taking the rear. The only person missing is their prisoner, but Cal can't say he misses Uri Levy.

One crash follows another against the metal door behind them as they move away. Cal begins to wonder if the creatures will lose interest, as Cassie assumed. They are very persistent at the moment. Perhaps they have no desire to wander the pitch-black tunnels either, for what could be an eternity in their case.

The narrow tunnel bends around to the left and then takes them up a flight of stairs into yet another spooky ticket office. Idle machines stand lurking above them after Locke has led them to climb over the inevitable access barrier. Cal calls for them to stop when he feels his phone vibrate in his pocket. The signal has returned.

Dawn is beginning to break, Cal decides, as he retrieves his phone. The sun is still weak, but daylight is definitely leaking into the station from somewhere. His hand in front of him isn't only lit by torch power any longer. Cal finds some comfort in the sun returning and his thoughts are concerned with Kim.

The first message he sees on his phone is from Kim's father, Tom. He tells Cal that he can't sleep, which isn't surprising, but that Kim, thankfully, is still resting. Cal sends a quick message back thanking Tom for keeping him up to date and to please tell him when Kim wakes up.

"Fuck me!" Cassie states whilst looking at her phone.

"What is it?" Cal asks, concerned that she has received some bad family news or something.

"Cities across the world have been hit," Cassie informs them all miserably. "Glasgow, Paris, Berlin, New York, Los Angeles, Mumbai, Beijing and Melbourne have so far reported outbreaks." Cassie lists off the cities stunned.

"We knew it was coming from what that prick confessed," Locke insists.

"So many places," Cal says. "We've got to act on Levy's information."

"This is all-out war, my friend," Locke insists. "We can't fuck around with search warrants and police procedures. We've got to take them down by any means necessary."

"You won't hear another argument from me, Sergeant," Cal replies in shock.

"It's gonna get brutal," Locke adds.

"It's already beyond brutal," Cassie insists.

"So, where do we go from here?" Neal asks.

"We hit them where it hurts and come down on them like a ton of bricks," Locke salivates.

"Agreed, Sergeant. But, before that, we need to regroup and form a plan of attack. Mercury House is out of action, so we need a base of operations," Cal insists.

"And you will have one, my friend," Locke replies without embellishing.

The mention of Mercury House fills Cal with worry for the people trapped inside the building. Their whole team, but especially Agent Morgan… and Tilly. He quickly returns to his messages and sees that he has multiple missed calls from various numbers, but Tilly's name is listed more often and, without delay, he returns her call.

"Thank God, Detective," Tilly answers almost immediately. "We thought we'd lost you!"

"It was close, Tilly, but we managed to escape and we're currently in Crosskeys station. What's happening there?" Cal replies.

"Crosskeys station. How have you ended up there?" Tilly asks.

"It's a long story, Tilly, and not important. What's your situation?" Cal asks again.

"We're still holed up on the seventh floor," Tilly replies.

"Any sign of a rescue coming?" Cal asks.

"Commissioner Jackson told me over the phone that help is on the way. We've seen helicopters circling and we think that some have landed on the roof. But nobody has arrived on this level yet," Tilly informs Cal.

"Where is the commissioner?" Cal asks.

"When he phoned, he was still in the building," Tilly replies. "He demanded to know where you were."

"What did you tell him?" Cal asks.

"I told him that I don't know where you are," Tilly replies. "He wasn't very impressed with my answer."

"I bet he wasn't," Cal says. "I have missed calls from him."

"I'm not surprised," Tilly says.

"I'm sure they will come for you. Just hold tight," Cal assures, hoping his confidence isn't misplaced.

"I hope so," Tilly replies nervously. "We have carried on working and have uncovered more intelligence. I've detailed it all in emails to you and Agent Sutton. I didn't want it lost if the worst happens here. We have kept it all private for now, as you ordered. Agent Morgan wasn't so sure we should, but I convinced him."

"Well done, Tilly," Cal congratulates her, his words seeming insufficient for her dedication in the face of such danger. "We must keep this to ourselves. We can't trust anyone."

"I understand," Tilly confirms. "The information in the emails is pretty damning and, you're right, nobody can be trusted."

"We have extracted information too," Cal says without elaborating. "Just between us, Arnoult Pharma and its CEO, Doctor Francis Arnoult, are now our prime suspects. See what you and Agent Morgan can dig up on both."

"We are already on to them," Tilly announces. "What we've found so far is contained in the emails. We are concentrating our research on them as we speak."

"Really?" Cal replies, thinking of the torture they put Uri Levy through.

"Yes," Tilly interrupts Cal's thoughts. "We think they play a vital role in this, if they aren't behind the entire plot."

"Then we're on the same page, it would seem. That can't be a coincidence," Cal says.

"It isn't, Sir. Read the information in the emails," Tilly suggests.

"I will, as soon as we're sorted and I can concentrate on them," Cal promises.

"Okay. What's your plan now?" Tilly asks.

"That's what we're just deciding. I'll let you know as soon as we're sorted," Cal assures. "I'll also be using whatever remaining influence I have to get you to safety, Tilly. All of you trapped there."

"Thanks, Sir," Tilly replies.

"Speak soon." Cal ends the call.

"Is she going out of her mind?" Cassie asks as the call ends.

"No, she is surprisingly calm. She and Morgan are still working, despite the danger. They've unearthed new intelligence, which she's sent us both via email," Cal replies. "They seem to be coming to the same conclusion as us though... Arnoult Pharma."

Chapter 21

"So where do we go from here?" Neal asks.

"Whatever we do, we need to keep it off-grid. We can't afford to let these people know that we're on to them or they will disappear like the darkness at dawn," Cal insists.

"The first thing we need to do is get to somewhere secure before we decide how to proceed," Cassie states.

"Sergeant, what have you got in mind?" Cal asks Locke.

"It's not pretty but me and my men have commandeered our own little corner at Riley Airbase. No one will bother us there," Locke replies.

"Of course they will, Sergeant," Cassie insists. "As soon as they know where we are, they'll be all over us like a bad rash."

"How would they know where you are if we don't tell them?" Locke counters.

"How are we going to get onto an airbase without anyone knowing?" Cassie asks.

"I'm working on that," Locke assures.

"I can see if Monks is available to fly us in," Cal offers.

"Negative, Detective," Locke states. "If we fly in, everyone's ID will be taken the moment we land. Security is too tight on that. We need to be more subtle."

"So, what do you suggest, Sergeant?" Cassie demands. "How are we even going to get to the airbase? It's a few miles away at least, isn't it? And, right now, we're stranded in zombie territory."

"And please don't suggest any more tunnels, Sergeant," Cal insists, only half joking.

"We drive,' Locke says surprisingly. "There's a car park above this station. I looked on my phone while you were on your call. We jack some wheels and drive in. I can smuggle you onto the base that way but not if we fly in."

"This sounds dodgy to me," Cassie says.

"Have some faith, Agent Sutton. I haven't let you down yet, have I?" Locke grins.

"We're not a couple of hookers that you want to smuggle onto base, Sergeant," Cassie grins in return.

"I don't know. With a bit more make-up, a short skirt and some heels, Agent…" Locke's grin widens.

"Careful, Sergeant! You're on thin ice," Cassie chuckles.

"When you're finished." Cal rolls his eyes.

"Sorry, Detective," Locke says. "Are you in agreement?"

"What do you think, Cassie?" Cal asks.

"I can't think of a better plan, as much as it pains me to admit," Cassie replies, eyeing Locke. "But we don't know if the streets are safe to drive around here. Judging by how many infected chased us into the metro, there could be swarms of them on the roads."

"I agree," Locke admits. "We need to get to the car park and check out the terrain."

Cassie shrugs her shoulders noncommittally, leaving the final decision up to Cal.

"Okay, Sergeant. Let's get up to the car park," Cal decides.

"The exit to the car park is over there," Atkins points. "Past that vending machine."

"Vending machine!" Locke repeats, turning eagerly.

The locking mechanism on the vending machine stands no chance against a hangry Special Forces officer and a police officer well trained in breach tactics. Neal has the machine's door broken open in quick time and nobody dares stand in the way of Locke as he plunders the machine.

Neal's skills are called back into action immediately when they find the exit door to the car park locked. This door resists Neal's attention for longer but succumbs in the end.

A few flights of stairs up is the car park, with sides opening out over the streets below. Everyone's rifle is up and ready to fire as they venture out into the car park, just in case any creatures have found their way up the entry ramps. A few emergency lights are still active above their heads and the dawn gloom is spreading with every passing minute. Fresh air is welcomed into all of their lungs, even if it contains a tinge of smoke, which has penetrated the entire city centre.

An eerie stillness hangs over the concrete space. Nothing moves, but the sounds of the traumatised city leak in through the car park's open-sided perimeter. Chilling wails of the undead confirm that the infected are in the vicinity before Locke leads them over to the closest opening to look out over the terrain below.

Peering over the side of the car park and past the station below is like looking over an alien vista. Power fluctuations have extinguished most of the street lighting but, inexplicably, the odd streetlamp remains active. Only one thing moves, save for the trees dancing in the breeze, and that is the ominous dark figures that have infected the area. Some travel in packs, searching for food, whilst others stumble around on their own and there are too many to count.

"Are we sure we shouldn't contact Monks to fly us out of here?" Cal asks.

"If we do, we'll be back in the system, Detective," Locke replies.

"He's right. If we want to keep the element of surprise when we hit them, we must stay off-grid," Cassie adds.

"Driving out of here it is then," Cal concedes. "I was just thinking I could do with some more excitement!"

"I can definitely guarantee you that, Detective," Locke grins.

"We don't want you getting bored," Atkins adds.

"God forbid," Locke says. "Now, let's find some wheels."

"What sort of thing are we looking for?" Cassie asks, looking across the half-empty car park.

"Something that can conceal two people," Locke confirms.

"Why two?" Neal asks.

"We don't want Detective Chambers and Agent Sutton having to show their IDs when we enter. Theirs will raise a red flag in the system. The rest of us shouldn't raise any eyebrows," Locke replies.

"A large SUV-type vehicle then?" Cal reasons.

"Preferably with blacked-out windows in the back. Something easy to hot-wire, so the older the better," Locke specifies.

"Something like that?" Stack interrupts, pointing through the gloom.

"That will do nicely," Locke replies, making a move towards a larger, older four-wheel drive parked a few rows into the car park.

"Toyota. At least it should be reliable," Atkins says, as they go.

The vehicle is broken into and the engine fired up in no time. There is no doubt that this isn't the first time Locke has helped himself to someone else's transport whilst out on manoeuvres. He takes the driver's seat, with Atkins next to him, whilst the other four squeeze into the back. Cal and Cassie will have to switch to the space behind the back seats when they get close to the airbase.

Before they set off, Locke and Atkins distribute some of the ammo they are carrying to whoever is out. Cal and Cassie reload their rifles eagerly; neither of them was keen on heading out with empty weapons. Ammo is limited but some is better than none.

"Everyone set?" Locke asks.

Locke hits the accelerator before anyone has the chance to answer. The Toyota lurches forward before turning hard towards the exit, with its tyres squealing. There is no thought of taking things easy as they head out. Locke speeds down and around the exit ramp, barely slowing as he smashes through the barrier to take them into the city's streets beyond.

Morning has definitely broken as they leave the car park and the cold light of day shows just how far the city has fallen. No other cars are on the roads to slow Locke down and the only pedestrians turn ferociously towards the interloping vehicle in their midst.

"Here they come!" Locke announces, as soon as he has straightened up onto the road out of the car park.

The infected move like ghouls towards the magnetic pull of the Toyota, the sound of its engine roaring around the streets, which only play host to the undead. Like moths to a flame, they come to attack, driven on by the gnawing hunger in their transformed inhuman bellies.

Locke swerves around the first one that steps out in the street, with no concern for its own survival it would seem. Even as the car sweeps past, its fingernails scratch into the side of the vehicle, its mouth gaping desperately to feed.

Atkins positions his rifle to aim out of the front windscreen as others launch themselves at the vehicle. A crash against the back quarter jolts them all where they sit. Locke swerves to avoid contact as best he can but the undead are beginning to swarm. The front of the car ploughs straight into a creature, its evil eyes fixed on its quarry right up until it is smashed into the air. The body spins up and over to the side of the road, where it smacks into the pole of a streetlight, its body breaking against the steel strut.

"They don't fucking care, do they?!" Locke bellows as more creatures are mashed against the front of the car and he tries not to lose control.

Some of the bodies are launched upwards to land on the roadside, whilst others bang onto the vehicle's roof before they're ejected off the back. Some are dragged under the wheels to be squished or dragged along, torn to shreds against the road's tarmac.

No matter how many Locke ploughs into, and how much carnage he leaves in his wake, more beasts are there to replace them, ready to attack. One somehow manages to ride up the front of the car to become caught on the windscreen directly in front of Atkins. Atkins prepares to fire at the hideous face twisting not a few inches from him, but he waits for Locke's order.

"Let him have it!" Locke barks.

Cal's hands land on the side of his head to protect his ears just as Atkins releases a controlled burst of gunfire. Bullets crack through the windscreen, the burst filling the beast's face with bullets. The gunshots ring around the cabin of the Toyota, penetrating through Cal's hands and into his eardrums. Locke tweaks the steering wheel to the side and the creature slides off the car and into oblivion.

"We can't keep this up, surely?!" Cal shouts as his hands leave his head.

"It'll get better, Detective," Locke says confidently and calmly.

"It can't get much worse," Cal protests.

Just as the words leave Cal's lips, the window next to him explodes inwards. Stifling a scream of terror as the head of a ferocious creature almost lands in his lap, the body halfway into the vehicle's cabin, Cal goes into panic mode. Without thinking, he grabs the beast's hair to try to lift its teeth away from the parts of his body no man wants bitten into. Thankfully, the blow to the creature's head has stunned it for a moment but the lull in the attack doesn't last. Cal's grip on the hair slips when the creature goes berserk.

Next to him, Cassie recoils in fright for a second. Her shock stops her from processing what is happening. She stares frozen at the matted hair in Cal's hand for what seems an eternity until suddenly she acts.

Her hand releases her rifle and rises to a position next to the left side of her ribcage, where her sidearm nestles in its holster. She does not need to divert her eyes to find her weapon, the movement is automatic, and her hand curls around the gun's grip. The gun slides out and, in one rapid motion, she places the muzzle of the gun against the side of the beast's head. She takes a millisecond to ensure the trajectory of the bullet won't hit Cal, or Locke in the front seat, and then pulls the trigger.

The opposite side of the creature's head explodes in a volcano of deep-red blood, grey brain matter and bone, together with a sprinkling of hair. The exhaust from the gunshot splatters onto the back of the driver's seat and the car, whilst the bullet continues its trajectory and hits the side of the car.

In a daze of confusion and fear, Cal feels the creature go limp in his hand. Somehow, he manages to gather himself enough to lift the head back up and also to push with his other hand until the disgusting mess slides back out of the shattered window.

"Are you injured?" Cassie asks, through the ringing in Cal's ears from the gunshot.

"I don't think so," Cal manages to reply, as he gulps down the air.

"What's happening?" Locke bellows.

"Just an unwanted visitor, but it's dealt with," Cassie replies, panting.

"Good. I think we're through the worst of it," Locke announces, as he rides over yet another body.

Cal becomes transfixed by the contents of the creature's head that are sliding down the back of the driver's seat in front of him. *How much more of this can I take?* his mind pleads. *As much as is necessary until the war is won,* he tells himself, as he blinks and pulls his focus back and away from the gore.

Air billows in through the shattered window and Cal turns his face into its stream, hoping it might blow away the remains of the horror from him. The wind feels refreshing against his face and he breathes it down to nourish his mind. *I must keep fighting,* Cal orders himself, *for Kim and my unborn child, if no one else.*

"Cal, are you okay? You're not losing your marbles on me, are you?" Cassie's voice says.

"No, Cassie, I'm not losing my marbles on you. I'm in this until it's over," Cal assures, turning to his partner.

"Good, because I don't think I can do this without you," Cassie replies.

"Yes, you can, and you will if you have to. Just the same as I will, if it comes to that," Cal tells her. "Giving up isn't an option for either one of us."

"No, Cal. No, it isn't," Cassie agrees.

"It's not an option for any of us," Locke pipes up from the front seat. "Unless we want to say goodbye to everything we know and hold dear."

"Well said, Sergeant," Cal says.

Locke is correct: they are through the worst of it. A few creatures on the periphery of the city centre show themselves in the hope of finding a meal, but Locke shoots straight past them with little concern.

The cabin relaxes and things go quiet as they make their way to the airbase. Everyone becomes lost in their own thoughts as they try to process what they have all been through. The odd bottle of water is passed around but nothing much is said until Locke slows and pulls over to the side of the road.

"Time to switch around, I'm afraid," Locke says, as he pulls on the vehicle's handbrake. "The airbase is two or three minutes away."

"I haven't been in the back of a car like this since I was a child," Cassie says, as she climbs in.

"In the days before safety-belt laws and health and safety bullshit," Cal adds.

"Many moons ago," Cassie says, as she scrunches up to let Cal in beside her.

"You're showing your age," Locke grins, waiting to shut them in.

"I'm feeling my age, Sergeant," Cassie admits.

"Aren't we all?" Cal says, as he squeezes in next to Cassie.

"It won't be for long," Locke assures. "Keep your heads down and keep quiet. Okay?"

"Yes, Dad," Cassie jokes, as Locke, with a wry smile, pulls down the back to shut them in.

A moment later, the Toyota pulls away. Locke has decided not to play silly buggers and speed off with two people in the back. Even he knows that there's a time and a place and, after what they've all been through, this isn't it.

True to his word, it isn't long until Locke is slowing down again as he approaches the security cordon at the entry to the airbase. Cal and Cassie glance at each other as they duck their heads lower to ensure they can't be seen over the top of the back seats.

"Back again, Sergeant Locke?" Cal hears a voice say, encouraged by Locke's familiarity with the guards at the entry.

"Like a bad penny, Private," Locke answers. "Much happening around here?"

"It's madness, Sarge, as you'd expect," the voice answers. "What are you doing now?"

"Come back for a refuel and to await orders," Locke replies.

"Never ends for you SF guys, eh?"

"You know it, Private. No rest for the wicked," Locke replies.

"Who are your associates in the back?"

"Police officers, I'm afraid, so best behaviour, Private," Locke warns. "Do you need to see their ID?"

"That won't be necessary," the voice says after a moment's pause.

In the back, Cal has the feeling he is listening to a real-life version of Obi-Wan Kenobi using his mind games on the stormtroopers on Tatooine. Locke has the private wrapped around his little finger. Cal assumes that most junior ranks are awestruck when they come face to face with the fearsome Special Forces sergeant.

"Thanks, Sarge. I think it's Italian tonight in the mess hall," the private says.

"Perfect. I'll smash that if I get the chance, Private," Locke replies, and a moment later they are moving forward again.

"Keep your heads down until I say," Locke orders, as he drives away from the security gate.

After a short time, the vehicle stops again and, this time, Cal hears doors opening.

"Welcome to La Casa Riley," Locke says, as he opens the back to let Cal and Cassie out.

"La Casa Riley, eh?" Cal says.

"Yep, our home here at Riley Airbase," Locke replies.

"What, smelly socks and cups of tea?" Cassie asks.

"Something like that, Agent Sutton. A home away from home," Locke grins.

"Men!" Cassie scoffs.

From what Cal can see on initial inspection, La Casa Riley consists of not much more than a few Portakabins arranged around the outside, together with some shipping containers. Nothing very 'special' for a Special Forces unit.

Cal is sure that Locke will tell him that it is all they need, and that it beats sleeping in the dirt of the desert or in the jungle, but Cal was expecting something more elite. He had visions of premium lodging, training and tactical facilities, perhaps with state-of-the-art equipment and communications. What they have arrived at reminds Cal of an ad-hoc travellers' community site. One that suddenly appears overnight on waste ground, as if by magic, to stir the local residents up into a frenzy.

"Is this it?" Cal says without thinking, as other men in uniform emerge from the Portakabins to see who's arrived.

"Yeah, we're having the swimming pool installed later this week." Locke rolls his eyes.

"I just meant…" Cal tries to backtrack.

"I know what you meant, Detective," Locke cuts Cal off. "We don't like to be interfered with and this keeps us out of sight while we're here. For the most part anyway."

"I know. Stupid of me," Cal replies.

"You said it," Cassie agrees.

Cassie smirks at Cal, teasing him, and he wonders how many of these black-ops type of sites she has visited around the world. More than him, that's for sure, so he ignores her bait.

"We thought you'd gone AWOL, Sarge!" Bubba grins as he approaches with Locke's other team member, Ken.

"Missed me, did you, boys?" Locke replies, whilst fist-bumping his men.

"I wouldn't go that far," Ken replies. "We were just worried we'd be pressed into another unit of squaddies."

"We'll, I'm back now and we've got work to do," Locke announces.

"What work?" a gigantic man with black skin and muscles bursting through his shirt sleeves asks as he approaches.

"Something right up your team's street, my friend," Locke replies, and he slaps hands with the newcomer.

"That's what I like to hear," the man replies. "I take it it's off-book and that there'll be a court martial when we're finished?"

"Too fucking right," Locke grins.

"I see you've been making new friends. Who are the civilians?" Locke is asked.

"This is Detective Chambers, he's in charge of investigating this shit show," Locke replies, his hand indicating Cal. "Then we have the lovely Agent Sutton, a spook from S.I., and Sergeant Neal and Officer Stack. They are police firearms officers and very capable men."

"And you are?" Cal asks.

"How rude of me," Locke says, not embarrassed in the slightest. "This is Sergeant Touré, the second badest sergeant in the unit."

"You wish, Locke. My team would eat yours for breakfast any day of the week," Touré replies.

"Shall we get down to business?" Cassie interrupts the banter.

"Absolutely, Agent Sutton," Touré says with a wide smile. "How can I help you?"

"You'll have to forgive Sergeant Touré, Agent Sutton. He thinks he's God's gift to women," Locke grins.

"I don't think it, Locke," Touré's smile widens.

"Whatever," Cassie rolls her eyes, exasperated. "We've got a raid to plan, Sergeant. Are you in or not?"

"Whatever you need," Touré replies seriously.

"Is there somewhere we can use?" Cal asks.

"Let's head into the briefing room," Locke replies.

"What's in the container?" Cal asks, as Locke leads them towards one of the Portakabins next to a shipping container.

"Weapons, Detective. Lots of weapons," Locke replies proudly.

A jumble of tables and chairs are ranged around a large whiteboard inside the Portakabins that Locke leads them into. The room is rearranged so that Cal and Cassie, together with the two Special Forces sergeants and Sergeant Neal, are in the centre. Nobody is left out of the discussions though. Atkins and Locke's other men pull up chairs around him and Stack is on Neal's shoulder.

Before they get underway, Cal and Cassie read through the emails containing the intelligence that Tilly and Agent Morgan have compiled. Thankfully, Locke sends men off to commandeer refreshments while they are reviewing the intelligence. The emails are comprehensive and detailed. They outline new evidence together with Tilly and Morgan's working theories, which Cal and Cassie discuss as they go.

The refreshments arrive and they finish reviewing the emails while munching on much-needed bacon sandwiches.

Other men wander into the briefing room during this period. Some of whom, Cal assumes, must be Touré's team members but there are also others. All the men appear to be rugged Special Forces combat troops and all of them have a deadly serious demeanour.

Cal has already all but decided how their fightback must begin and he is positive that Cassie is of the same mind. They just need Locke and his associates' expertise to plan and then execute their next move. Cal is more than confident that they have somehow stumbled on the right team of men for the task at hand. It almost feels like their coming together was fated.

As Cal finishes his sandwich, he seeks assurances from Locke and Touré that all the men inside the room can be trusted to keep what is said to themselves. Locke guarantees that he can vouch for each and every man present, which is good enough for Cal.

The whole room looks to Cal to get proceedings underway, but there are two important people that Cal wants to be involved. Their input will be vital. The only question is are they still able to continue to help, or have things deteriorated at Mercury House?

Guilt weighs heavily on Cal that Tilly and Agent Morgan have been left behind inside Mercury House in the face of such horrendous danger while he sits in relative safety. *Needs must*, Cal tells himself, as he looks at his phone to dial Tilly. She will be desperate to continue to help if she can and her phone begins to ring.

"Hello, Tilly," Cal says when the phone is answered.

Supplementary

"I have brought you a drink, Michael, darling," a sultry female voice says in a Caribbean accent.

Janus opens his eyes to be greeted by a vision of beauty standing over him. Carmel waits for Janus to stir himself from the snooze he has fallen into whilst relaxing by his villa's infinity pool. He has little trouble rousing himself as his eyes wander across Carmel's soft, dark skin. The gold bikini that he presented her with this morning has the desired effect of doing little to cover her long, slender body.

"Thank you, Carmel," Janus says, as he pushes himself up in his sunlounger. "I hope you haven't been too bored while I've been relaxing."

"Don't be silly, Michael. Wendy and I have been entertaining ourselves while you relaxed. We let you sleep. You will need all your energy later, after all," Carmel smiles seductively.

Janus looks over to the outside bar where Wendy, dressed in another of Janus' expensive, but tiny, gifts, stirs another cocktail in the shade. Janus takes his cocktail from Carmel and raises his glass towards Wendy to say thank you. Wendy pops a glazed cherry into her mouth directly from a cocktail stick and waves back at him, smiling.

"While you are relaxed, would you like Wendy and I to give you one of our special massages?" Carmel offers.

"A tempting offer, my dear, as you can see," Janus replies, indicating an aroused mass in his lap. "Unfortunately, I have business to take care of this afternoon. I will make it up to you both later though, I promise. Will you and Wendy be okay with your own company until I'm finished?"

"Of course we will, but we will miss you," Carmel smiles, moving from one hip to the other. "Don't work too hard now, Michael. We will have a busy night tonight."

"I will be ready. Don't worry," Janus assures.

With that, Carmel winks at Janus before she spins to walk back over to Wendy and the bar. Janus stares at Carmel as she walks across the patio, feasting on her sumptuous swaying curves. He continues to stare as Carmel picks her drink up off the bar and takes Wendy by the hand to lead her inside. Janus watches them both longingly until they disappear inside the villa.

Calming himself for a moment before he gets to work, Janus looks out at the luscious turquoise Caribbean Sea beyond the infinity pool. His motor yacht is anchored just off the coast of the Cayman Islands, and he can see the yacht's staff going about their business on deck.

The trappings of great wealth have become the norm for Michael Spalding. Things were not always like this, however, but long gone are the days when people referred to him as simply Mike. He can barely remember his deprived youth growing up on a run-down council estate in England. That world was a lifetime ago and he often wonders if it happened on a different, alien planet entirely, as he continues to look at his beautiful vista. Even the hard work and illegal activities it took to arrive in his position of wealth and power are becoming nothing more than a hazy memory, lost in the annals of time.

Janus has achieved everything in life that he ever dreamt of and far, far more. Everything he desires is catered for and women like Carmel and Wendy are the icing on the cake. Why have one when you can have two? Three is too many, that was decided a few years ago. Arguments and jealousy between three friends are just too much to deal with. He no longer has the time or inclination for that triangle. He was also forced to admit to himself that his energy levels aren't quite what they once were.

Every now and then, Janus will log on to one of his many bank accounts, just to remind himself how far he has come. He still finds it hard to fathom how many figures his bank balance includes. He has to count the number of figures individually and that will be for just one of his accounts. His liquid funds are but the tip of the iceberg: the majority of his wealth is invested in untold numbers of international businesses and other assets. His stock portfolio is longer than both of his arms combined.

As with many wealthy people, businesses and financiers, the COVID pandemic represented a veritable gold rush for him. Michael Spalding was wealthy before the supposed pandemic, but when the dust settled following the biggest con in history, Janus was super-rich. Wealthy beyond even his wildest dreams.

The governments of the world kept printing money out of thin air without a thought for the long-term effect on their economies or their citizens. The public will be suffering from their governments' disastrous economic policies for decades to come. Money is printed and its value decreases, sending inflation skyrocketing, which is then closely followed by hikes in the interest rate percentage points. A vicious circle of economic misery and, as always, the buck stops with the ordinary taxpayer. They are the ones footing the bill for

Janus' life of luxury and it is their money that has been transferred into his bulging bank accounts.

Janus sips on his delicious cocktail, with no pangs of guilt for having profited from other people's misfortune. A government's economic policy isn't under his control... Well, not directly. He was just in a position to benefit handsomely from its folly.

That's what Janus continues to convince himself of anyway. He has managed to discount the inside knowledge that he was privy to from one of the world's largest drug companies, Arnoult Pharma. It is a partnership that has proved exceedingly profitable for Janus, a partnership that flourished and one that will now change the world forever. Individual finances will be the least of problems for the world's population in the very near future.

Janus checks his watch. The morning of rest and relaxation that was afforded to him only by the time zone he is currently residing in is nearly over. Janus decides to try to reach Mr Easter once more while he finishes off his cocktail. He holds out virtually no hope that Mr Easter will answer his phone. Janus has concluded that Mr Easter has expired from proceedings., the operative either having been apprehended or possibly caught up in his own explosion on the industrial park.

Either way, as expected, Mr Easter doesn't answer his phone. Janus is confident that Mr Easter will remain loyal to the cause if he has been captured. He was meticulously selected. The more favourable scenario is that Mr Easter was killed along with the multiple police officers in the explosion. That would be a cleaner ending to his involvement. Not that any information was divulged to Mr Easter that might compromise Foundation Day's success or threaten Janus' identity.

After sucking up the last dregs of his cocktail through the straw, Janus puts the empty glass onto the table next to him and gets up from the lounger. The heat of the Caribbean sun hits him as he steps from beneath the protective orange parasol fitted next to it. As tempting as it is to swing by the bar to mix himself another cocktail, Janus walks straight for the door off the patio that leads into his office. One morning cocktail is enough today; he is going to need his wits about him for the afternoon's business.

Janus' thumbprint disengages the lock that allows him into his villa's office and the air conditioning inside immediately cools him down, ready for work. He sits down at his desk, which has a direct view of the infinity pool and the Caribbean beyond. *Not a bad environment to conduct business in*, Janus tells himself.

Following his snooze, he hadn't realised how short the time was until he is scheduled to make his report in the run-up to the second phase of Foundation Day. No matter. He is in plenty of time to log on to the system and update his fellow stakeholders. Janus and Doctor Francis Arnoult are the only two stakeholders who know the identity of all their other fellow believers. Doctor Arnoult, referred to simply as SH1 (stakeholder number 1) on the system, is the mastermind behind Foundation Day. He is the visionary that Janus and all stakeholders owe so much to and most of them don't even know his true identity.

Janus sees that all stakeholders are logged on to the system, no matter the time of day or night in their locations around the world. This is a meeting for stakeholders only; Janus will be holding a separate meeting with high-ranking operatives later in the afternoon. That meeting will include high-profile politicians, civil servants and members of the authorities from across the globe, all of whom will need to be brought up to speed with the latest phase as it unfolds.

Unfortunately, Mr Easter will be missing from that meeting and Janus is forced to report that fact to the stakeholders, as the first meeting begins. Janus assures everyone that Mr Easter's disappearance will not have a detrimental effect going forward, but some stakeholders insist on further clarification, especially SH1. Janus assures them that Mr Easter didn't possess intelligence that might compromise either the project or, indeed, their security. He also explains how contingencies are already in place to ensure that Mr Easter's disappearance will not hinder the imminent planned expansion of Foundation Day.

Eventually, his fellow stakeholders' minds are put at rest and Janus can move on to the task at hand and the main reason for the meeting. All stakeholders must register their approval to move Foundation Day into phase two at 20.00 Coordinated Universal Time today. Once their approval is received, Janus will hold the second meeting before finally issuing the go-ahead order to Foundation Day's operatives around the world.

Janus thinks of the cities around the world that the next stage of the earth's cleansing will rip through as he waits for the stakeholders to register their approval to proceed. Many of the cities are ones that he has had cause to visit over the years and some of them he even enjoyed. The culture of Paris, the vibrancy of Melbourne and the sheer organisational structure of Tokyo. So many cities will suffer terribly but things cannot continue as they are. Earth simply cannot withstand mankind's continued assault on its resources, which escalates with every passing day. Every continent will endure pain for a time until the cleansing is over. Only then will they and the planet begin to flourish again.

Rapidly, Janus receives approval from the stakeholders, just as he expected. None of them registers an objection and no abstentions are logged on to the system.

Janus now has the authority to proceed to phase two of Foundation Day and he feels both excitement and dread as he realises what this means. The planet will be a very different place tomorrow for humankind: one of chaos, suffering and destruction.

Foundation Day will conclude with -

FOUNDATION DAY

– BOOK 3 –

If you have enjoyed **FOUNDATION DAY – BOOK TWO –** be sure to leave a review. Amazon reviews only take a minute and are so important in building a buzz for every book.

Many thanks, every review is appreciated!

CAPITAL FALLING – THE SERIES

As Black Smoke Rises, Order Disintegrates...

Former SAS soldier Andy Richards is no stranger to horrors, but no training could ever have prepared him for the nightmare unfolding at home. While a viral epidemic hammers London, Andy finds himself trapped in the epicentre, forced to protect his family. Together with his young daughter, he leads a small group of survivors toward latent refuge, all the while searching for his missing son and infantryman; this is the ultimate game of survival.

With those infected displaying brutal, inhuman behaviour and caught up in a climate of martial law, no one can be trusted. Old connections may help to unravel this mystery virus, but the resultant hellscape means Andy and his group meet danger at every turn.

Stakes are high, and failing means a fate worse than death...

The perfect tale for troubled times, *CAPITAL FALLING* delivers dark thrills and surprising sentiment—twisted, cerebral fun. You'll race to the end like your life depends on it...

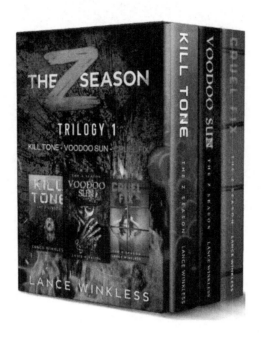

THE Z SEASON - TRILOGY 1

3 Novels - A #1 Best Seller - 650+ Pages

- Infectious to its Very Core

A trilogy of standalone and unique novels that don't hold back and all with a zombie - undead twist.......
YOU HAVE BEEN WARNED!

KILL TONE

A festival of feverish, exhilarating tension with a rock 'n roll crescendo that unleashes hell itself, this is not for the faint-hearted. KILL TONE proves the perfect blend of decadence and undead carnage, whilst never losing sight of its predominant humanity.

VOODOO SUN

Caribbean Voodoo may have caused this nightmare, and nothing short of a miracle will help Max get out alive.

A tale of undead carnage and mayhem, VOODOO SUN embarks for bliss but lands in true perdition.

CRUEL FIX

CRUEL FIX is a terrifying trip through the labyrinth of loss and lunacy. Bleak and sinister it may be, but spirited humanity retains a twisted shard of hope …. Though all that glitters isn't gold, and all that walks is not alive.

Read these novels in any order, you choose. Each is a tale of its own and completely unique but. be warned they are not for the faint-hearted or easily offended!

Praise for THE Z SEASON TRILOGY

GREAT BOOK ★★★★★

"Just read the Kill Tone what an amazing book. the story had me captivated from start to finish. great author, love his books."

JUST A BRILLIANT AUTHOR ★★★★★

"Another great book by the author Lance brilliant from start to finish kept me on the edge like the others so will have to wait for next one now… hopefully."

ANOTHER GREAT READ ★★★★★

"Action packed from the beginning. So realistic that you could actually imagine this happening! Just wish it didn't end so soon. I would like to see how the virus spreads so roll on the next one."

PAPERBACK – KINDLE & KINDLE UNLIMITED

For more information on Lance Winkless
and future writing see his website.

www.LanceWinkless.com

By Lance Winkless

FOUNDATION DAY

CAPITAL FALLING - THE SERIES

&

THE Z SEASON – TRILOGY

KILL TONE
VOODOO SUN
CRUEL FIX

Visit Amazon Author Pages

Amazon US- Amazon.com/author/lancewinkless
Amazon UK- Amazon.co.uk/Lance-Winkless/e/B07QJV2LR3

Why Not Follow

Facebook LanceWinklessAuthor
Twitter   @LanceWinkless
Instagram @LanceWinkless
Pinterest www.pinterest.com/lancewinkless
BookBub www.bookbub.com/authors/lance-winkless

Printed in Great Britain
by Amazon

14426224R00173